The Ghost of Ravenswood Hall

By H. B. Diaz

Literary Wanderlust | Denver, Colorado

Published in the United States by Literary Wanderlust LLC, Denver, Colorado.

www.LiteraryWanderlust.com

ISBN Paperback: 978-1-956615-31-9
ISBN Digital: 978-1-956615-32-6

Printed in the United States of America

Dedication

For my late mother, who lingers in these pages
despite her passing.

For her mother, who always told me I'd get here.

And for my son, who made me a mother, too.

Prologue

Dear Inspector Gerard,

In accordance with your request, we have placed these documents in as cohesive and chronological an order as possible in the hope that you might know the truth as we know it. Portions have been omitted to avoid repetition, though I am glad to provide these sections according to your wishes. On the whole, I trust this fractured narrative may elucidate a few peculiarities, which have no doubt troubled you these past months. Whether you can believe it or not is another matter entirely.

Your humble servants,

Dr. William Garrett

Miss Charlotte "Lottie" Garrett

Witnessed by Constable Charles Devlin
June 11, 1889

Chapter I

WILLIAM GARRETT'S JOURNAL

The Catskills, New York
January 9, 1889

I ought to have taken it as an omen.

Darkness unfolded across the night like a bolt of damp wool, winter clinging to its fibers and stiffening its edges. I had, however, inherited my father's obstinacy, and since I'd begun this journey in the crisp morning sun, I instead took the poor turn in the weather as nothing more than a touch of innocent misfortune.

Had I known the toll this crossing would take upon my spirits, I might have obliged the driver to return me to Baltimore, or to a port or railway station, so long as I was away. Alas, though, I am my father's son—God rest his miserable soul—and my current predicament requires it, so we drove on. Sleet battered the carriage as though wailed upon by a poltergeist, and our wheels sank into cracks, rattling the very brain inside my skull.

The blanket across my lap did little to warm me. The cold ached in my bones, in my heart, and I missed my daughter dearly. A man does not know true loneliness until he has traveled this part of the country in wintertime, when he has only the cry of the fox and the hoot of the owl to remind him that he's not fallen into purgatory. In the summer, there are fledgling sparrows and fawns for company, but January is a cruel month, reigned not by man but by the savage earth, by the mountain spirits and an eternal ration of superstition. It puts down any creature that survives the yuletide season, my father among them.

I withdrew a crumpled sheet of newspaper from my greatcoat. This, my father's final blow, ought to have been written in blood, for it sealed my fate as effectively as a devil's pact. I needed no candle by which to read it. Every word was etched into my mind, the headline as boldly printed behind my eyes as it was in ink. As the moon skirted behind churning snow clouds, I read nonetheless.

BALTIMORE — WEDNESDAY—NOVEMBER 26, 1888
ESTATE OWNER LEAVES FORTUNE TO ESTRANGED SON
HEIR YET TO CLAIM INHERITANCE; ACCUSED OF
MURDER

OUR CORRESPONDENT IN ROCHESTER HAS RECEIVED NOTICE THAT OLIVER GARRETT, NOTABLE OWNER OF THE VAST RAVENSWOOD HALL ESTATE IN CATSKILL, NY, HAS PASSED ON, JOINING HIS WIFE AFTER A LONG SEPARATION. HIS LONE HEIR AND SON, WILLIAM GARRETT, WHO PRACTICES MEDICINE IN OUR GREAT CITY OF BALTIMORE, HAS NOT YET APPEARED TO CLAIM HIS FORTUNE.

THE ELDER GARRETT HAS, IN ACCORDANCE WITH HIS LAST WILL AND TESTAMENT, SENT THE FOLLOWING LETTER TO OUR CORRESPONDENT FOR IMMEDIATE RELEASE. WE

HAVE HONORED HIS WISHES, AND ARE GRATEFUL TO THE MANY CONTRIBUTIONS MR. GARRETT HAS MADE TO THE SUN OVER THE FINAL YEARS OF HIS LIFE. HIS LETTER IS AS FOLLOWS:

DEAR WILLIAM,

YOU HAVE RETURNED ALL OF MY LETTERS UNREAD, REFUSING ME AT EVERY TURN, SO I KNOW NO OTHER METHOD BY WHICH TO COMMUNICATE BUT THIS NEWSPAPER IN THE CITY IN WHICH YOU'VE CHOSEN TO BUILD YOUR LONESOME LIFE. I HAVE REMAINED SILENT ALL THIS TIME, OUT OF RESPECT FOR YOU, BUT YOUR MOTHER'S BLOOD CRIES OUT TO ME. HER SPIRIT LINGERS HERE, UNABLE TO REST, AND SO I MUST SPEAK THE TRUTH.

I KNOW WHAT YOU HAVE DONE.

YOU CAN NO MORE DENY IT THAN YOU CAN DENY THE BONES OF YOUR MOTHER ROTTING IN THE GRAVE. WHEN YOU STOLE MY PURSE FROM MY BEDSIDE AND TRAVELED ALONE TO DR. JOHNSTON, WHEN YOU RETURNED WITH THE LAUDANUM IN YOUR POCKET—BY GOD, IF I HAD KNOWN THEN YOUR INTENT! I MIGHT HAVE KILLED YOU MYSELF, BOY. BE GRATEFUL TO GOD THAT I HAD NOT IMAGINED WHAT YOU WISHED TO DO WITH THAT DIABOLICAL TINCTURE.

WHEN YOU PREPARED TEA FOR YOUR MOTHER THAT EVENING, AS WAS YOUR WONT ON A THOUSAND NIGHTS BEFORE, I COULD NOT IN MY MOST HEINOUS NIGHTMARES HAVE SUPPOSED THAT YOU ALSO CALLED UPON HER REAPER. I KNOW, BOY. I KNOW EVERYTHING, AND NOW THE WORLD MUST KNOW IT, TOO. GOD FORGIVE ME, I BIT MY TONGUE ALL THE WHILE. I CANNOT TAKE THIS SECRET TO THE GRAVE.

YOU RUINED US ALL THAT NIGHT. THE LIFE YOU HAVE BUILT UPON THESE LIES SHALL CRUMBLE TO DUST, AND YOU WILL TURN TO ME ONCE MORE. I HAVE SEEN TO THAT, AT LEAST.

I crushed the article in my fist for the hundredth time, my face afire. A letter from the family attorney might have sufficed to inform me of his death, but I'd been unable to reach him for an explanation, or indeed any information at all regarding the matter. No, my father meant to ruin me to the last. He meant to cast me, and all that I had built, under his boot like in the days of old. It was the work of nigh on twenty years to escape the clutching, covetous influence of Ravenswood Hall, and a single page of newsprint rendered all these efforts for naught. The power my father held over me had weakened only in my mind. He was correct on that point in the very least. I had built my life upon a lie.

I was no more responsible for my mother's suicide those many years ago than I was for the impending storm overhead, and I had no memory whatever of visiting the family doctor, but his slanderous accusation met its mark. I'd lost nearly every one of my patients to this blasted article. My daughter and I carried on for as many weeks as we could, but my father won out in the end. When the time came this month to pay the landlord, I could not.

I brooded on these matters for a long while. With no moonlight to show the hands of my pocket watch, I lost all concept of time, as if I'd been traveling this road all of my life and might for a lifetime more. I slid the sleeve of my greatcoat across the frosted glass and peered out into the night in a feeble attempt to orient myself.

Thick with hemlocks hunched like trolls beneath shawls of snow, and the stark skeletons of sleeping birch, the forest gathered us into its darkness as we pressed on. Our lantern lit the eyes of a creature along the road, but it slunk away into shadow before I was able to identify it. There was a time long ago when these beasts did not fear man, with his weak legs and dull teeth. Now we have guns and our qualms with one another are no longer settled justly.

The horses sensed perhaps what lurked among the snow-shrouded pines. As my driver brought the carriage to a halt, they snorted and pawed the frozen earth, their voices high in protest. I heard no creaking of the carriage, no footfalls. The horses fell silent, and only the groaning wind reached my ears as it moved like a wraith through the trees. I waited, the breath held in my throat.

A pale face appeared at my window.

Even as my fingers tightened around my fountain pen, the only weapon available to me, I recognized Wilson, my driver. Despite an innumerable collection of wool scarves shrouding his neck and shoulders, he shivered fiercely, his face as bloodless as a corpse. I opened the window to hear him better.

"Good God, man," I said before he could speak. "Let's call it a night."

"We ought to keep moving, sir," he said, and sent a troubled glance toward the heavens. "The weather may not hold."

"Let the weather do what it will," I answered. "You must warm yourself."

My insistence was driven only partially by concern for this man, whom I had known since boyhood. Although my hand had been dealt, I clung still to resistance. The dread that wrung its wiry fingers around my throat released its grip. Perhaps a messenger was on his way at this very moment to relieve me of this terrible burden and to tell me it was all a mistake.

"Would that be too much of an inconvenience for you, sir?" Wilson asked. "There's an inn what lies up the mountain just a ways. We might rest the horses there."

"And yourself, Wilson," I answered. "You're frozen to death."

"Well-nigh, sir, well-nigh." He laughed, rubbing his hands together in the old way, back when I would sit up in the box with him after church, flicking the poor horses with the whip to drive them faster while my father hurled threats at us from the carriage.

Reaching our respite took the work of another half hour, though I suspect it couldn't have been more than a mile's journey, for the ice had so built up on the steep road that we would have been better suited in a sleigh. The sight of the old place warmed my heart, and so the cold was of little import.

Nestled against the forest with a candle burning cheerfully in each window, the Oak Mill Tavern held its old ground at the corner of a crossroads. Catskill lanterns shone through the trees like will-o'-the-wisps to the east, and to the west, only darkness.

This place had been a haven for me as a boy. Indeed, I spent more time with the old regulars there than I did with my own father, who spoke with a switch of birch instead of his tongue.

Beyond the window, a pair of drunken old men laughed and leaned on their canes, pipes bobbing beneath their mustaches. Pellets of ice crunched beneath my feet as I stepped out of the carriage and approached the walk lined with cheerful bushes of holly, Wilson close at my heels. Despite the many years that had separated us, the man was as loyal as an old dog and as skilled at conversation, but his presence was a comfort.

So familiar a place reminded me what a stranger I am to this life. The boy in me recognized the sign above the door and the bell that heralded our entry, but the man William Garrett had become was a foreigner there.

When Wilson closed the door behind us, expressions akin to horror dragged down the lines of every face in the room, as if a great hand had run itself down a slate.

"Christ Almighty," a woman carrying a plate of mutton exclaimed, halting so abruptly that gravy splattered onto the floor. "Oliver Garrett, as I live and breathe."

"You've mistaken me for my father, madam." I removed my hat. "My name is William."

"Willie? That little devil we caught chasing the chickens into trees?" She approached us and looked me over, her gaze somehow motherly and lewd at once. I recognized her, though the years had not been kind. "I'm sorry to see you back here, love. Indeed I am."

"Forgive me," I replied. "I don't understand what you mean."

"Your father's place isn't fit for anyone but the ghosts, and believe me, that miserable estate has its share. Better leave it be, Willie." She set the plate down before a man in a hunting cap and ambled back into the kitchen, nary a goodbye. Wilson stretched his neck so as to speak in my ear.

"That's—"

"Mrs. Peasley," I interrupted, looking after her. "I remember."

"I had better be seeing to the horses," he said, nodding dutifully and then turning to leave, but I set my hand on his shoulder and bade him join me by the fireplace.

"The horses are no good without a driver," I said, and sat at a table within the warmth of the cheerful flames. An expression of uncertainty narrowed his eyes, already drooped by fatigue. "Sit, man. Before you fall."

"Very well, sir. Thank you."

As he slid sheepishly into the chair, the pair of old men beside the window ceased making merry and approached us. One of them, a hairy man who had been sucking on a stained ivory pipe, clapped me on the back as if we were compatriots in the army.

"Here to avenge your father's death, are we, old boy?" he roared, puffing out his chest and swinging his arm across his heart like a knight.

"Avenge his death?" I repeated, laughing with more gaiety than I felt. "Shall I challenge the widow's walk to a duel? Run my sword through gravity, then?"

The man leaned toward his friend and whispered, "He thinks he fell!" and they both burst into laughter, their faces red, mine redder.

"What the devil do you mean by that?" I demanded, standing.

"Bah, we're only having a bit of fun," the other one said, his voice thick with ale. Before I could press the matter further, I felt a gentle tugging on my coat sleeve. When I turned, a young boy stood before me, large eyes as dark as coffee.

"Do you believe in hell?" he asked.

I was so taken aback by this seemingly random inquiry that I did not immediately know how I should reply. As a man of science, I had largely rejected the teachings of my childhood in favor of those set forth by Gray, Bunsen, and others. My tongue worked behind my lips to answer the child. He scratched his head and stood on his tiptoes until I bent to hear him.

"Mother says your papa's gone to hell."

"She said what?" I straightened and glanced over him, meeting the eyes of a pale-faced woman in the corner of the room. A shawl covered her head and shoulders, but I could see her hands wringing in her lap. She crossed herself and looked away.

"Have you ever seen a ghost?" the boy continued, louder. I could not properly answer this either. "Don't believe in them myself, but Mother does. She says you'll need this." He opened his hand to reveal a small silver medallion. He shrugged, dropped the trinket in my palm, and then scampered back to his mother, who gathered him beneath her shawl like a hen.

I hadn't time to give this singular interaction a moment's thought, for Wilson cleared his throat and looked up at me. Some color had returned to his face.

"Perhaps we ought to keep moving on, sir," he said, and then smiled. "I'm warm as wool now. Mr. Murdoch will have something for you to eat, sure as the sun."

All this talk of ghosts and devils had rather effectively subdued my appetite, so I agreed.

Once restored to my place inside the drafty carriage, the strangeness of our short visit weighed upon me. The silver trinket bore the relief of a man clad in robes. Some saint perhaps, but try as I might, I could not deduce the meaning of it. As I brushed the pad of my thumb over its surface, I thought of the woman in the shawl. Why should she give a thing of such worth to a stranger? It might have been her most valuable possession in all the world. A better man might have thanked her, but she had given me something else, which I resented. A spore of fear had been planted in my heart, nourished by the gloom and fog that had descended upon our journey. It bloomed inside me like so much fungus as the horses pressed on, steam rising off their backs.

I looked at my reflection in the glass, but my father peered back—the sharp cruelty in his black eyes and the strength of his jaw. Was this the man Mrs. Peasley had seen? In a moment, my breath softened his features and my own emerged again. Yet the scent of his tobacco filled the carriage, lifting the hairs on the back of my arms.

"How much farther, Wilson?" I called, but I could not hear his reply. I could bear no more of this. I longed for the warmth of my library and the clean, clinical air of my medical office, but Baltimore was a world away.

I felt Ravenswood in my soul before I beheld it in the distance. It came upon me as a terrible suppression of spirit before settling into gloom as we approached like moths, drawn to its skeletal light.

I fear this place instinctively, the way a child fears a spider. I do not recall the exact moment when Ravenswood became a monster to me, only that one morning I was a child, and when the evening arrived, my mother was dead and I was a man. I no longer knew William Garrett, the respected medical doctor. I'd inexorably become Will again, the child who had seen his mother's ghost on the widow's walk. The boy whose father had no patience for tears.

I clutched my blanket and watched with a sort of feverish dread as the carriage brought us through the rusted iron gates, now suffocated by long tendrils of dead ivy. Two stone wolves stood in the lamplight, laden with shadow and lichen, long neglected but guarding the place as furiously as in the days of old. When I was a boy, I had given these creatures silly names. But they were buried deep within my memory, beneath the ever-present whispering. *This place is diseased. Leave at once.*

We continued up the gravel drive, the *clop, clop* of hooves dulled by recently fallen snow. The stars no longer spit their ice down upon us, and Ravenswood rose up before me in the ghastly moonlight. It was not how I remembered. It seemed smaller and somehow more menacing. Gone were the rose gardens and lilac bushes that once lined the pebbled walk and perfumed the air. Gone was the wooden trellis I had climbed during long summer days. Gone was my father, his countenance drawn in resentment as he stared down at me from the window, my mother's body barely cold in the ground. I recalled that last day with bitterness in my heart. What a fool I had been to believe I could be free of him. While I had felt his presence with me after leaving the inn, I felt his absence now, hollow and heavy inside me at once.

Instead, old Murdoch stood inside the open door with a candlestick in his hand, the flame blown out. He appeared grim and frail beneath the archway of this monstrous old house, preposterously so, as if he were only a sketch or a memory faded by madness. He had been ancient even during my boyhood. The grace of God alone must have kept him from collapsing into a heap of bones on the stone.

"A sad sight, sir," Wilson muttered, and I was uncertain if he referred to Murdoch or the degree of ruin into which Ravenswood had fallen. Withered tendrils of ivy climbed walls held together not by expert masonry but by sheer force of will, for hardly a fingernail's worth of mortar remained between the crumbling stones. It gave a man the impression of suspension somehow, as if the house were holding its breath, waiting for permission at last to surrender to the forces of nature.

My eyes rose, perhaps instinctively, to the window of my mother's boudoir, which had once been a place of warmth for me. I tasted licorice and remembered the crinkling of the paper sack where she kept the candies, saving them for me when Father was away. The memory soured on my tongue as it lingered. He'd locked her door after her death, and I suspect it had never been opened again.

Now, the wind sucked moth-eaten lace curtains through the broken window, the delicate fabric snagging on shards of glass. A phantom hand gripped my throat. I had expected decay but was unprepared for ruin. I'd imagined my mother's space as unchanged through time as my memory of her. The truth was cold.

My father told stories of the spirits of our ancestors guarding the gates of Ravenswood Hall, stone wolves among their ranks. As I stared up at the dead eyes of the house, I realized he had it wrong. My long-dead kin do not protect me, nor have they ever prevented evil from thriving here. Indeed, it seems they've welcomed it.

In any case, it is of little import now. No one tells these stories. Not anymore.

Chapter II

WILLIAM GARRETT'S JOURNAL

Ravenswood Hall
January 9, 1889, continued

I lingered on the porch as the clopping of the horses' hooves faded behind me. Old Murdoch stood within, his ancient arm stretched to bid me enter. The old man neither smiled nor admonished me. He simply motioned into the darkness of the house, the extinguished candle quivering in his hand as his cataract gaze fell upon my face.

"I trust you had a pleasant journey, sir," he said. I had not heard his voice since I was a lad of seventeen, and the sound of it cast my mind headlong into the house, although I remained firmly outside in body. I thought of his tattered copy of *Robinson Crusoe* and the scent of soot and lemon polish as we read together in the kitchen. I heard the sound of my mother's piano, and then the gentle clicking of her knitting needles.

When I summoned up my courage and stepped inside, I steeled myself for the weight of grief or the opening of the floodgates of memory, but nothing of the kind occurred. Only silent barrenness greeted me, only absence.

"Where is everyone?" I asked, shaking the ice pellets from my hat. No scullery maid or housekeeper darted into the kitchen, no footmen or underbutler waited quietly to be called upon. There was only Murdoch, his clouded expression as empty as the house itself. I ventured farther into the foyer, beneath a chandelier laden with cobwebs, and looked about as he took my coat and draped it over his arm.

Candles burned brightly in the sconces lining the staircase, illuminating the Garrett family portraits. The empty space on the wall at the bottom of the stairs, reserved for my father, remains so even still. He couldn't be bothered to sit for a portrait in life and had not suffered me to sit for one either, so the set remains incomplete. The portrait of my mother was missing, and I have resolved to locate it and restore it to its rightful place.

"I'm afraid you'll find no one, sir," Murdoch said. "It's been difficult to keep help since—"

"Has he come?" a voice called. A man flew from the kitchen, his apron dusted with flour. He halted when he saw me and quickly untied the apron, casting it over a small table beside the doorway. I did not know him until he smoothed his hand across his hair, a nervous habit of an old friend.

"Peter?" I cried. A smile crept across my lips, the first since I'd left Baltimore.

"The beard fooled me somewhat," he said, his lanky frame bounding toward me. "It is Will under there, surely?"

I barked a laugh, taking his hand and shaking it fervently.

"My God, man," I said. "You look just the same."

"I'm glad to hear that," he said. "This old place has made me uglier, I think."

Although he said this in jest, he had landed on the truth. He must be near forty now, and the years had stripped him to the bone, giving him the appearance of emaciation. His hairline had gone back a great deal, and creases crowded his eyes, though they still retained the insolent spark of boyhood that I'd known.

"Peter will bring your trunk upstairs," said Murdoch, his expression as stern as ever.

"Yes, Father," he answered, and then slipped outside. A moment later, he returned with Wilson, my trunk between them.

"What's this, then? Only the three of you?" I asked. "What of Mrs. White and her daughter?"

"Mrs. White passed on some time ago, I'm afraid," Murdoch answered. "Young Lucy went on to the city after her mother's death. I never did find another cook who could prepare as good a roast duck." He sighed with a nearly imperceptible shake of his head, and then added, "The groundskeeper attends to outdoor matters in spring, but he lives in town, sir."

"Why does he not remain on the property?" I repeated.

Peter opened his mouth to answer me, but footsteps sounded on the stairs, and we turned to find a young girl descending, fingers clutching an apron covered in soot.

"You've set the fire in Master William's quarters, then?" Peter asked. She stopped at the bottom of the steps and nodded. Peter turned to me. "Will, this is my daughter, Christine."

"A pleasure," I said, but she only curtsied, and then she scurried back up the stairs.

"She's a quiet little sprite," Peter said. "Hasn't said a word for months."

"Is she all right?" I asked.

"I've brought her on to help with the cooking," Murdoch said before Peter could answer. He and Wilson followed her upstairs with my trunk. "You'll forgive the liberty, I'm sure. She and Miss Laveau take on additional duties as required."

"Mrs. Laveau?" I asked.

"Yes, sir. She's retired for the evening."

"Is there anyone else?"

"No, sir. That is all."

I lifted my gaze, noting the blistered wallpaper and soiled, threadbare rugs.

"That explains the look of the place, then. It's just as well," I sighed. "I'll see to it." He looked offended, but the wrinkles smoothed to his usual plain, albeit pained, expression a moment later.

"Will you be dining tonight?" he asked.

"No, thank you. If you could have the child heat some water for a bath, I'd be grateful."

"It is done." He bowed gallantly and turned away. Laughter tugged at the corner of my lip. Murdoch took his position as seriously as an undertaker, and he was just as grave. A young boy could have found no better victim for tricks.

"It's good to see you, Mr. Murdoch," I called after him, and he turned to bow his head toward me, a small smile creasing his face. Nay, perhaps I'd imagined that. I doubt he had ever looked at me fondly. I was such a devil to the old man.

I wandered alone into the sitting room, marveling at the terrible decay that had taken hold here. It seems an impossible task to restore it to its former grandeur, especially in comparison to the grand hotels that have appeared in this part of the country as of late. I have seen their advertisements in the papers. That any man would travel into so remote and wild a place for no greater purpose than leisure is beyond my comprehension. Still, these terrible mountains must appear marvelous to those who've never before beheld them.

The Murdochs kept decay out of the sitting room, at least. My mother's ruby-red curtains hang still upon the windows. My father's books line the great shelves against the wall, all atlases and business manuals, yellowed by tobacco. Someone had taken pains to repair the rat-chewed holes in his smoking chair. I dragged it to the fire and sat to rest and take in my surroundings.

I sat there quite still, remembering, and trying not to

remember.

My mother's piano held its customary position at the edge of the room, its surface gleaming with polish, and I fancied I could hear her play one of those French compositions she so adored. How my father despised them! This sweet memory, however, rotted in the face of my renewed mourning.

Her basket of embroidery remained beside the fireplace, as if she'd only gone outdoors to watch the falling snow. How strange that I should find it here still after all this time. I half expected her to walk through the door with my father on her arm. There had been happiness here, long ago. There had been laughter despite the harshness of my father, and I had forgotten it. Perhaps I'd left it behind deliberately, as it brings me pain to recall even as I write this.

There was much to be done. I had letters to write, people to visit, assessments and arrangements to make, but it all seemed so trifling for some reason, so utterly unimportant now that I was sitting in my father's chair, *my* chair, before the fire in *my* sitting room. Tomorrow, the burden of all that I had to do to relinquish my rights to this place would fall squarely upon me, but tonight I was master. Master of the forest, the brook, the mausoleum. It all belonged to me. This dreary pile of rubble and faded memories was now entirely under my control.

I allowed myself this conceit for only a moment, for upon its heels came a disturbing realization. As I stared at the crackling fire, I knew I was horribly wrong. It is this house that exerts its control over me. I am not a superstitious man in the slightest, and I feel foolish writing such a thing. Even still, the feeling remains, and in the name of honesty, if nothing else, I put it to paper.

Before I could fall too deeply into misery, Peter brought me coffee and cakes, the latter of which I could only nibble. My appetite had not yet returned, though I made some effort to eat so as not to offend him. He inquired after my health, seemingly unaware.

"Rather worse for the wear, I suppose," I answered with a smile. "Sit down and have a drink with me." I removed a flask from my pocket and passed it to him. We had long forgone social graces, and Peter had once been as much a brother to me as a friend despite his station in life. My father had discouraged our play as children, but having neither brother nor friend of my own, I disobeyed him as I was wont to do. Peter became my only ally in all the world, and it feels so still.

"I cleaned the guns," he said. "If the weather clears, we ought to go out. Molly could use the exercise."

"What? Is that ugly, old dog still alive after all this time?"

"Christ, no," he laughed, but it fell away quickly. "She died after you left. I think losing both you and Lady Garrett so near one another was too much for her to bear. We've a tradition of passing down her name to a new pup." He whistled loudly, and we waited only a few moments before the gentle pat of paws sounded in the hall. A petite Irish setter trotted into the room, feathery red tail waving behind her.

"Gets her good looks from her father," Peter said. The dog stopped in her tracks when she saw me and let a low growl issue from deep within her throat. "You two have that in common, apparently," he added.

Even the dog mistook me for my father.

"Easy, girl," I cooed, extending my hand toward her. She approached me cautiously, growling all the while, and then sniffed my hand. My biology, at least, if not my face, is mostly my own, and the little creature realized I presented no great threat to her. After a wag of the tail and a brush of her tongue across my hand, she curled up before the fire and promptly fell asleep.

"Do you remember when my mother brought old Molly home?" I asked.

"Like it was yesterday." Peter smiled and took another drink from the flask. "Father was furious. He was worked enough without another 'miserable flea-bitten dog,' I think he put it."

"You never told me that."

"Well, you know my father, Will. All business."

For the second time tonight, I frowned at my own name. I did not feel like Will. No one had called me so in ages. Perceiving the turn in my spirits, Peter sobered as well and set the flask on the warm stones of the hearth.

"My father's body," I said. "Where is it being held? I will need to make arrangements."

Peter looked away, adjusting in his chair and drawing his hand down his face before answering.

"Christ, I thought someone had told you. Your father fell onto the outcroppings beneath the balcony. That's nearly fifty feet, Will. The wolves…"

I did not immediately know how to reply to this news, and I tried not to imagine the beasts of the forest quarreling over scraps of my father's body. These thoughts belonged only in nightmares, but they came unbidden nonetheless.

"Well…" I stammered. "Well, I suppose we shall have to have a funeral in any event."

"No one will come." He said this only as a statement of fact, without malice or cruelty. He was right, after all. "Much has happened since you went away, Will. Your father fell into such a state after you left. He never left the house, became prone to fits, and then when—"

"I've heard as much." In truth, I knew nothing of how my father whiled away his time during my absence, but I wished to hear no more.

He looked at me sharply. "You've heard then—the gossip?"

I leaned toward him and was about to inquire what he meant when Murdock appeared in the doorway and cleared his throat.

"Your bath is growing cold, sir," he said. "It would be a shame to heat the water twice."

"Right," Peter said. He stood with a whispered promise that we would continue our conversation at a later time, but I was no longer interested in bathing.

"Wait a moment. What gossip?" I asked.

"Peter." Murdoch folded his arms behind his back and blinked slowly, which told us both that he meant to offer up one of his lessons. We braced ourselves and he did not disappoint. "A gossip is the worst kind of villain," he said at last. "I trust you aren't making the master of the house an accomplice in your transgressions?"

Laughter crept into our throats, but we held our tongues. Suddenly, I was a schoolboy again, facing the threat of the paddle. Thoughts of sinister rumors and my father's corpse were gratefully forgotten.

I was obliged at last to retire to my quarters, lest the bath grow cold. I bid Peter and his father good evening and made my way up the stairs, my ancestors marking my progress until at last I reached Wilhelm Von Garrett, our family patriarch. Time had cracked the paint of this portrait, lending my great-great-grandfather a leprous countenance. I once flattered myself that I'd inherited my features from him, this powerful, unsmiling figure at the top of the stairs, but tonight I saw only my father, who has no portrait at all.

The room at the end of the hall had belonged to me all of my life, and so it was as familiar to me as an old friend. I knew the four-poster bed with its powder blue curtains, now faded and moth-chewed. I knew the sound of the birches tapping against the window and the wind that whistled down the chimney to hail me. It breathed life upon the fire, brightening the room. And yet, even as I stepped through the threshold, I sensed something unfamiliar, something foreign.

The scent of lavender mingled with the burning of cedar, but decay lingered beneath. A dead rat in the walls, perhaps. I had expected the room to feel vacant after my long absence, but it did not. On the contrary, I would not have been surprised to find my volume of *Robinson Crusoe* beside the bed, a scrap of paper marking some favorite passage or another. The fact remained, however, that I *had* left, and my poor, exhausted mind perceived this singular flicker of nostalgia as a senescence about the room itself, rendering my own presence unwelcome, or worse, unnecessary.

The strange sensation manifested only as a slight prickling of the hairs on my arms. No ragged breath caressed my ear. No shrouded figure awaited me behind the bed curtains. Yet I searched the room, scarcely daring to breathe.

Lavender clung to everything. My daughter has often asked me why I cannot drink tea steeped in the stuff and refuse bouquets of it in my examination room, and I have always neglected to answer her. The truth, safe in these pages for no eyes but my own, is that I cannot bear the memories it exhumes. My mother's lavender gardens had been well regarded in town, prized for their color and quality of scent. She fashioned wreaths of the dried twigs for midsummer, made hair oils for the men and candles for the women. The summer she died, my father set the garden afire. The smoke curled into the forest, the flowers' fragrance permeating all it touched, the oak trees and the sunflowers, the pastures, and the stables. The town smelled of her for weeks.

Surely Murdoch must remember this event. He must know how deeply this memory would wound me. I cannot pretend to know his mind when he scented my room, but I plan to give him a piece of mine tomorrow. Gone are the days where he can do as he pleases. This is my house now.

I suppressed the memory of my mother and, satisfied the room contained no ghouls but my own, I entered the bathroom and unbuttoned my shirt, tossing it across a wicker chair. The feeling of strangeness grew. Something, some small disturbance of air or light, drew my attention to the mirror. Had I seen a flash of white there? Had I heard the rustle of a woman's dress?

Surely fatigue conjured the image of a woman and reflected her into my mirror. Perhaps only hunger summoned the soft swish of silk outside the door. Murdoch had overstimulated my senses with his blasted lavender, and I saw spirits where there were only meddling housekeepers.

I had been touched by madness before, so I would recognize the warnings if it were to pounce upon me again. I cannot write more on the terrible interval of illness that befell me in the winter of 1880, the same that took my wife and young son. I have journals filled to the brim with this hideous period of my life and I can expend no more thought upon it, except to say that disease resurrected my own mother and carried her to my sickbed. I possessed a sound enough mind then to know she was a fever dream and nothing more. Tonight, I was wide awake and aware of my surroundings, cognizant of every drop of lavender oil in the bath, every crackle of wood in the fire, every hooting owl and screaming fox. I stood like a fool in the center of the room, bare feet planted on the cool floor, listening but unable to move.

"Sleep," I muttered to myself at last. That was all that I required. Still ill at ease, I continued with my tepid bath. I felt eyes upon me all the while, utterly exposed, and so hastened to dry myself and dress, but I could not find my trunk. I was ultimately obliged to rummage around in the wardrobe until I found an old robe from my youth, abandoned in the back behind a variety of women's dresses. Most unusual. Who the devil knows what went on here in the absence of a master. And some master I was with sleeves to my elbows and a hem that barely fell to my knees. Very dignified indeed.

Thus clothed, I made up my mind to wander about in search of my trunk and set my mind at ease with a bit of writing. Although I required no light in this room but the dying flicker of the fire, I lit a candle and the shadows slunk back behind the furniture. Armed with my candlestick, I fished my journal out of the pocket of my travel slacks and set out into the dark hall.

My fingers slid across the smooth wooden panels on the walls until I came to the locked door of my mother's quarters. Some demon tempted my hand to the knob, the cool beveled glass bringing to mind the summer sunlight. As a boy, I'd always marveled at the rainbows it refracted upon the floor. Footsteps down the hall stilled my hand.

A woman lifted her hand to my chamber door, and she became so still upon seeing me she might have been wrought by Corradini. Her silk dressing gown, buttoned all the way to the throat, shimmered in the dim candlelight. The shadow of dark hair tumbled down her back, and her skin gleamed ghostly pale, as if lit from inside. Large black eyes regarded me with an expression of horror, her hand on my door, and my hand on my mother's.

Neither of us stirred.

A warning, offered to me in passing during my journey, came abruptly to mind. *Your father's place isn't fit for anyone but the ghosts.*

Surely my eyes deceived me. It simply wasn't possible. And yet, I lost my breath merely looking at her, this strange and beautiful creature in my father's house. Before I could speak to her, she fled down the hall and vanished into the darkness. No footsteps sounded on the boards, no creaking panels or slamming doors broke the dismal silence of the night.

A drop of wax fell onto my thumb and returned me to my senses. Bah! I must have dozed off and been sleepwalking. Yes, yes, of course. I'd woken from the conjuring of my own weary brain to find I'd wandered out into the hall. Seeing no reason to disturb Murdoch with my foolishness, and not wishing to enter my quarters a second time, I took my candle downstairs to the sitting room where I managed to coax a few coals back into a small flame.

Angling my father's chair to view the garden, I placed the candle on the mantel and set to writing this entry, and to thinking, brooding really, about the mysterious woman I had seen in my dream. Surely, she can be nothing other than a product of my imagination, for she hadn't a single flaw. She was the most beautiful creature I had ever seen in my life, her black eyes as dark as the starless night beyond this window and somehow as bitterly cold.

The moon breaks now through the fabric of the sky, permitting me small glimpses of the skeletal remains of my mother's garden. Tomato cages pierce the earth like the white ribcages of vultures, and the glass chimes she had hung in the willow swing ever so slowly, without sound, refracting moonlight onto the shriveled husks of chrysanthemums. And overlooking all, the cemetery upon the hill, and the stark, gloomy structure of the family crypt.

My mother's loss is still as sharp to me as the spikes atop our gates, though she has been gone from this world for decades. My father, whose passing occurred little more than a month ago, has been dead in my heart for so long that his loss is only a crusted scar, improperly healed.

The candle has burned down to a guttering stump. Deep, malevolent shadows now dance across the whole of the room, but I do not feel the passing of time.

Sleep has always eluded me in this old house. I have grown accustomed to life in Baltimore, to the clatter of horse hooves on the street, to the cheerful shouting of children and the barking of dogs. Nestled within the silence of Ravenswood Hall there is disquiet. There is moaning and gnashing of teeth that a man feels deep inside himself. The years cling to the walls, weighing upon them so the stones groan and shudder like old bones.

Insufferable emptiness hollows out my chest as I sit, watching the stillness of ruin that has worked its evil here. My life in the city seems impossibly out of reach. I have lost my reputation, my medical practice, my colleagues, and the very ability to provide for my daughter, and for what, this vast wilderness that stretches out cold and savage beyond the glass?

Chapter III

A LETTER TO MISS CHARLOTTE GARRETT

*Ravenswood Hall to 14 Albany Square, Baltimore, Maryland
Postmarked January 10, 1889*

My dearest Lottie,

You asked me to write once I'd arrived safely, and while I can say I am indeed here at Ravenswood Hall, I cannot in good conscious relay any feeling of security. I don't wish to alarm you. I am safe enough in body, though my mind is ill at ease. I suppose I am as comfortable as a man can be in these circumstances, excepting that I'm rather the worse for lacking your company.

I'll spare you the details of the journey, largely because I don't wish to recount them save for a most peculiar interaction with a young boy at the Oak Mill Tavern. He offered me a silver trinket, and with it a grim warning.

I will enclose a rudimentary drawing of the thing. Do write me your thoughts when you've a moment? Beyond this, it was a cold and troubling ride, and I was grateful to have it over until I saw the state of this wretched place.

I cannot express to you the utter ruin that has befallen my childhood home, Lottie. Rats scuttle perpetually behind the walls, the floorboards bow like bones bent by rickets, and cobwebs gather insects as well as darkness into the corners. As my memories of it decayed and blackened over time, so too has it become in life. I was only about your age when I left here, and it pains me to think that its infernal influence has reached beyond me to you.

Forgive me, but I fear I may be required to stay here longer than I'd hoped. There is much to do before I can return to you. I've scarcely had a moment to inspect the place, but my list of repairs is long. The roof needs patching, the floors and banisters need refinishing, and the furnishings must be replaced, and this is only inside. Nature has had her way with Ravenswood Hall, and I've no doubt that if given a few years more, she would consume all, no trace left but a crumbling spire or a cracked headstone covered in moss. My father, your grandfather, has left us both a great burden, and I am sorry indeed to leave you so that I might make things right again.

Do not be afraid, my dear girl. I will have these unsavory matters settled soon, and I will return with funds sufficient to pay both the landlord and the grocer. Indeed, we shall never want for anything again. I swear it. Give my regards to Mrs. Olsen, whom I trust is treating you kindly and not plying you too full of those raspberry cakes.

All my love,

Papa

P.S. There is no need at all to accept another invitation from the Landons to perform one of your confounded séances. You know my feelings on this so-called spiritualism, and our present financial situation is no excuse for swindling those kind people out of their savings. I'll say no more about it.

WILLIAM GARRETT'S JOURNAL

January 10, 1889

Much has occurred in the hours after sunrise, so I have stolen away to record the details of all that has transpired, lest my memory fail me at a later time. I do not feel entirely master of myself and hope to find my voice again in these pages.

I did not sleep last night until the first fragments of dawn scattered through the naked oaks. It was a deep and dreamless slumber, blessed oblivion cut short by Murdoch and his cursed idioms about early birds and worms.

"Are you ill?" he asked, looking down at me. I blinked like a mole in the sun, but was grateful for it. Part of me believed I might never see the daylight again, so endless last night had seemed.

"Nothing a hearty breakfast can't cure, Mr. Murdoch," I answered, with as much cheer as I could muster, but I must have been a sight. I stretched my half-naked legs, and he huffed at me before walking out of the room. Pretty little Molly trotted in with a wagging tail, cheering me despite the strangeness of the night before. I patted her between the ears, and she thanked me by licking my knee.

"Breakfast is served at eight thirty, sir," Murdoch called from the doorway. The clock on the mantel read that time exactly, so I bothered not with dressing. I had no one to impress and only Murdoch to disappoint, so I cinched the belt of the preposterous robe around my waist and strode into the dining room, Molly close behind.

Murdoch had outdone himself. The polished tables and chairs, the silverware, and the china all shimmered in the morning sunshine. Fresh flowers from the greenhouse sat in a crystal vase situated exactly in the center of the table. My plate was set at the head, my father's place. Peter walked into the room with another place setting and arranged it at my right side before banishing the dog with a click of his tongue. She obeyed dutifully, if a bit dejected.

"I'm hardly dressed for company," I said to him.

"You're not dressed at all, Will," was his laughing answer. "It's good to see that city life hasn't dampened your sense of propriety. Miss Laveau will be down in a minute. You can take it up with her."

His gaze shifted to the doorway and the fork in his hand chimed against one of the teacups. I couldn't fathom why he had set a place for one of the servants. I turned to look.

The spirit from last night!

She stood beneath the threshold with her pale hands folded, either unwilling or unable to meet my gaze. Her hair, which last night had fallen freely to her waist, was now pinned up in the common fashion, and she wore a dress the color of cornflowers. I rose to my feet out of shock more than any sense of etiquette. When Murdoch first spoke of this Miss Laveau upon my arrival, I had imagined an old, portly housemaid. It never occurred to me last night that this creature could be her.

"Miss Laveau," Peter said, bowing and rescuing us both from a sort of horror-stricken paralysis. "May I present Dr. William Garrett, the master of this household."

Master of the household? I was barely master of myself. The woman recovered herself enough to curtsy, but she did not speak.

"Your father commissioned Miss Laveau's artistic talents," Peter said. "She is widely regarded in Spain." I waited for him to explain.

"His portrait," Miss Laveau answered. The delicate taste of Spain upon her tongue bewildered me. Her name was so clearly French that I once again presumed to know more than I reasonably could. This trait had greatly perturbed me in my father, and although I was its only witness now, its presence in me was a great humiliation.

"My father's portrait?" I repeated dumbly. I could only remember how adamantly he had refused to sit for one. My father did not have changes of heart. It was not his nature.

"*Pues*, I am having some difficulty with it now," she said, but I could not tell if she said so in jest. There was no humor in her voice. "You are his very likeness, Mr. Garrett."

Her gaze traveled the length of me, regarding my child's robe and bare feet with amusement alighting on her lips. Heat bloomed in my cheeks. She had been no specter, no dream. One of the most perfect examples of the female sex stood before me and I had not even combed my hair.

"F-forgive me," I stammered. "I was not expecting company."

She smiled and walked to her chair with the fabric of her dress clutched in her fist. Peter stifled another laugh.

"Perhaps Mr. Garrett would be more comfortable if I dined elsewhere today," the woman said, and then turned to me. "Your father often insisted on my company at his table, but I am pleased to eat in the kitchen if you wish." We both stood before our chairs, I waiting for her to sit and she awaiting my reply.

"Nonsense," I managed. "If my appearance is not offensive to you, we shall dine together."

"Will's appearance is offensive to everybody," Peter whispered, and Miss Laveau covered her mouth with long, delicate fingers. I imagined them working over embroidery or wrapped around a porcelain teacup. The slightest tinge of blue darkened her fingernails, and I wondered if she might be cold, though I did not have the courtesy, or perhaps the courage, to ask. Her warm, lighthearted laughter did not ripple in the black pools of her eyes.

"You forget your station, Peter," I said, smiling despite myself. He paid me no mind, as was always his custom. I motioned for the woman to sit, and she did so with a graceful dip of her head.

"I suppose we are, ah, *igual*," she said as I sat, the edge of her lip tilting upward.

"I don't know what you mean."

"We have both seen each other in our dressing gowns, so now neither of us is at a disadvantage." When she met my eyes, the whisper of suggestion upon her glance, Peter cleared his throat.

"I thought I was sleepwalking when I saw you," I said, but the heat in my face became so unbearable that I nearly reached for the vase of water at the center of the table.

"And I you," she replied. "It is a wonder we did not cross each other on the staircase. My bath had grown cold, so I went down to heat a pitcher of water. You were there when I returned."

"That was you in my room then? In the mirror?"

"Your room?" she exclaimed. "Peter, did you not show Mr. Garrett to his quarters last night?"

He served us overcooked strips of bacon and then turned to me sheepishly, answering, "A miscommunication. Your father gave your room to Miss Laveau. It does have the best view of the forest, and the drafts aren't so bitter as they are in the other chambers."

"And where shall I sleep, then?"

"We arranged the guest bedroom for you down the hall. I saw no reason to trouble Miss Laveau with relocating herself after all this time." The expression on my face must have conveyed my annoyance. Here I was, returned home after all these years, to find my own bedchamber had been given away to a stranger?

"My father should have told you," Peter said, sighing. "Ah, you had better have it out now. Am I to have my references?"

"Peter, the words I have to say to you cannot be uttered in the presence of a lady."

I could not remain angry with him anymore than I could blame this woman for our strange meeting last evening. Perhaps she thought I was a spirit, the ghost of my father returned to the halls he haunted in life. The horror in her eyes had been plain enough.

I dropped a sugar cube into my coffee only to occupy myself, for I preferred coffee bitter, and said, "I can only imagine what you must have thought of me, a strange man entering your bedroom, dirtying your bathwater. My God, I am sorry."

"I admit," she said, "I thought you were a nightmare. Peter told me of your coming, but I did not expect you to look so like your father. When I encountered you again in the hall, I am afraid I was overcome, and I fled to one of the guest rooms."

"You were frightened of him?"

"If you knew your father as well as I, you would not ask."

She stood, so I did as well, and she added to Peter, "I think I will breakfast in the studio. The shape of Mr. Garrett's brow has inspired me, and one cannot ignore inspiration when she strikes." She turned to me and curtsied again. "You will forgive me?"

I nodded, still taken aback by the abruptness of her departure, by everything. The strangeness of last night bled into the morning, made all the more stark and bizarre by the bright light of the cold winter sun. When the sound of her footsteps faded, I looked to Peter for explanation.

"Your father hired Miss Laveau not long after his sixtieth birthday," he said, as I sat. "A contract was drawn up between them affording her lodging until the date the portrait was completed. My father did not believe it proper to ask her to leave since the painting remains unfinished."

"He died before she could complete it, then. Surely his death voided the contract? Why does she remain?"

"Your father died before she was paid, Will. Perhaps she assumed his heir would make good on the contract?"

"I've no need of a portrait," I said.

"She brought a bit of light back into the place, if you ask me, and she has a fondness for lavender that reminds us all of your mother. You may wish to honor your father's bargain once you know her better."

I nodded again, pressing my finger to my lip. "Well, I've made quite a fool of myself in any event."

"Don't fret, Will," he said, and clapped me on the shoulder. "It's not the first time."

"I really ought to give you those references and be through with you."

"Perhaps you ought." He laughed and tilted his head to my full plate. "But not on an empty stomach."

I picked up my fork as he left the room, but I was not hungry. I could smell nothing but oil of lavender, and in my mind, I saw Miss Laveau before my mirror, dabbing a drop in the gentle hollow of her neck. These imaginings stirred something inside me, something I'd believed long dead. I twisted my wedding ring around my finger. Nine years, and I'd never once removed it. Somehow this morning it felt tighter.

She has utterly bewitched me and I do not even know her Christian name.

I hastened to dress after breakfast, as I wished to speak with our elusive family attorney who held an office in town. He had not answered my letters following publication of the article in *The Sun*, and so I had little choice but to appear before him in person.

I inspected my sleeping quarters while making my toilet, taking pains to comb my hair so I might resemble the master of the house, even if I did not feel it to be so. Perhaps once I'd made some effort to order my appearance, Miss Laveau might see me as the respectable doctor that I am and not as my father.

I walked around the comfortless room, bitter cold pouring down the chimney and dampening the spent coals. Strips of pale-yellow wallpaper clung to the walls like jaundiced flesh, which gave the room as a whole a rather ghastly and dismal quality.

Even still, my trunks had been unpacked, my clothing hung in the wardrobe, and instead of lavender I smelled only the faded cedar of the furniture, which I preferred. I would need to have the shutters repaired. One had fallen into the garden below and the other swung against the window in the wind. Perhaps I might find a craftsman in town.

Wilson had known my mind and readied the horses without instruction, so I needed only step into the carriage and be off. The gloom unwrapped its heavy shawl, a crystalline sun shining upon me as we carried on through the gates. Only the desolate aspect of the Hall suppressed my spirits, for my burden grew lighter by degrees the farther we traveled. The skeletal hemlocks that greeted me upon my arrival were now magnificent, shimmering beneath a glassy coating of ice. Only birdsong and the slick churning of our wheels cut through the stillness.

When we reached Main Street, the frigid air had so exhilarated me that I was almost merry. Wilson drove the horses past the general store, where I had often stolen away to plead for a morsel of licorice as a boy. The shopkeeper, a kind old man whose name I have forgotten, always had a handful to spare for me.

This blessed town looked just the same. I felt like old Scrooge with the Ghost of Christmas Past. I could walk it blindfold. Looking out the filthy carriage window, my boyhood flashing before my eyes, I momentarily forgot my father's plot to ruin me. It reared up after only a short while, when the horses stopped before a narrow building, set at the end of the street where the road turned sharply toward the river.

Wilson opened my door. "Here we are, sir. The offices of Mr. Hawkins, esquire, attorney at law."

"Thank you, Wilson," I answered, emerging from the carriage. I pulled my hat down over my eyes and squinted as the sun glared off a large window, rendering it impossible to see inside. The sign above the door, while small, had been recently polished, its golden lettering gleaming.

"Shall I wait for you here, sir?" Wilson asked.

"Come 'round in an hour, would you?"

He nodded, climbed back up to his post, and drove off, leaving me alone with my duties. I pulled open the door, but no bell heralded my entry. Instead, an emaciated gray cat wound itself around my legs, its patchy fur clinging to my trousers. I muttered a curse and tried to step away from the thing, but it seemed intent on tripping me.

"Fezziwig!" an old man shouted, his voice booming in the small space. My hand flew to my heart. I must have cried out in surprise because the cat slunk beneath Mr. Hawkins' desk, which was situated beneath the improperly stuffed bust of a moose. It was preposterously too large for the space and jutted out so far into it that one had to duck to sit at the desk. The creature's glass eyes bulged, and a portion of its jaw hung loose, exposing a shriveled tongue.

"Forgive me," I breathed, but I could find no other words but these.

"The apologies are mine," he said. I remembered his accent from the few times he had visited the house but could not have picked him out in a crowd. He was perhaps English, for remnants of the accent were old and stale on his tongue. He must not have seen his homeland in many years. "Old Fezziwig hasn't realized he ought to be dead already. Bastard keeps clinging onto life."

I cleared my throat, unsure how to begin. He pushed his spectacles up the bridge of his nose, and it occurred to me how bitterly cold his office was. Indeed, it might have been warmer outside in the sun. I shivered, glancing at the stove that had but a single glowing coal.

"The cold is cheap, Dr. Garrett," he said.

"You recognize me, then, sir?"

He smiled, smoothing hair as patchy and gray as the cat's with his palm.

"Why, you're a regular bull, just as he was. Pity your tailor, having to fit those shoulders." He chuckled to himself, and then frowned, adding, "You've grown into his brow and grim countenance as well, I see. Of course, I suspect your inheritance is the reason you've come."

I resented his evaluation of me. I saw the same each time I looked in a mirror and did not need reminding.

"I'm sorry to arrive without an appointment, Mr. Hawkins," I answered. "I've tried to reach you via messenger and post and have had no reply."

"Yes, you will forgive me. I am bound by your father's wishes." He motioned for me to sit. I bowed beneath that ghastly moose and slouched into the proffered chair across from him. "Your father went to a great deal of trouble, you see, to ensure your arrival here in the Catskills. He was certain you would not come unless—"

"I had no choice in the matter," I finished.

"Quite right, sir. I could have cleared up many matters if I'd been allowed, but your father's will forbade me from answering your letters."

I reached into my pocket and withdrew the article, asking, "You've read his message to me, then?"

"Certainly. It was I who sent it to print."

"I must tell you that none of it is true. It was a lie told to draw me back."

Mr. Hawkins removed his glasses to polish them with a handkerchief. I waited, my impatience growing.

"May I be frank with you, Dr. Garrett?" he asked at last.

"Please."

"It is of little consequence to me if your father's accusations regarding your mother's death are true. I have known your family a long time, and I watched Oliver descend, if you will, into madness, as surely as I watched your mother. This letter was written long before lunacy sullied his mind."

"What do you mean, 'lunacy'?" I asked. I was all too aware of my mother's collapse into herself. I had witnessed with my own eyes the ruin that madness wrought upon her soul, and I had watched as my father tired of it. Mother's fall into lunacy had been a slow, painful meandering, as if she had only lost her way. Somewhere on this path, my father began to resent that she could not find it in herself to carry on. I still bear the scars he had intended for her. A particularly ugly one on my back burned as I sat before Mr. Hawkins' watery gaze.

"My father was a cruel man, but he was not mad," I said, but even as the words left my mouth, it was too easy to believe he could succumb to such a thing.

"Over time your father lost his ability to see reason," Hawkins replied. "Each letter you returned to him unread hardened his heart against you. Years passed. He became reclusive, and the only living soul who could comfort him seemed to be that painter he brought on."

"Painter?" I asked, Miss Laveau's features blossoming behind my eyes like a beautiful mirage.

"Yes, that whole nasty business with the painter," he said. "I think that's what did it, that's what cast him down into the maelstrom once and for all. In any event, I often asked him to reconsider that letter. It would be easy enough to send a messenger to retrieve you, but I could not persuade him in the end, and so here you are."

I found myself unable to speak. Too many questions crowded my brain, and I could not sort them.

"There is something else you should know," he said.

"Yes?"

"Your father made an appointment with me before he died." Mr. Hawkins opened a leather-bound appointment book and traced the dates with a long, bony finger. "Here it is. Yes, we were to meet January fourth at nine o'clock."

"When did he make this appointment?"

"Coincidentally, the day before his death. I thought at the time that perhaps he'd had a change of heart, but I suppose we'll never know."

The cat mewed under the desk and then sprung up onto my lap before bounding to the floor. A moment later, the door opened, and the beast assaulted the pant leg of the poor fellow who entered.

"Ah, Watson. You've arrived," Mr. Hawkins said, standing. He turned to me. "I'm afraid that's all the time I can give you at the moment, Dr. Garrett. Ah." He rummaged through his papers, extracted a single sheet, and handed it to me.

"What's this?" I asked.

"Your father's last will and testament. It was last amended several years ago, but I think you'll find all in order. You are the executor of his whole estate. There is no other heir. Do visit me again if I can be of any further assistance."

I stood, nearly hitting my head on moose's hanging jowl, and he shook my hand, but I was too dumbfounded to offer him any answer. The visitor tipped his hat to me as I walked by him.

"Mr. Hawkins," I said, turning again to the attorney. "Can you point me in the direction of a craftsman or skilled laborer?"

"Certainly. There's a Texan on the river. Goes by the name of Walter. If there's a job to be done, he's a fine choice."

Nodding my thanks, I walked back out onto the street with my father's will grasped in my fist. I was uncertain what I ought to do with the information I'd been given. Had my father foreseen some portent of his demise? And what of Miss Laveau? I'd met her only hours ago, but I doubted she could play any great role in his descent, as Mr. Hawkins called it, into madness. Certainly no greater role than I, who abandoned him to it. The seed of guilt that sprung up in my heart quickly shriveled as my scars ached with cold.

At length, my feet carried me toward the river, knowing the way despite my mind's presence elsewhere. I asked a young boy where I might find the man named Walter, and he pointed a grimy finger toward a workshop near the wharf.

As I neared the workshop, the river a rippled sheet of glass beside me, I beheld a man laboring over a small, beautifully wrought cabinet. He polished its intricately carved door with a cloth, and then wiped his hands on his apron when my footsteps sounded on the gravel.

"What can I do you for?" he called, but rather than offer me his hand, he engaged himself in affixing a metal pull to one of the drawers. A wad of chewing tobacco bulged in his lower lip.

"Good morning, sir," I answered. "Are you the craftsman named Walter?"

"Well, I ain't a dancer," he said, motioning to the cabinet. I was in no humor for games.

"Forgive me for interrupting your work, but your name was given to me by Mr. Hawkins, and I'm in great need of a man who can quickly make repairs to my estate."

"Whereabouts do you live?"

"My name is William Garrett. The place is Ravenswood Hall, up the mountain. Do you know it?"

I could see by the stiffening of his shoulders that he did. He set his box of nails on the ground and straightened, leveling his gaze to mine for the first time.

"That woman still boarding there?" he asked.

"Woman?"

"The Spaniard."

"Miss Laveau? Yes."

"Then I 'spect you won't find a man in the whole state willing to do work for you long as she's livin' there."

"I beg your pardon? She's only a painter."

"Don't give a damn what you say she is, but she ain't right with the Lord, comin' back from the dead like she done."

"From the dead? What the devil do you mean?"

"You ain't from around here, are you?" He spat his tobacco into an old coffee tin and wiped his whiskers.

"Not anymore."

"That whole place is full of devils, Mr. Garrett. I once sent my boy up there to help the old man fix up the stable door, said he saw a lady ghost out on the widow's walk. Won't go near it no more. Can't say I blame him."

The mention of the widow's walk chilled my heart. It had been my mother's favorite place in the whole house, and the place she had chosen to die. The image of her lifeless body, slumped in a chair facing the forest, came unbidden into my mind, and I closed my eyes to rid myself of it. I had not seen this terrible vision in so long that I believed it had been forgotten. I resented the craftsman for recalling it so efficiently into the forefront of my memory.

"Sure as hell hope you know how to use a hammer," he added, turning his attentions back to the cabinet. "Only man who'll work up there is you."

I bid him goodbye between my teeth and left him alone with his work, chiding Hawkins for directing me to such a superstitious and ignominious man. What a fool's errand this had been.

I wandered the town for another hour, searching for a man I might hire, but I was unable to find even a chimney sweep who would set foot on the property. Feeling dejected and piteous, I turned at last toward the livery, where Wilson waited for me, and I read my father's will as I walked. He had indeed left the whole of his earthly belongings to me, but when I arrived at an article near the end, I stopped cold.

Only after the house shall be inhabited for the length of one year may the heir retrieve allowances, a sum of ten thousand dollars, from the bank. No access shall be afforded to these monies prior, under any circumstance, nor shall any items or heirlooms be sold from the estate until the allotted time is completed.

It was fortunate that I'd reached the square and coincidentally a set of benches, for I had no more strength in my legs to continue. I dropped down onto the seat, the damp wood seeping through my trousers, and read the passage again and again.

I had intended to use my father's account to restore the estate so some unsuspecting bastard might take it off my hands. What in God's name was I to do now? I hadn't even credit with the grocer. My father had so efficiently ruined me that I could see no way to sort it out.

Hot, angry tears burned my eyes, and I yearned to see my wife, to hear her steady voice and feel her cool hand on my cheek. I did not allow this weakness to spill down my cheeks. Control over my own sentiments remained mine, in the least. I should not surrender it all so easily to him.

"Are you unwell, sir?" Wilson asked, leaning over me with an expression of distress. I straightened, pulling my hat down low over my eyes. "You often came here as a boy to feed the ducks. I thought you might find your way here again."

"I'm at a river I can't cross, Wilson," I said by way of reply. "Nor can I turn 'round."

"It's not so hopeless as that, sir, is it?"

"You would do well to stay out of matters you cannot understand," I replied, but I heard my father's stern voice. I cringed as Wilson fell back and mumbled an apology, and I immediately wished to call back the words. What had come over me to speak so wickedly to this man, who had only ever shown me kindness?

The recollection of all these matters weighs too heavily upon me, and the dinner bell has rung. I shall continue once my strength has been restored.

Chapter IV

WILLIAM GARRETT'S JOURNAL

January 10, 1889, continued

Wilson drove the horses down a road I'd not seen in many years and almost did not recognize but for the massive oak. My cousin, Anna, had broken her arm after falling from the tree's branches. A burr of regret clung to me as we passed. I'd buried the bones of this place so completely that I'd nearly forgotten Aunt Meredith and Anna.

"I thought we might call upon your kin, sir," Wilson called from his post. "She always lifted your spirits, she did!"

I could not admonish him for the presumption. Visiting them ought to have been my first order of business, but admittedly I was so ensnared by my own misery I could not see beyond it.

Wilson slowed the horses as we reached what had once been the gravel drive. Tangles of weeds and dried grasses choked the path and climbed the dilapidated fence posts. Decay pressed down upon the once cheerful farmhouse, stripping the paint and sitting upon the wooden porch until it sagged at the center. Burlap curtains hung limp inside the windows.

Perhaps my aunt and cousin had gone away for the winter. The windows of the nearby greenhouse, once perpetually clouded with the warm moisture of Aunt Meredith's many plants, were filthy and cracked. I exited the carriage into a sudden downpour of sweeping rain and traipsed through the grasses, wondering if they had abandoned the place.

"Annie?" I called, approaching the porch. The curtain to my right swept aside, and a pale face peered out at me.

"Will?" the lips mouthed, and then the curtain fell. A moment later, the door flew open and my little cousin stood before me, very much a woman now, but somehow less of a woman than she had been before. She stood with bare arms wrapped around her waist, her figure so frail I feared she might collapse, so I was prepared to catch her when she fell, sobbing, into my arms.

"Oh, Will," she murmured into my shoulder. This was not the greeting I had expected. I would have been more prepared for a slap across the cheek and to be turned away from the house unseen, but tears I could not manage.

"What the devil is the matter?" I asked, and she lifted her head to meet my gaze. The decay had invaded her gently, the way it blackens the soft edges of a rose before it withers. A subtle hollowness took hold beneath her hazel eyes. I had once likened the color of these eyes to cattails, but time had somehow darkened them. It sharpened the angle of her jaw and drew lines around her mouth.

"Look at us," was all she said, and she needn't say more. I could tell by the sight of her that her mother, my aunt, was gone from this earth, and with her everything she'd ever held dear.

"You never came back," Anna murmured into my chest.

"I'm sorry," I said again and again, embracing her, but the words did little to express the guilt that weighed upon my breast. In the entirety of my life, I had never seen Anna cry, not even after she injured her arm. She had the nerves of a man, and all the softness of a woman. This life, the one I had abandoned her to, had broken her, and I held the pieces in my arms.

She pushed me away, the tiniest spark of the girl I knew flashing in her swollen eyes, and then wiped her face on a kerchief. "You've become a regular old man, haven't you?" she said, smiling and touching the gray at my temple.

"I'm not yet eight and thirty," I laughed, but I felt my age. This place added years to the marrow of my bones.

"Well, you had better come inside before your rheumatism flares up."

My God, I had missed her.

The exterior of the house had deceived me. My dear cousin had not let ruin inside. She'd held it at bay with a warm fire cracking in the grate, a teakettle hanging over the flames, and her mother's shawl draped over the wing chair in the corner, where it had always been. It warmed my heart to see it so, and I smiled. I could tell by the blankets upon the sofa that my cousin had been sleeping in the sitting room where it must have been easier to tend the fire. She poured us both a cup of tea and placed the china on a small table, which she dragged to the sofa where I had settled myself.

"For God's sake," I said, rising again. "Let me help you." As expected, she set her thin hand upon my shoulder and pushed me down, never one to accept assistance from a man, nor suffer one to complete a task she could do on her own. I wondered how long she had been here alone.

"Aunt Meredith..." I said, after a hesitation. She met my eyes with a long sigh, and then collapsed beside me on the sofa, her teacup rattling against the saucer.

"It was her heart," she answered.

"How long ago?"

"Last year. The land's been sold. The gentleman was kind enough to let me remain on the grounds as a tenant. I still grow a few flowers to sell in town, enough to pay my dues, but I am no botanist like my mother. He's built a grand house in the upper field, where you and I used to swing from the birches." Tears welled up in her eyes again. They were angry tears, the burning kind. "You're soaked to the bone," she said, her voice thick. "You won't catch cold?"

"You always were a worrier." I smiled, leaning toward the fire and wrapping my half-frozen fingers around the teacup. "My daughter takes after you, I think."

"Your daughter?" Her eyes widened in what I presumed to be surprise, but the blood left her lips.

"Yes. Lottie," I replied. I could only interpret her expression to mean that she believed I'd be a poor excuse for a father. Judged by my father alone, I suppose she had reason for it.

Some of the color returned to Anna's cheeks, and she shook her head as she brushed a blonde ringlet away from her face, sighing deeply before murmuring, "I gave you up for dead, you know. When I heard the Murdochs were making preparations for you, I could hardly believe it."

I listened to the sleet against the windowpanes for a long while, cold to my bones and utterly ashamed of myself.

"I can't ask you to forgive me, Annie," was all I could manage.

"I wish you would."

I sat my cup on the table and took her hands in mine. "Cousin, would you? Could you ever forgive me? Come stay with me. Leave this old house. I'll have Murdoch make up one of the guest rooms for you."

She held my gaze, her eyes awash with tears. "I could not ask such a thing of you."

"Then do not ask, only accept." I pressed her hand. "I will not leave you here alone. Not again."

"That house is a dark place," she said instead of answering. She withdrew her hands from mine and set them in her lap before leaning back against the sofa. "Momma and I went to live with Uncle when you went away, has anyone told you that?" I shook my head. "She managed the servants, and I tended the garden. Uncle's grief hardened to hatred, and it made him so cruel that most of the help fled in tears. No one ever returned, and no one ever sought new work there. Momma worked herself to the bone. She was master of the house in every aspect, but Uncle treated her like a scullery maid."

"Why did she stay?"

"He was her brother. That's what you do for family."

Anna lifted her eyes to mine for only an instant, long enough to reveal that the comment bore more weight than the words alone. The disdain in her eyes, darkened by an infection of Father's hatred of me, lingered there. She had every right to loathe me, but it cut straight to the bone.

"Don't mistake me, though," she continued. "Momma held her own. I suspect their shouting matches were heard all the way in town."

"They argued?"

She nodded and gulped her tea as if she were dying of thirst. "In the beginning I think he was glad to have her. He retreated into himself as the years passed, but the loneliness wore on him. I brought the post to him every day, Will. He was always holed up in his study, running his hands down his face and mumbling to himself. You never wrote him, not once, but he never stopped waiting for your letter."

"He abused my mother until she was only a husk of herself," I said, a shiver creeping down my arm so violently that my hand trembled. "Until there was nothing for her to do but end her life. My mother is dead because of him. That's why I left. How could I stay?"

"We have that in common, then," Anna replied, her eyes on the burning fire. "Your father had a way of sucking the life from people, didn't he?" When I didn't reply, she added, "I think we might have got on all right if Momma hadn't convinced him to sit for that portrait."

"What do you mean?"

"She found him a painter, who I suppose you've met now.

When she first arrived, she woke something in him, but her disappearance was too much for him to bear."

"Disappearance?"

"Oh, yes. There was an inquiry."

"Into what?"

Anna looked down at her teacup, examining the remaining leaves like a soothsayer.

"Murder," she answered, her voice sharp. She set the teacup down on the table and stood, warming her hands over the fire with her back to me.

"Whose murder?"

"Why," she said, turning. "Miss Laveau's."

"But she obviously returned." When she did not reply, and instead turned back to the fire, I added, "Quite *alive*."

"Not before Constable Devlin investigated your father for her murder. Many of the people in town still believe she did it." Anna's shoulders rose and fell with a great breath. She returned to the sofa but did not look at me.

"I don't follow."

"When she returned, her influence over your father became too great," she continued. "We begged him to release her from her contract. Instead, he turned us out. Momma was dead a month later. I think she was living for him, for Ravenswood. And now she's gone. Everything's gone."

"Not everything."

"Yes, you've returned, haven't you?" This was not spoken with kindness.

"Surely if Miss Laveau is here now, she wasn't murdered, least of all by my father."

"That was sufficient for the constable," she said. "But your father believed it to the last. He thought she was a ghost, in the end."

I laughed, believing the remark a poorly told joke, but her frown revealed otherwise.

"Forgive me, Annie, but it's absurd. You can't possibly

believe this nonsense."

"Don't take it from me. Dr. Johnston has records of your father's delusions. Whether I believe in it or not is of no consequence. The townspeople can be terribly superstitious. I can only tell you the facts, and the fact is that Miss Laveau disappeared for months. When she returned, your father went positively mad."

"And you're certain Miss Laveau played a role in this?"

"I am as sure of it as I was of your demise, but then again, here you are."

I did not know how to respond to this, so I ran my hand over my beard, finishing my tea as the logs popped and cracked in the grate. The chill had gone from me except for a portion of my spine, where it thrived and slipped along my vertebrae like a salamander.

"She haunted him, Will, until he could bear it no longer."

"She's only a woman, Anna."

"Yes, well, I suppose your father had forgotten that. Take care that you do not."

I stayed at Anna's house until dusk, much of that time spent convincing her to leave it. At length, she yielded, and after assisting her in the packing of a small trunk, I obliged poor Wilson to take us back up the wicked mountain. The clouds had cleared away and constellations of stars speckled the darkness with their faerie dust. My spirit might have been glad for this happy change in the weather, but Anna's warning resounded in my mind even as my lungs breathed in the clean, frozen air.

Once restored to my quarters, with Anna secured at last in the guest room at the end of the hall and my conscious slightly sated, I sequestered myself to write these pages, leaving only upon the tolling of the bell for dinner. When I stepped into the hall, the door to my mother's boudoir opened, and Miss Laveau emerged from the room.

"Do you require something of me?" she asked, perceiving my bewildered expression.

"That door is to remain locked at all times," I said. I had imagined I would be the first to cross the threshold of my mother's room, the first to look upon her things, shut up for so many years. That a stranger had come before me was an inconceivable violation. "Who opened it for you?"

"Pardon," she said, and she closed the door behind her. "Your father gave me the key."

"I can't believe that."

"*No soy una mentirosa.*"

Some madness struck me then, for I opened the door with such haste that she was forced to step out of my way. I heard the gentlest inhalation of breath, but she did not admonish me, nor appear in the slightest bit disturbed, as though this behavior was expected from me. Thus far, I had given her no reason to fear me less than the ghost of my father. I was a brute, and it embarrasses me still to think of it.

I stood not inside my mother's boudoir, but in an artist's studio. Bottles of paint lined the windowsills, and brushes of varying sizes were laid out on a silver tray, drying in the meager rays of sun. A wicker table took the place of my mother's favorite chair, no doubt cast into a seldom-used room to gather cobwebs. Easels and trays stood in every corner of the room, the largest before the pair of windows that overlooked the garden and gravel drive. This puzzled me, for I clearly recalled the left window being broken. The curtains were not lace, but emerald velvet drawn aside and held by heavy woven tassels. What state of mind must I have been in when I arrived here to imagine a thing so far from the truth?

"Where are my mother's things?" I asked.

"Your father and the younger Mr. Murdoch moved them to the attic. If I have offended you, I beg your forgiveness. Your father was a cruel man, but he did afford me a lovely room in which to paint."

"He was cruel to you, then?" I turned to face her, expecting perhaps to see trouble in her expression, or sadness, but such impassioned hatred blazed in her dark eyes that I was taken aback. It fell into a sort of sublime bemusement so quickly that I wondered if I had imagined it.

"Does that question amuse you?" I asked.

"Yes," she said, but I did not know which one of my questions she answered. She traced her fingers over the back of a velvet wing chair and then looked at me with narrowed eyes.

"*Santa Maria*, you are his exact likeness," she whispered, and a moment later those fingers lifted my chin toward the light. I daren't even breathe. No mere specter laid her warm hand upon my cheek, but a woman of flesh and blood. How innocently she conjured all within me that was *man*. I could not step away, though I wished to, for she had summoned my wife's easy smile with one of her own.

"Your nose is slightly less offensive," she said with finality. Her hand fell again to her side. "You must have inherited it from your mother."

"Yes," I replied, not comprehending the insult she had paid me.

"Do you want to see it?" Miss Laveau asked, unaffected by my bewilderment. A moment passed before I understood her meaning.

"My father's portrait?"

"Is there another?"

She removed the sheet, and I beheld the unfinished figure of my father. His broad shoulders and chest, clad in his old army uniform, filled the entirety of the canvas. Where anyone might have seen muscle and bone that had carried me to church or set me atop my first horse, I saw only arms that had wielded a switch of birch. She had portrayed the strength in him valiantly but none of the cruelty. That, I suppose, was all in his face, which remained a vacant ring of spectral white.

"You are very talented," I said. She folded the sheet quietly and set it upon the sofa.

"Thank you, Mr. Garrett. I am sorry to show it to you incomplete, but your father doesn't sit for me anymore."

Her smile slid through the somber atmosphere, and I laughed without meaning to.

"He was a bastard." I don't know what came over me to speak in such a way. There was something about her manner that made a man easy, as if he were speaking to a dear friend or a cousin who already knew all of his secrets. She replied with the gentlest upturn of her lip. Even in spite she was beautiful.

"Mr. Garrett," she said, her eyes examining my face, but somehow not all together looking at me.

"Will, please."

I still do not understand why I said this. This shortening of my name often aggravates me, but I could not call it back once spoken. Her eyes met mine, her expression suspicious.

"That is hardly proper," she said. "We are perfect strangers."

I bowed, begging her pardon in a blundering sort of manner, which she gave without pause. She set her hand over her mouth gracefully and there was as much laughter in her eyes as blood in my face.

"Dinner will be getting cold," I said. "I trust you will notify Murdoch should you require anything?"

"Thank you, I shall."

I nodded, my hands folded behind my back, and made my way with long strides to the door.

"Mr. Garrett," she said behind me.

"Yes?"

"You are so like your father, in the jaw and the hairline. Might you consider sitting for me?"

"For my father's portrait?"

"Yes. And if you are pleased with the result, perhaps I could paint yours as well. Then you should have your empty frames filled."

"Yes, perhaps."

I had no desire to sit before this woman's gaze for hours on end, pretending to be my father. There simply wouldn't be time for idleness. Why, then, had I agreed? Silence settled between us. There was nothing more to say. When I could bear it no longer, I turned again to take my leave.

"One last thing," she called after me, and her face brightened when my eyes met hers. "My name is Lenora."

I bowed and left her with my faceless father.

Chapter V

WILLIAM GARRETT'S JOURNAL

January 10, 1889, continued

The attic door at the far end of the hall called my attention before I could turn to the dinner bell, which rang again. I could not bear the thought of my mother's belongings moldering up there, and I wished to see them. A quick look to confirm their condition, I decided, and then I could sup in peace.

A shadow passed beneath Anna's door as I walked on down the hall, and she opened it an instant later as though she had been waiting for me.

"Cousin," she breathed with a smile, clutching a tattered quilt to her throat. "I thought I heard you in the hall."

"Shall I have Peter tend your fire?" I asked, for frost had settled in her voice and alighted on her skin, drawing the blood from her cheeks.

"Just a chill from the carriage," she answered, wrapping the quilt tighter. "Where are you off to? Are the Murdochs serving dinner in the attic now?"

I snickered at this absurd remark and revealed the fate of my mother's things. "Would you like to accompany me?"

"Not on your life or mine," she answered, and the ice cracked again in her throat. "You haven't seen them yet, have you?"

"Seen who?"

A pregnant hesitation, and then, "This is not the place you remember, Will. Things linger here."

"I don't understand your meaning."

At least, I wished I had not understood it. I wished she would tell me with her schoolteacher's grin that there was nothing in the attic but the sturdy rafters and a trunk of dusty blankets.

"Forget I mentioned it. Just the fancies of a lonely girl with too grand an imagination." A smile and a quick exhalation of breath cleared her countenance. She kissed me on the cheek, and then asked, "Will you ask Peter to save a plate for me? I heard the bell, but I'm not quite settled."

"Of course," I said, but this exchange troubled me. As a child, Anna feared nothing. That she had succumbed now to superstition spoke more of the years she'd passed here than even the wasting in her face or the haze of grief in her eyes.

She bade me goodnight, a weary smile lifting only one side of her mouth, and I continued on. Before I reached the attic door, however, a rustle drew my attention back toward the staircase, halting my journey a second time. I glanced over my shoulder to find young Christine standing quite still at the top of the stairs, her hair in loose curls all around her face. The dog stood beside her, motionless but for a slight wag of her tail.

"Good evening, Christine," I said as pleasantly as I could manage. A little chirp squeaked out of her throat and she flew back down the stairs. Molly cocked her head and must have decided I was unfit company, for she followed the child down and out of sight.

Bah. A strange dog for an even stranger child. They could

have each other.

The heavy attic door made no sound as I pushed it into the darkness. I lit the candle I'd taken from the hall table and ascended.

The flame flickered as I rose higher, a bitter draft drawing shadows from the wick and casting them all about me. So thick was the darkness that my light illuminated only those few steps ahead and nothing beyond. Surely there must be some chink in the boards, some crack in the roof after such a time of disrepair that might permit a shard of moonlight into the place. I held my candle up high over my head, searching for the glint of a lamp on one of the old desks.

I know every part of this house, and this attic, by memory, as familiar to me as my own face in the glass. I know the wooden beams that crisscross over the ceiling and the broken mirrors in their gilt frames, which seem to reflect the fractured faces of long-dead ancestors. I know the strange forms of dust-softened curtains, which appear at once as nothing more than piles of old fabric, and then as hunchbacked beasts. While imagination had been my dear friend in childhood, it became my enemy as I reached the top of the staircase.

I swept a lamp off a clawed night table and lit it with the candle flame. I've never lit a lamp with so much haste in all of my life. Enough oil remained to light my way for perhaps a quarter of an hour, though I had no intention of staying so long. I could send Murdoch and Peter after my mother's chair and her other belongings. Surely, she wouldn't mind abandoning them for a day longer if it meant saving me from the contraction of pneumonia. The bitter air settled deep inside my lungs, and I feel it still even as I write. Perhaps the illness has already taken hold.

Whether the tremors in my hands were a result of the terrible cold or of fear, I know not. The lamplight swung about the room and splashed upon the walls in such a maniacal manner that it might have possessed its own volition. I wished to leave. Yet, inexplicably, I walked farther into the room, my shadow an amorphous lump of darkness behind me. The lamp cast the halo of light upon an old wardrobe, which I remembered had once been in my father's study.

Drawn inexorably toward it, I continued. A trick of light gave it the appearance of movement, a slight shifting of mass first to the right, and then to the left. I watched as if from above as my trembling hand reached for the knob.

"Enough, boy," a voice whispered behind me. I spun, holding the lamp high. I saw no one. I knew the voice with as much certainty as I knew that it was impossible to hear it.

"Hello?" I called into the darkness. Only the groaning ceiling beams replied, no match for the ceaseless wind. Good God, what demon had driven me here? I fled from the room and down the narrow staircase, certain that some dark and malignant creature pursued me.

The light from the hall shone bright, as sweet to me as summer sunshine, and so great was my hurry to escape the monsters of my own imagination that I ran directly into Miss Laveau, knocking her and my candle to the floor.

"My God," I said, dropping to my knees by her side. "Are you hurt?" She shook her head and accepted my proffered hand. Her fingers were colder now, mine enormous and clumsy.

Spanish slipped out under her breath as I helped her to her feet. The words, though unknown to me and likely disparaging, I found rather beautiful.

"You've torn your dress." I pointed to the hem around her left foot, which had ripped, exposing the lace beneath.

"It seems you have torn my dress, Mr. Garrett," she said, though her smile revealed that she held no real ill will against me. She brushed herself off and said, "You have seen a ghost up in your attic?"

"Not exactly."

I was hardly certain I had *heard* a ghost. My diet had been disrupted, my whole life in fact. The disembodied voice was surely nothing more than a morsel of poorly cooked bacon. In the words of a certain Ebenezer Scrooge, there was more of gravy than of grave in my strange hallucination.

Miss Laveau nodded solemnly, retrieving the pieces of my candle. "Hamlet's father, perhaps?"

"Perhaps."

"He visits frequently to ensure my continued progress on his portrait, you know."

"Surely you're joking."

"Surely." She turned back toward the stairs. "We haven't been properly acquainted, Mr. Garrett. Come and dine with me, if you have the time."

I followed her downstairs, my wits returning to me. The scent of roast duck mingled with smoke from the crackling logs in the fireplace below, and it steadied my hands. I put my father's voice out of my mind as we entered the dining room and took our seats. Murdoch, sour for having kept the food warm so long, set our first course before us. I'd had my fill of oysters in Baltimore and the little morsels bobbing in our soup appeared as appetizing as slugs.

"You must think me such an intruder," she said, and sipped her soup. I assured her that her presence here was no intrusion. "Thank you. I won't forget your hospitality."

"I've hardly been hospitable," I said, laughing. I picked up my spoon but could not bring myself to eat. "You'll have to forgive me. I think I've been too long in the city."

Her laugh reminded me of sparrows in the spring—cheerful, full of natural confidence, but somehow busy.

"I am sorry about your dress," I offered. "Perhaps Christine could mend it for you."

"Never mind," she said with a wave of her hand. "It will give me an occupation when my muse is otherwise engaged."

"Do you paint often?"

"As often as I can. The forests are a lovely subject in the spring, when the daffodils are all abloom. They remind me of our garden in Málaga."

My mother had loved the daffodils, so much so that she would spend all day wandering the woods, gathering the blossoms in her basket. I did not tell this to Miss Laveau. The memory was sacred to me, a piece of parchment that would crumble when exposed to the light.

"In Spain?" I asked. "Your name is French, is it not?"

"Yes, my father was French. My mother was born in Málaga, near the sea, where we were raised."

"You have siblings, then?"

"A sister," she answered, and her spoon clattered against the porcelain.

Christine appeared from the kitchen, wheeling a cart much too large for her. Miss Laveau rose to help, but after darting an anxious glance in her direction, the child ignored the offer and set a silver tray of roast duck and peas before me. I was no longer accustomed to such beautifully prepared and lavish meals. Lottie and I ate only what we required, and we were as satisfied with rye bread and soup as we were with mutton cutlets. I could not help but imagine how she would have enjoyed all this, though.

Mem.: I must speak with Murdoch about this. No doubt my father has provided him a certain allowance for these meals, and I should think it would be better spent elsewhere. I am master now, after all, and decisions are no longer made according to Father's will, but my own.

Miss Laveau sat again beside me, carrying her own plate, but Christine lingered. She twisted her braids between her fingers, as if gathering courage, and then leaned toward me.

"She's not real," she whispered in my ear at last. Miss Laveau's mouth fell open, and the child ran from the room.

"She hasn't said a word in months," Miss Laveau said. "What did she say to you?"

"What a strange girl," I said, but I did not repeat her words. They had chilled me, as nonsensical as they were. We allowed the seeping quiet to invade the table, each of us feigning hunger but doing little more than scattering peas over our plates like children.

"You are married?" she asked, nodding to the golden band on my finger.

"My wife passed some time ago," I answered. *Charlotte.* Her name resounded in my ears, but I could not speak it.

"*Perdóname,*" she said, turning her eyes to her plate. "I did not intend—"

"It was a long time ago," I said, but in my mind, it had been only moments. My wife's inelegant but merry spirit remained with me always, in my daughter. I felt both Charlotte's loss and her warmth each time Lottie spoke, each time she left bread out for the crows or comforted my ailing patients with gentle words.

Miss Laveau asked me why I still wore the wedding ring.

"It...ah...it is very valuable," I stammered, and I set my fork on the tablecloth to rest my hands in my lap. She only smiled and graciously pretended not to notice.

"Do you have children, then?" she asked.

"I lost my young son to tuberculosis, the same that took my wife. My daughter, Lottie, and I have only each other now."

I could not dwell on thoughts of my son. The memories were so sodden with grief, with his small, wasted form and tiny cough, that speaking of him opened a seeping wound inside my chest. I looked down at my duck, the sliced breast appearing somehow grotesque. I pushed this away, too.

"You are not married?" I asked, eager to direct the conversation away from myself.

"Only to my canvases. It is just as well. A woman should belong only to herself and none other."

"Peter tells me you're highly regarded in Europe," I said. "You've found success in your art?"

"It is astonishing how much money a man will pay for a likeness of his own face," she said, and I laughed, but she did not. "I was very successful in Spain, but I wanted something more, something new. My family begged me not to come here. America has a way of stripping one to the bone."

Murdoch came around again to clear our china before I could ask her to elaborate, and Christine wheeled in another course, resolutely avoiding my gaze.

"Does the food not meet your expectations, sir?" he asked. "Peter and Christine prepared all of your childhood favorites, it being your first proper dinner home."

I smiled. "It's been a long while since I've had such splendid courses before me, Mr. Murdoch. It seems a shame to ruin them with eating."

"Always too kind, sir," he said, and exchanged my plate for another laid with whole, roasted fish. "Do try the trout, if you fancy it. Peter caught it just this morning."

I thanked him, and picked up my fork as he left, his granddaughter close behind. Miss Laveau set her hand on my arm.

"You must eat," she said. "You will need your strength. Nothing comes easily here."

My skin burned beneath her fingers as she slipped her hand into my own. It was, perhaps, a gesture of solidarity, or of new friendship, but my stomach somersaulted against my will. I felt her touch deep inside my bones, thrilling me and troubling me at once. Her thumb brushed across my ring, and I pulled away, my cheeks afire.

"Lenora," I said, my voice raw. "Your contract was with my father. I have no means of honoring his debt. Return to Spain, to your home. There is nothing for you here."

"You wish me to leave?" she asked, her eyes wide and lovely. I looked down at my plate to find the trout staring at me as well, its shriveled eyeball unblinking and hideous.

"On the contrary," I answered. "I am quite fond of you already, but I cannot keep you here under false pretense. My father is dead, and with him, your contract. He has made it impossible for me to access the monies I require to pay you."

Lenora bit down on her lip, her elegant fingers tracing the pattern on the china.

"I have nowhere else to go, Mr. Garrett. The money was meant to purchase my fare home." She lifted her eyes to mine, her distress creating only the tiniest of creases around her eyes.

"Perhaps we could come to an accord," I offered, but she furrowed her brow in confusion.

"I do not know this word, *accord*."

"An agreement," I said, and I continued upon her nod. "My father, you see, has forbidden access to his accounts until I've lived on the property for the whole of a year. I've no intention of staying so long, but we need money to sell the property so we can both return to our lives. I cannot do this alone."

There was nothing in my father's will specifically prohibiting the sale of the estate, only its contents. I had lived nearly half my life without his money, and I'd be damned if I would turn to it now. I'd take the money from the sale, pay his debts, and return to Lottie. That was all. Only the matter of my tarnished name remained, and that could easily be cleared up by word from Dr. Johnston that I hadn't called upon him before my mother's death.

"How can I help?" Lenora asked.

"Stay and paint," I said. "Not my father's portrait, we've no use for that. Paint the house, the garden, and any place you like. Paint it as it ought to be, as it was, so people might see beneath all of this wretchedness that there could be happiness again."

"And you believe this will help to sell it?"

"I am good with a hammer. We can clean, and mend, and repair, but I can't restore it without a craftsman or my father's money, and I have neither. Our only hope is to appeal to the buyer's fancy."

"Are there no craftsmen in town?"

Surely, I couldn't tell her they all believed the place was haunted, least of all by her. Nor could I ask her to explain how the whole thing had come about. The question was so ridiculous

I couldn't fathom how to articulate it.

"None willing to do the work I require," I said at last. She considered this for a moment, her gaze lost in a glass of port she hadn't yet touched.

"Very well," she said, and then extended her hand the way men do when agreeing upon a business venture. I took it in my own and shook it. "I will help you so we may both go home."

January 11, 1889

I had not planned to write again so soon, but sleep escapes me still. This evening, when I had bid goodnight to Lenora and sequestered myself in my room with the bed curtains drawn around me, my thoughts turned toward the wardrobe in the attic. How could I account for its curious movement? How still could I account for my father's voice that prevented me from inspecting it?

The evening stretched out before me, long and misshapen in the dim moonlight, my journal propped open but the page empty. I ran the pad of my thumb over the trinket, which I kept always in my pocket. The thing was as confounding as it was comforting—a talisman to keep away the darkness, though it possessed no real power.

When I at last I fell into a disquieted sleep, my head was full of strange dreams. I awoke in the middle of the night with the memory of only one, which I will relay here to be referenced in the future should it hold some subconscious understanding of my current situation.

I stood on the balcony with Lenora, looking out across the garden. It did not look as it did in life, but was instead a wasteland of scrub grass and quicksand. Smoke thickened the balmy air, like the rail station in June, and the dried husks of willow branches whispered names into the coming night. Animal carcasses attracted vultures and insects alike. Crows, foxes, and deer rotted under a dying red sun, the air abuzz with flies.

"What has happened here?" I asked her. She looked at me with her large black eyes and pointed to my mother's lavender garden. There, down among the dead things and the withered grasses, stood my mother. Her dress clung to her, stained pink in the strange atmosphere, the hem dark with clay. The wind whipped a black silk scarf around her neck to strangle her.

I called out, but she did not hear me. A blossom of darkness appeared on her womb, growing and growing until the stain soaked the front of her dress—blood, as black as the wasted earth. I smelled it on the night air as it spilled like ink across the whole of the universe. Piano music poured over me, from everywhere, from nowhere. Louise Farrenc's *Etude*, Mother's favorite song.

The notes echoed in my bones as Lenora set her frigid hand upon my cheek. I turned to her. She kissed me without a word—an indecent kiss that set my blood afire. I slipped my arm around her waist to draw her closer, but a sudden and horrible stench overpowered me, and I shoved her away. Her full and lovely lips drew back from her teeth, shriveling and cracking, bits of flesh flaking off and fluttering to my bare feet. Her eyes clouded over and sunk into the depths of her skull. I stared in horror as her skin moldered, festering with fungus, and then the flies descended upon us both.

I awoke with a start, my legs entangled in sweat-dampened bedclothes. Although my wits gathered in the darkness and slowly chased away the hideous vision of Lenora, the song lingered still in my ears. With a weight upon my chest, like the Mora from German myth, I recognized the instrument upon which it was played. My mother's piano in the parlor.

Despite many professional tunings, one of the keys fell slightly flat. It gave the song an impression of disease, a rotting of the tune that disturbed my spirit. I thought I might still be dreaming, and yet these notes rang with such clarity that I rose from the bed and opened the door. In only my nightshirt and cap, I walked out into the cold hall and descended the staircase. I did not know what I might find, only that I wished to confirm or contradict my own madness.

I gained the main floor of the house with blood pounding in my ears. The song continued, louder. When I at last rounded the corner and stepped into the sitting room, terror and grief struck me to stone. I could not move nor breathe. My heart seized inside my chest.

With her back to me at the piano, fingers moving lithely over the dusty keys, sat my mother. Her hair fell down over her shoulders, as she had worn it in Father's absence, and candlelight flickered softly on the yellowed sheet music. She was warmth and hope, and everything lovely that had gone. Tears sprung up in my eyes, blurring the apparition before me into a mere impressionist painting.

"Mother?" I whispered. My voice shattered inside my throat, but I could not go to her. She turned.

"Mr. Garrett?"

Lenora.

My limbs broke free from this spell as though a chisel had struck me, and I grasped the doorframe for fear I might collapse. Lenora stood and wrapped her dressing gown tightly around her neck, the candle atop the piano flinging shadows across the keys.

"Are you ill?" she asked, but I could not answer. She took the candle and approached me as I stood in the threshold, warm light driving all the darkness behind me. Her eyes were coal, stoked orange by flame.

"I thought..." I said. "That song..."

"Forgive me. I found the music. I didn't mean to wake you."

After lingering for a moment before me, perhaps to assess my ability to stand freely, she moved to the side table and poured me a glass of water, which I gulped.

"Sit down," she said, and nodded toward the sofa. I obeyed,

falling into the cushions. She sat beside me, her eyes fixed on the piano.

"My mother played that song often."

"I am sorry to have distressed you."

A long moment passed away, nary a sound but the scratching of mice behind the walls. The details of my nightmare, though fading, moved about inside my memory like a wriggling worm, and I could not look at her.

"It's grown quite cold," she said at last.

I answered, "Yes."

Even when the silence stretched its long shadow over us, she stayed with me. I did not wish to be alone. Either she perceived this and was doing me a kindness, or she desired the same. She filled the space between us with grand tales of her world travels, and as my spirits lifted, I found my voice. I told her all about my daughter and the medical practice we had built together. She took particular interest in Lottie's studies of spiritualism.

"I forbade her from it, of course," I said. "She has a will of her own, though, and is wont to do as she pleases. You don't believe in such things as ghosts, surely."

"It would be foolish not to believe," she answered. "I have seen my father several times since he left this earth."

"You were not frightened?" I asked.

"Only your father's spirit frightens me."

"You have seen him then?"

"On the widow's walk. I don't go there anymore."

Lenora gathered the skirt of her dress to busy herself, and the satin brushed across my hand. The sensation summoned a memory, one so deeply entrenched in my mind that it had no neighbors. It existed alone, out of time. I remembered creeping into my father's quarters. I heard the creaking of a drawer and felt the satin of his purse beneath my fingers. And then, as quickly as it had begun, it was over. Try as I might, I could not recall the circumstances surrounding this event, or if it even happened at all.

"You saw him in the attic, didn't you?" Lenora asked, rescuing me from these maddening thoughts only to draw me into another.

"I thought I heard his voice." She only nodded her head absently, her eyes far away. "How did he die?"

"He fell." She did not look at me but picked at a frayed thread on her sleeve. "So they say."

"You don't believe it?"

Her fingers stilled. Fear and hatred hardened her gaze, as malformed as a poorly healed wound. She knows more about my father's demise than she tells, of that I am certain.

"It's almost dawn," she remarked. The sun struggled to break the horizon, a thick layer of fog dispersing the light like gauze as it crept up Lenora's face.

"I should like to paint the sunrise someday," she said.

It would have been polite to respond to this, but her eyes transfixed me. I searched the lines of her face, seeing only the unadulterated hatred she harbored. Even after my father passed on, he remained with her still, in this house, guarding his belongings and persisting where he ought not.

Hamlet's father indeed.

"I must seem strange to you," she said, smiling and breaking the spell. The sun continued its ascent.

"Are you certain you're not a spirit?" I replied. "One of my long-dead ancestors sent to teach me a great and horrible lesson?"

A rueful laugh crackled between us.

"Your father used to believe so," she answered, the humor gone.

I asked, "I'm told he went mad, in the end."

"Yes. Madness made him cruel, *agresivo*. He was only a shell when he threw himself from the balcony."

My heart slowed to a whisper inside my chest, holding my breath hostage along with it.

"He fell," I corrected.

"I have said too much already." She stood, smoothing a trembling hand over her wrinkled dressing gown. "And what would Mr. Murdoch think if he saw us together at this hour?"

"To hell with Murdoch," I said, standing. "You've told me my father killed himself as casually as if he'd eaten eggs for breakfast, and you're concerned about what my servant thinks of you?"

She turned to leave, and I wanted to seize her arm to stop her, but some better angel stayed my hand. The rigidness of her posture warned me that if I touched her now, she might never allow me do so again, and that would be a great loss.

"I am sorry," she said without looking at me, and then she was gone.

I write now with only the scratching of my pen for company, my spirits dim despite the sun's young rays upon my face.

My head is full of dangerous questions. I dare not put them to paper.

Chapter VI

A LETTER TO MISS CHARLOTTE GARRETT

Ravenswood Hall to 14 Albany Square, Baltimore, Maryland
Postmarked January 11, 1889

My dear girl, what a singular day I've had. I've been to see Dr. Johnston, and I cannot wrap my mind around what he has relayed to me. Forgive me if I am long-winded in the pages ahead, but I hope that you might help me make some sense of it all. I have written this letter twice already and cast the pages into the fire, for I could not set the words to paper in a comprehensive manner. This is my last attempt, and you shall tell me your thoughts.

You have not yet received the hasty letter that I posted this morning,[1] wherein I introduce your once removed cousin, Anna, and the enigmatic Miss Lenora Laveau's intimations of your grandfather's suicide. Pray, read that

---

1 Inclusion of this document in the narrative has been deemed unnecessary by its authors.

letter first so you might better comprehend all I write here. More information has come to light to harden my belief that Lenora—that is, Miss Laveau—has not been entirely forthcoming with me.

When I went down to breakfast, I discovered Miss Laveau and cousin Anna already at the table. Although their discussion died upon my entry, the grim expression they shared, and the heat in Lenora's cheeks, suggested a dispute of some kind. I thought it best not to meddle, and I kept to my coffee and toast.

We breakfasted, the three of us, making small conversation of the dismal weather, and then I set my course for the stables. I'd begun to feel rather ill inside that old house, plagued by bouts of vertigo and nausea, no doubt a consequence of the poor air and creeping mold. I wanted to feel the air on my face, cold be damned. I wished to breathe in the ice, to hear the gentle dripping of snow from the pine boughs. My suffocated spirit yearned to see colors other than the deep burgundy of velvet and mahogany paneling. So, despite the protestations of my loyal groomsman, Wilson, who had readied the carriage, I set off on one of my father's mares. The old girl whinnied, prancing and shaking the winter off her shoulders.

I patted her, laughing.

"There now, let us be free of this place for a while, eh?" This met with another snicker of approval, and she all but galloped past the stone wolves at the gates. We carried on down the muddy road, a low-lying fog flanking me on either side. My heart felt lighter despite the gloom, but the poor horse's gait slowed after a mere mile from the estate. Her hooves sloshed through the mud, and I spurred her but could not convince her to maintain a speed beyond a leisurely stroll, leaving me more time than I wished for pondering.

Stories abound here of both my father's cruelty and madness, Lottie. The former I am acquainted with, but the latter troubles me. Our family tree is now only a withered stump, with you, me, and your cousin Anna to maintain it. So many branches have been shriveled by lunacy that I am beginning to doubt my own mind, the very thing I have built my life upon. But I am getting ahead of myself.

Carry on with it, Papa, you say!

Yes, very well.

I held the conviction that the doctor could aid me in two ways. First and foremost, I needed him to confirm that the accusations in The Sun's article were as false as you and I know them to be. Second, I needed his assertation that some event brought about my father's madness, and not heredity. If such a thing does indeed run along the veins of our family tree, we must be vigilant—nip it in the bud, so to speak. I wanted only the truth. It is as simple as that, and perhaps as complicated.

As I carried on, I searched my mind for anything that might have foreshadowed my father's ruin, any condition that might drive him to madness, and thus to suicide. For some ungodly reason, the only memory I could recall was the day he took me out with him to hunt grouse, the day he taught me how to use his gun. I had taken a life on this day, a fledgling bird that had fled from Chap, our old spaniel.

"I'm proud of you, son," he'd said, as I held the twitching creature in my hands, its dark eyes staring up at me. I remembered the sting of tears, and the gripping fear that my father might see this weakness. It was the only time in my life he had been proud of me, I think. The bird was the first life I had ever taken, and the last. Perhaps this makes me less of a man, but it is of no importance to me. I may have inherited my father's face, but I did not inherit his propensity for killing. It is not remarkable to think that he would stand accused of cold-blooded murder, but I could not for the life of me surmise the events that must have unfolded during Lenora's mysterious absence. This would not do, all of this wondering and not knowing.

I fell into reverie as we trudged along, the lights of town only dismal orbs against the fog. In my mind's eye, my mother stood before the open window, her nightgown fluttering. Toward the end of her lifetime, she would spend hours there, looking out across the hemlocks, as silent as the night.

"Are you well, mother?" I'd ask.

"I'm waiting," she would answer.

"What are you waiting for?"

She would turn to me and smile. "My son. He went away."

The first time she said this to me, I locked myself in my chamber and wept. How could she have forgotten me? The pain of this dulled after repetition until I would only return her smile and leave her to her waiting. Father had no patience for this. I think he would have left her up there at that open window all the year long. After my father's cruelty drove away her lady's maid, it was I who drew the curtains at night, I who showed her to bed, and I who woke her each morning for breakfast. And on that singular day in January, it was I who could not wake her, I who felt the coldness of her skin beneath my fingers. Death had come in the open window and spirited her away. My life had been slashed into two pieces on that night—before and after. Everything that came after bore the gray dimness of sorrow.

The horse, somehow knowing my heart or else accustomed to visiting Dr. Johnston often, carried me to his door, snorting to herald our arrival. She could have taken me into Canada and I would not have noticed, so entrapped was I in my own mind.

The lamp burned in Dr. Johnston's window, stained glass refracting gemstones onto the snow beneath. As if through a kaleidoscope, I spied him nudge thick spectacles up his bony, hooked nose and turn the pages of a manual. He did not hear the hooves upon the drive, or even my footsteps as I dismounted and approached the red door. His name, once painted in brilliant white contrast, had faded to a pale flesh color, but there was no other indication he might have retired. Perhaps he wouldn't recognize me, or worse yet, refuse to see me. I lifted the frozen knocker and let it fall, once, twice, and then waited.

The doctor opened the door wide as if he had been expecting me.

"Ah, Mr. Garrett the younger," he said. "I heard you were back in these parts. Do come in."

Perhaps I hadn't changed as much as I'd thought.

The place looked exactly as I remembered. The same long wool carpet stretched the length of the hall—and the corresponding scent of unlaundered clothing—the old iron coatrack, worn smooth by time, and the portraits of his four daughters, all married and gone away. I'd never met any of them, but their faces had enchanted me as a boy, waiting for my father or mother to finish a consultation or retrieve a tincture of one kind or another. The tray of antique surgical instruments sat, as always, displayed in a case beside the fireplace. They were fearsome tools, with cruel hooks and darkened blades, and I wondered still to whom they had belonged and what poor bastard had gone under them.

"Here about your father, are we?" he asked.

"Why, yes, I am," I answered, stunned. "You are as astute as ever, Doctor." I followed him into his office and sat in one of the chairs opposite him. His white moustache drooped over his lip, obscuring the same good-humored smile that he wore perpetually when I was a child. It was as much a part of his aspect as his glasses or the snowy shock of hair atop his head.

"It pays to be astute, as you say, in our profession, Dr. Garrett." Then, upon my expression of surprise, he added, "Ah, I see you've forgotten the time you spent with my medical journals and instruments when you were a boy. Am I wrong that you became a doctor, after all?"

"I did, indeed," I answered. "Though my father has put my profession into purgatory, as it were."

He folded his great, wrinkled hands on the desk and studied me, no doubt looking for signs of my father in my hairline or my cheekbones, but I was weary and eager for answers.

"I've been to see my cousin," I continued, but he held up his hand, closing his eyes with a little tip of the chin that ceased my questioning.

His watery eyes opened, and he asked simply, "How are you, William?"

The question startled me, and I did not immediately answer. No one but Peter had yet inquired after my health or my well-being. I doubt greatly if anyone sees me at all here, so transfixed they are by my father's features.

"Fine, Doctor," was the only reply I could manage, and I admit I did little to convince him it was true. He hummed a note of dissatisfaction and nodded.

"Just as I thought."

"You see illness in me?"

"You're fit as a fiddle, my young friend, but if I could offer a bit of professional advice?"

"Certainly."

"Return to Baltimore." The humor had left his eyes. He delivered this to me as if he had diagnosed me with the plague.

"I beg your pardon?"

"I watched your father's decline into madness. I will not watch the same fate befall you."

"It's true, then. My father was mad?"

"As a hatter, my boy."

"Like my mother?"

"Heavens no. The case was nothing like your mother's." The doctor rose to his feet with some difficulty, likely due to rheumatism. As a medical man, I might have advised him to winter in some warmer clime, but I knew he would refuse.

He rummaged around in a cabinet behind his desk. "Your mother's illness was brought on by long periods of depression and hysteria after the miscarriage."

I stiffened in my chair. "The what?"

He turned back to me, but I could not read his expression.

"They didn't tell you, then," he said. "Before we proceed, what is the likelihood that you will heed my advice of leaving this miserable place?"

"None whatsoever."

"I feared as much." He drew a long, deep breath and released it. "Very well. You might as well have all of the facts." He turned his back to me again and extracted a small leather-bound notebook. "When you were a young man, about sixteen, your mother became pregnant but miscarried. She nearly died."

"I-I," I stammered. "I didn't know."

"I imagine they wished to keep it from you." He paused, his finger to his lip. "But I suppose you should know all now. A man can hide his wickedness from his friends, even from himself, but never from his doctor. He told me she fell down the stairs, a tired excuse, and one he employed for you many a time. The truth is that your father, in one of his rages, beat Mrs. Garrett near to death. I could not save the child."

I remembered this night vividly. I'd accompanied Anna into town to collect an order from the feed store, and I returned to a house in the throes of chaos. My mother's lady's maid tore down the stairs, bundling blood-soaked sheets as she passed Murdoch, who climbed with a bucket and soap. The kitchen servants were huddled in the dining room, whispering among themselves. Mother and Father were gone, and no one would answer my questions. I never knew about the child, only the beating, which was not the first and would not be the last.

"I remember," I muttered to myself. I nearly forgot the doctor's presence, so garish were these images in my mind. "When they returned home in the morning, Mother was a ghost."

She was never the same after that night. The light in her dimmed, and then finally flickered out but one year later. Knowing all I know now, it is a wonder to me that she clung to life so long.

"I was obliged to shut my eyes to it," the doctor continued. "It was no business of mine. Still, I continued to treat your mother in secret, despite your father's protestations. I could do nothing for her. It was as if he had broken her spirit, and no tincture could heal the break."

"A son," I said. It was not a question. I understood now that the child she was waiting for at the window every night was not me at all. It never had been.

"Yes," he answered anyway.

"I am sorry to be the one to tell you all of this, William. It's a hard thing to return to after all these years." When I could not respond, he continued. "There's something else I wish to tell you, something I should have said many years ago."

"Yes?"

He leveled his gaze on me, and said, "You are a good man."

I lifted my brow, a mordant smirk tugging at my lip.

"You don't know me."

"You were but half your father's size, and still you bore the brunt of his rage. Bruises meant for your mother fell on your back, broke your bones, and I set them all. A bad man would not sacrifice himself at so young an age to protect his weakened mother. Whatever has happened these many years, you are still him in your heart."

I was prepared neither for these accolades nor the hideous memories they restored to me. My hands trembled as a stone formed in my throat, but the doctor simply patted my arm.

"Strong and sturdy," he said, nodding. "The breaks healed. Seems I did a fine job."

He leaned back and tapped his fingers on a leather-bound book, inhaling deeply.

"But," he went on, "you came to speak about your father. I recorded his case in my journal. I was never able to make any sense of it. Maybe you will have more success than I. As I said, your father's case was nothing at all like your mother's. Some men cannot withstand the wiles of a woman." He shook his head gravely but would not elucidate.

"You don't mean Miss Laveau?" I prompted, hoisting myself out of the mire.

"Indeed, I do."

"What do you suspect? That she deliberately drove him to suicide?"

I'd not yet spent a week with her, but I could not believe there was any truth in it. If my father had lost his mind, surely there was a medical cause, leaving Lenora only a bystander, a scapegoat for superstitious farmers and town gossips. Gloom descended upon me again like a great London fog. I might have choked on it as it suffocated the words in my throat. I took the book from him and flipped through pages filled with curling, illegible shorthand. I could make out body temperature readings and a few phrases here and there such as complaints of pain, vivid hallucinations, and strangely, my own name. As a doctor myself, my hand is not the neatest, (you can attest to that), but I should have asked him for a legend.

"You found no sign of fever? No illness?" I pressed, when

he would not answer my question.

"None whatsoever. It was as if he had aged thirty years in only a matter of months, an old man in the grips of dementia. Paranoia has that effect sometimes. Paranoia and guilt."

"Guilt?"

"Read the notes, my boy. I can offer you no further explanations."

All of my inquiries frustrated, my attempts thwarted by nonsense and allusions to mystery, I stood and tried to keep my temper.

"Surely you have a hypothesis. You cannot expect me to believe that my father's demise was brought on by some supernatural entity, woman or otherwise. I won't have it."

"Supernatural? What are you going on about, boy? The facts are plain enough. Your father grew so enamored with the painter that he simply couldn't bear it when she went away."

"But where did she go?"

"I heard she went to visit family in Spain, but it matters little. Your father's mind conjured a cause for her absence that could not exist with her return at the end of the summer."

"My cousin said he was accused of her murder," I said. "You mean to tell me he confessed to it because it was easier to accept than a holiday? It's ridiculous."

"The absence of a great love is easier to bear if it's been expunged entirely from the earth. He clung to the fantasy of her death so desperately that when she returned, his delusion unraveled, and along with it, his mind. Now, I'm in no position to extrapolate on matters of law. You'll need to speak with Constable Devlin if you require details of the inquiry."

I dropped back down in the chair, exasperated, and so befuddled by the whole thing that I asked him to begin again. Dr. Johnston scratched his head. Deep creases crowded around his eyes and tremors shook his hands as in men who've returned from war.

"William, please. Devlin can fill in the details. Please go home and try to rest. This dogged pursuit is not healthy."

All the fire left me then, and I sat in the chair quite dumbfounded, numb to all I had seen and heard, and more muddled than when I'd begun. I longed for a draught of whiskey.

"Let me give you something to help you sleep," Dr. Johnston said, but I refused him, heaving myself to my feet to take my leave.

"There's one more matter, Dr. Johnston," I said. I'd nearly forgotten it in the confusion of all he'd relayed to me. "Did I come to see you shortly before my mother's death?"

He frowned, appearing puzzled. I relayed the matter's importance to him but did not explain the details in the letter.

"Why, yes," he answered. "Why do you ask?"

This was not the answer I was expecting. It staked me through the heart and I could not move.

In a weak voice, I asked, "Did I purchase anything?"

"A tincture of laudanum for your mother, as I recall."

The hairs on the back of my arms rose, prickling up my neck. I have no recollection of this, Lottie. I can't make sense of it. There's no truth in my father's letter, of that I am certain, but how then can I explain this?

I left quickly, wishing only to return to my ruined home and write to you, and I've exhausted myself in doing so. Now you know all. Tell me, what do you make of it? Have you had any luck with the trinket I described in my first letter?

All my love,

Papa

Chapter VII

WILLIAM GARRETT'S JOURNAL

January 11, 1889, continued

My God, what madness is this?

I have not lost my senses. I cannot, *will not*, fall into lunacy as my father and mother did before me, but what other explanation is there for what I have seen? How can I account for this humming between my ears, this terrible gnawing inside my skull, like so many rats come to feed? I am a man of science. A man of science, by God!

If I am not mad, the other possibility is equally troubling. I dare not acknowledge it, not yet. I must write, this candle glowing by my hand, for I've worn holes in my slippers already and can pace my room no longer. I shall begin when I returned home this evening, utterly exhausted from my travels. Ah, this—I am simply fatigued. Is a hallucination beyond the realm of possibility for a mind as weary as mine, a mind as troubled with these tales of murder?

Well, I digress.

When I returned, as I was saying, I found Lenora toiling over a piece of needlework in the sitting room, three tall candles lighting the details of a few beautifully wrought black irises. Murdoch must have given her my mother's sewing basket. He had no right to do so. These were not his belongings to give away. As he was only lingering in the hall, according to his custom, I turned to give him a piece of my mind.

"First my mother's belongings are discarded to the attic, and then I find you've given away her needlework?" I began, my voice low enough that Lenora would not hear. "You've done as you pleased during my father's absence. I am master now. If you meddle with my mother's things again, I shall turn you out."

His eyes widened for a moment, and then he bowed his head, the way I'd seen him do under my father's barrages. When I opened my mouth to apologize, I found I could not.

"Begging your pardon, Master Garrett," he said. This, the name he used only for my father, struck my ears like a mallet and I winced.

"Murdoch," I whispered, but all I managed to say was, "That will be all."

He shuffled toward the dining room, his hands clasped tightly behind his back. Well, I'd done what I'd meant to. Why did it feel so wretched?

"You've been away quite a while," Lenora said to my back. I turned to her. She weaved the thread through the delicate fabric, her hands so like my mother's, the peculiar combination of dexterity and grace making quick work of it. My initial desire to tear the materials from her hands subsided, for I so enjoyed watching her work that it would be a great shame to interrupt her.

Instead, I shook the rain from my hat and draped my greatcoat over Father's chair, eager to warm myself by the fire. Molly, whom I had not noticed, lifted her head from her paws and yawned. Such an easy life dogs have, to while away the day with no care at all but the occasional scrap of meat from the kitchen.

"I'm sorry for worrying you," I said to Lenora, but I was not. It had been so long since I'd been in the company of a woman—excepting my daughter, of course—that I admit I rather enjoyed the concern that creased her brow. In a moment, though, it had smoothed again to alabaster.

Ultimately unable to stop myself, I asked, "Have you been waiting for me?"

She looked up at me with laughter in her eyes as I sat in the chair, though her fingers continued over the fabric.

"I thought your old horse had stranded you," she said, her face warmed by candlelight. I could find no malignancy in her, even as the flame licked its reflection into her dark eyes. If my father had gone mad, it was due to no wrongdoing on her part, of this I am unalterably certain.

"And Anna?" I asked.

"She has gone to bed. It was kind of you to offer your home to her."

"I hope her presence here does not make you uncomfortable," I said. "Am I wrong to presume there is antipathy between you?"

A cloistered smile moved behind her lips but did not part them. But for this curious expression, she did not answer me. Nearly a quarter of an hour passed in silence as I gathered the courage to ask the question that had been upon my tongue all day.

"Lenora," I said, my voice weaker than I expected. Her name tasted sweet, but also somehow foreign, like my first sip of communion wine as a boy. My tone must have told her that I meant to speak seriously because she set the needlework on the cushion beside her.

"Is something the matter?" she asked.

"I've been to see Dr. Johnston."

"Are you feeling ill?"

"No," I answered, though in that moment I rather did. "No, nothing like that. He's confirmed my father's condition."

Lenora looked down at her hands, now folded delicately in her lap. "I am sorry, Mr. Garrett."

I knew not how to accept these condolences, so instead I removed the journal from my pocket and handed it to her, asking if she could read shorthand.

"Yes, of course," she answered, turning through the pages, frowning. "Why must doctors always have such a tedious hand?"

"That's simple enough. We're always in a terrible hurry." I said this lightly, but my heart wasn't in it. And then, finally, "May I ask you something?"

"Whatever you like, though I reserve the right to withhold the answer."

"Very well." I cleared my throat. "Dr. Johnston and my cousin both report that you went missing for a time last year." Her lips hardened to a thin line. Her shoulders stiffened, and yet I pressed on. "There was an inquiry. Some believed you'd been murdered. I spoke with a man in town who thinks you're a spirit."

"*Pues*, here I am," she answered with a gentle lift of her shoulder. "I only returned to España to visit my sister. I longed for the sea."

"My father," I pressed. "He was in love with you?"

The dark sibling of laughter passed through her lips, an ugly sound. She made no further reply.

"Dr. Johnston believes his love for you drove him mad," I said. "Drove him to suicide."

"It is of no importance to me what the town believes." She stood. "I wish to speak no more of this."

"Please," I pleaded as she turned to leave. "Forgive me. It is not curiosity that motivates me. I am lost and trying to find my way. If my father was ever capable of love, if he at any point gave it to you—" I turned my eyes to the fireplace, the boy in me so starved for my father's affection that he clawed up to surface even after all these years.

"How could he have had no love for you?" I could not tell by her tone if this question was rhetorical. When I did not speak, she said, "What your father felt for me was not love. It was possession."

This answer did not soothe me as I hoped it might.

"You were free of this place, with your sister by the sea," I said. "Why in God's name would you return?"

"I was bound by a contract. What binds you?"

I did not at once know how to answer this. And then, with a great sinking sensation in my chest, I answered, "My father."

"Your father is dead."

"Is he?"

"You have allowed yourself too much pity, Mr. Garrett, and that is very like your father indeed. If he still lives, it is because you keep him so."

She turned to leave, but I rose, taking her fiercely by the arm.

"Do not presume to know me," I retorted, my voice so low that ice crackled in my throat. Fear sparked in her eyes. I knew it well, for I had seen it many times in my mother. She tore herself from my grasp and lifted her chin.

"Do not touch me again."

Her dress whispered on the stairs. I ought to have gone after her. Peter entered the room moments later with bleary eyes, stocking cap in hand, as I paced.

"What did you do?" he asked. "I passed Miss Laveau on the stairs. I've never seen her so cross."

"We had a misunderstanding." The cold lingered deep within my chest, as if the frost upon the windows had encrusted my lungs. "It was nothing. We will set it right in the morning."

I could not imagine her ever wishing to speak to me again. Peter patted me on the shoulder and said something classless about the better sex, but I did not hear him or even notice that he'd gone. I retrieved Lenora's abandoned embroidery from the cushions and set it upon my mother's basket. Beneath my misery rose another concern.

She had taken the doctor's journal.

I paced the sitting room for a long while, and when that did not sate my anxious mind, I paced my bedroom, hands clasped behind my back until they grew numb. I'd made a grievous error in approaching Lenora with my troubles. All this talk of phantoms and murder had affected my judgment. I didn't even believe in ghosts.

Why, then, had I lit every lamp in the room?

I paused at my window, looking out over the garden and the forests beyond, black with shadow on the moonless night. I wondered what horrors might have forced my father to leap from such a height.

Myths abound in these woods, stories that instilled such fear in me as a child that I dared not be caught outside after sundown. Even now grown men tell tales of trolls and ancient Indian witches still performing their nefarious rites down among the hemlock groves.

The widow's walk at the back of the house overlooked the whole of the mountain, and from its balcony one could see even the serpentine Hudson as it carved its way through the trees. The wolf, hunted now nearly to death, still clings to this harsh landscape, and I imagined I could hear its eerie music. In the summer sunlight though, the forests echo with the song of a thousand birds, bear cubs splash in the streams, and fox kits chase field mice among the ferns. Men long their whole lives to own a tract of land as magnificent as that upon which Ravenswood Hall sits.

Surely no monster had driven my father to his death, no witch had cast her spell upon him. What then? How, in the presence of such beauty, could my father have ended his life?

Driven by this final question, and a momentary lapse of sanity, I snatched up a lamp before my courage could fail me and left the warmth of my bedroom for the dark hall. My heart galloped in my chest as I neared my father's chamber, the shivering candlelight leaping upon the door ahead of me. I do not know what I hoped to gain by this mad errand.

The doorknob turned freely in my hand and I stepped inside. I'd rarely entered this room, except to sit with my mother in the adjoining boudoir. She would help me with my French lessons while she pinned up her hair.

The four-poster bed stood tall and oppressive in the flickering light, the curtains drawn around the mattress, keeping darkness within. My father's hairbrush and pocket watch still sat upon the vanity before a mirror from which, out of some kind of childish fear, I averted my eyes. The door to the dressing room remained closed, and on another night, I may have entered to find the remnants of my mother's belongings packed away in boxes, or perhaps I'd have found her things laid out as they had always been, every hairpin and ribbon in its place, but I did not enter.

The old Indian rug had been taken away, leaving behind a dark square in the floor where it had protected the hardwood from the sun. Strangely, this rug had been one of his most prized possessions. If his story was to be believed, he had purchased the piece in India during his extended honeymoon, and it had cost a great deal. My mother didn't care for it at all, but he would not be thwarted. It reminded him of *One Thousand and One Nights*, a favorite tale from his boyhood. It was difficult to think of him as a child, perhaps with happy dreams and aspirations, for I understood at least in part how truly dismal his end would be.

Excepting this missing magic carpet, nothing else appeared out of place. I approached the balcony doors and lifted my hand to pull aside the heavy velvet curtains that hid the glass from my view.

William.

I stilled, not daring to move.

William.

The curtain rippled as if by breath, as if my father stood just behind the folds, for I knew his voice as I knew my own. I grasped the curtain with trembling fingers.

Another voice, one I did not recognize, spoke in a language I did not understand. In a moment there were others, like a large party of people gathered suddenly in the adjoining room, but I could discern no words. There were women and men, their voices raised in argument, and a child screamed. Then, out of the cacophony of sounds arose a verse from an old Irish folk song called Lovely Molly, once sung to me by my mother.

"Stop," I pleaded, releasing both the curtain and my lamp. The latter shattered across the floor, leaving me in darkness. I bowed my head, palms pressed tightly to my ears, but the singing continued all the while, heedless of my prayers and the tears that burned in my eyes.

And then, all at once, silence reigned again.

Trembling and gasping for breath, I opened my eyes and looked about. Nothing but shadow, nothing but the cobwebs of memory in a disused room. When I at last summoned the courage to cast aside the curtain, a part of me believed that I might find my father standing there beyond the glass, his back to me with the winter wind in his hair, but only the dim image of my own haggard face looked back at me.

I turned the knob.

"Will?"

I cried out like a fool, spinning toward the voice as light filled the room. It was only Peter.

"Christ," I murmured. "What the devil are you doing in here in the middle of the night?"

"I was about to ask you the same."

He wore the same bloodshot, weary expression that I had seen earlier in the sitting room.

"Did you call my name?" I asked.

"Yes, just now," answered he.

"And not before?"

"Just the once. Why? Is something wrong?"

"No." I closed the curtain with a quick yank and collected

the broken pieces of my lamp. We walked together out into the hall. I added, "I should like to have this room, and that widow's walk, set to order once the house is ready to be sold. It's in as poor a state as the rest of it, I'm sure."

"You still wish to sell it?"

"Why shouldn't I? My life is in Baltimore."

"Your family has been here for generations."

I did not consider at the time that this inquiry had not been about my family at all, but his. The Murdochs had lived on these grounds for nearly fifty years, with no other prospects to sustain them in the area but one of the hotels that attracted tourists in the summer. With weight upon his shoulders, he closed the door behind us. Although I had not inspected the widow's walk, I had achieved my aim. Fear is a powerful thing, an almighty thing. I now believe that it had been this, and not madness, that drew my father to the ledge.

January 12, 1889

This habit I've acquired of wandering around the house in the middle of the night is beginning to wear upon me. When I woke in the morning from another strange and fitful sleep, while the house was quiet but for the chirping of a brave sparrow, I became certain that the episode I experienced last night must have been merely a dream or some flight of fancy. This old house had always delighted in playing tricks on me. Rereading last night's account proves it so. Surely the episode could be explained by little more than the cries of a fox poorly translated by an overtaxed mind. I shall leave it thus rationalized for the time being.

I woke nearly an hour before breakfast, another consequence of the broken shutter, and so busied myself with my morning rituals. When I came to the mirror and regarded my face in the glass, I had the overwhelming impulse to shave my face bare. My beard, the same chestnut hue as my mother's hair, had shaped my profile for over a decade, but I suddenly needed to see myself as I had been before I left this place, before my mother left it.

I shut out the maddening knocks against the window, for I had the distinct notion that something wished to be let in, and ran the blade across my skin.

When I was nearly finished, I nicked myself with the razor. A drop of blood bloomed from the small wound, and I reached into my bag for a kerchief to blot it away. When I returned my eyes to the mirror, they deceived me. My chin had no cut at all. The razor, which I thought was in my hand all the while, sat in the washbasin, still lathered. I ran my fingers over the place, as fascinated as I was unnerved.

The shutter crashed against the window.

"Christ," I muttered above the pounding of blood in my ears. I leaned toward the mirror and wiped away the residual lather, half expecting to discover blood beneath or feel the sting of soap. Instead, the wilted memory of my father's voice unfurled in my mind.

Take care with the blade, my boy. Hold it thus to shave, and thus should you be threatened.

Instinctively, my fingers closed around the razor as he'd taught me. With the shaving done, I held it backward, blade toward the mirror as if I meant to open the throat of my own reflection. I recalled then why I had grown the beard, and why I'd hidden myself behind it all these years. My father's face glared back at me.

Coming to my senses, I dropped the razor in the basin and fled to the relative security of my room where I hastily dressed.

At length, I crept down the stairs and headed outside into the frozen, milky dawn to either repair the blasted shutter or else tear it off entirely. I needed somewhere to begin the work, and since not a soul would help me, this was as good a place as any. My father kept a supply of workman's tools and materials in the garden shed, where a groundskeeper could obtain them easily enough for repairs. I drew up my coat against the bitter wind and set out down a weed-ridden gravel path to fetch a ladder. A wolf sent up his melancholy howl toward the heavens, the chill mounting.

I passed by the barren lavender fields, and I fancied for a moment that I could still smell the sweetness of my mother in the blackened earth. Even if I searched every last inch of these one hundred twenty acres, I knew only her bones remained, laid to rest in the cemetery on the hill. It kept watch from its perch—I could feel its immortal gaze upon me, but I did not look.

Behind me, the bloody sunrise poured itself onto the house, its shadow chasing me as I quickened my step. As I rounded a bend, the dark woods rose up before me. Nestled therein was the shed. A light glowed within, oozing through the slits between the boards.

Odd.

The shadow of a figure passed by the sagging door. The whole structure ought to have surrendered to nature and been done with it. It leaned precariously to the left, trembling with the footfalls of whomever occupied it, both choked and supported by the thicket of blackberries behind.

A vagrant perhaps, searching for something of value.

Having no weapon, I snatched a large stick from the path and held it at the ready. The shadow stilled, curling out from under the door. I wrenched it open. One of the hinges snapped, sending the door banging against the side with a crash that echoed into the hills.

Someone cried a curse, and although I blinked in the lamplight, my eyes aching as they acclimated, I recognized Peter's voice.

"Peter?" I asked. My vision adjusted at last. He clutched a canvas tarp, which he then draped over a workbench cluttered with items, including a broken easel, a number of gilt-framed mirrors, and a phonograph.

"Jesus, you look just like him," he said, and coughed as the dust whirled. "Why the hell did you shave?"

"What are you doing?" I asked instead.

"I thought I'd help clear out some of the rubbish. This here won't fetch much."

"Was all this my father's?" I asked, nodding to the now amorphous lump. "Anyway, he's forbidden us from selling it."

He sent me a sheepish smirk, and replied, "The phonograph is mine. I saved and scraped for it, intending to give it to a lady, but she found a fine sailor to run off with."

I laughed, and then tossed my stick to the ground. "You had me ready for battle."

"You needn't have come out here, Will. Tell me what you need and I'll see it's done."

"The shutter on my window is driving me mad," I answered. "If you know where I can find a ladder in all this, we shall see to it."

He smiled at this, seemingly happy to be of use, and then turned toward a rickety ladder tucked behind a dusty silk ficus. Once he extracted it, the pair of us plodded back to the house to stand it beneath my window.

I climbed, hammer in hand, the rungs creaking under my weight. My reflection in the windowpane, split by a hairline crack in the glass, gave me pause. There was something not quite right about it, something untrue, but try as I might, I could not determine the cause of this oddity. It was as if an artist had painted my portrait there but had misread the shape of my eyes or used the wrong hue.

Before I could raise the hammer to the shutter, such a wave of vertigo overtook me that I was forced to cling to the climbing ivy for support. This gave way as a single curtain, tearing from the stone with the strange peeling sound of flesh. The ladder trembled.

"Easy now," Peter said, steadying the ladder. Somehow, I regained control as pill bugs and the cocoons of moths spilled from the ivy and onto my coat. "Come down, Will."

I scurried down the ladder like a startled mouse, shaking off the debris as I went, and then leapt to the ground.

"Are you all right, then?" Peter asked. "You look like a ghost."

"This house is grating on me, Peter," I answered, and ran my fingers through my hair, shaking out withered ivy leaves. "Perhaps I need a bit of coffee."

"Better give me the hammer. You hold steady the ladder."

With Peter at the lead, the whole job was completed in less than a quarter of an hour, and it gave me hope that we might yet restore the place. That is, if I could set myself to rights.

January 14, 1889

My inspection of the estate has consumed the last two days of my life. I have trod over every inch of this festering pile—from closet to outbuilding. The company of starved rats and moldering memories at every turn has taken a toll on both my body and my spirits, for I am more dismal and ill at ease than before.

After filling nearly four pages of this journal with lists of all in need of repair, and the supplies required to do so, I went down to breakfast wishing only to be in the company of a lovely woman, or at the very least, a friend. I've not had time to become closer acquainted with Lenora, nor to tend my cousin during her stay here, and can only trust that Murdoch has seen to the needs of both.

At the table, I waited only a moment before Lenora's footsteps sounded on the staircase. She had seemingly forgiven me for neglecting her. At least, she did not seem to harbor any sort of ill will when she came into the dining room, clad in a lovely yellow housedress and muslin shawl, the doctor's journal and a ribbon-bound packet of papers beneath her arm.

"What have you there?" I inquired, standing as Peter brought a tray of teacakes.

"You needn't rise every time I enter the room, Mr. Garrett. This is your home. You shall do as you please."

I bowed, a needless courtesy that went unnoticed, and sat as she gathered her dress and settled gracefully into her chair.

"I've gone through Dr. Johnston's notes, as you asked," she said, sliding the documents before me. "I'm afraid you thought I meant to destroy them the other night. I had half a mind to do it."

"I'm grateful you decided against it. I have no excuse for the way I treated you, nor for being so absent these last days."

A rueful smile lifted the corner of her lip, and she answered, "Your father ensured I became accustomed to such things. It is no great shock to me."

"I am not him," I said, louder than I'd intended. I lowered my voice. "Please, forgive me."

She bowed her head in ascent and then tapped the doctor's journal.

"I think you will find the information herein enlightening."

Anna entered the room at this moment, her bearing more like the girl I remembered. That is, with a dash of rose in her cheeks and a warm countenance independent of emotion. Her gingham dress had seen happier times, as had we all, no doubt.

"Good morning," she said. "Has the post come today? I am waiting for a letter."

"Not yet," I answered. "Do join us."

She sat in the chair across from Lenora, but they did not address one another.

"I went to see Dr. Johnston as you suggested," I explained to my cousin. "Lenora was kind enough to transcribe these pages from his journal. Perhaps you can tell me what you make of it all."

"I'd be glad to," she answered. Both she and Lenora drew close as I untied the ribbon.

Chapter VIII

DR. A. JOHNSTON'S MEDICAL JOURNAL

Patient: Mr. Oliver Garrett, Ravenswood Hall
September 5, 1888

Mr. Garrett has been my patient for many years. The change I see in him today is startling and disconcerting. Much wasting in the face and shoulders, but no further symptoms of tuberculosis. No cough present, no wheezing in chest. Fever absent.

His fingers twitch like the antennae of an insect, a consequence perhaps of his elevated heart rate. I prescribed a tincture of whiskey, honey, and chamomile to ease his nerves. It seems like the poor fellow has been frightened half to death. We've made an appointment for Tuesday next, and I hope to see some improvement.

September 11, 1888

Symptoms have worsened. Garrett complains of headaches and joint pain. We had a peculiar conversation, and I've composed it here as far as my memory serves me:

Garrett: I'd like to know about hallucinations.

I: What do you wish to know?

Garrett: What causes them? Are they common?

I: They are cause for concern. Have you experienced a hallucination, Mr. Garrett?

Garrett: I saw someone yesterday, someone I shouldn't have seen.

This talk concerned me, and he would not offer any further insight into the nature of his hallucination. I offered him laudanum both for his pain and the paranoia that was beginning to make itself manifest. I hoped that it might help him to sleep and so chase away these delusions. No fever or other symptoms of disease currently present.

October 5, 1888

Having not heard from Garrett for more than a fortnight, I assumed his condition was improving. He appeared at my door this morning without an appointment and I saw in his face how horribly wrong I was.

Before I could invite him in, he asked, "Do you believe in ghosts?"

"I'm a man of science, Garrett. You know that I do not."

"I think," he said, rubbing his hand across the back of his neck compulsively, "I think I've seen one."

"A ghost? Whose?"

"She's dead. Oh, God."

"Who?"

He grabbed me by the collar with madness in his eyes, and sobbed. "What have I done? Oh, my God, what have I done?"

He would not come inside. I fear there is little I can do for him.

October 20, 1888

I received a letter from Oliver Garrett today, driven over by one of his men.

"He's in an awful state," he reported. "Just paces day and night, talking to himself. Please come, Doctor." And what could I do but promise I would? The letter said only this, written in shaky, ink-blotted script:

Come quickly, doctor. I am undone!

I've just returned from Ravenswood Hall. Garrett's condition has deteriorated, as I feared. I found him exactly as the man had said, pacing from one side of his room to the other, clutching his ears and whimpering in the most pathetic manner I've ever seen.

The look in his eyes haunts me still.

"They're everywhere," he whispered. "Do you not hear them? My God, this is the price I must pay!" He approached me, but I stepped aside for fear he might grab me again. "I wish to die. Please, have mercy. You're the only one who can help me." He fell onto his knees and latched onto my legs.

"For God's sake, Garrett, get a hold of yourself," I said, urging him to release me. I gave him opium to sedate him, but it had little effect. At length, we—Mr. Murdoch and I—were obliged to restrain him in his chair lest he harm himself. I sat with him for nearly an hour until he fell asleep. I fear the worst.

WILLIAM GARRETT'S JOURNAL

January 14, 1889, continued

I read these horrible details barely daring to breathe. When I'd finished, I looked up to find both Lenora and Anna watching me intently.

"Is this all?" I asked. "What of these final pages?" I flipped through the journal, noting additional entries. "There must be more."

"I did not see your father's name after this," Lenora said. "But if you wish, I will transcribe the other passages."

Anna unceremoniously snatched up the book before I could agree and shook her head.

"I know shorthand as well, Will," she said, casting a sidelong glance at Lenora, which was dutifully returned. "I am happy to take another look, if you like."

"Very well," I replied, casting Lenora's papers across the table like a petulant child. "If you find nothing more, I shall have to extract the rest of this miserable tale from Dr. Johnston in person."

"Leave it to me," Anna said, and then nodded at Lenora. I again wondered at the coldness between them, but perhaps Anna perceived my malaise and knew I required air. In any case, it prompted Lenora to take my hand.

She might have cast a spell on me, so powerless was I against her touch.

"The sun shines," she said, smiling warmly and drawing me to stand. "Enough of this. Come into the garden with me. Let us walk together."

I resisted her, albeit half-heartedly. Each hour I spent in idleness here meant another away from my daughter, another in the damp, close air of this God forsaken house. My head ached all the time, my stomach full of churning acid.

"Come," she said, and she leaned into me, threading her arm through mine. I could not withstand this sort of persuasion, and so I allowed her to lead me toward the door, leaving Anna alone to examine the journal.

"Time outdoors will restore you," Lenora said, and she released me as we approached the staircase. "I will meet you in the garden. I require something warmer."

Once she had slipped away upstairs, I stepped outside onto the warped porch boards. To my left, a rat scurried beneath a dwindling stack of wood, and I decided it would do me well to feel the sturdiness of an axe in my hand and hear the splitting of logs. I reached for a smooth-handled axe propped against the house, forgetting Lenora for one blessed moment. My heart leapt into my throat each time she glanced at me, and I yearned for peace. I thought of my wife, of how easy it was to be in her company, how quiet. My feeling for Lenora is a climb up the face of a mountain, loud with the calling of foxes and the ever-present danger of falling.

I touched the place where her fingers had rested on my arm. She is a bluebird in this house of spiders, and I have no choice but to follow her up onto the jagged rocks.

"I thought I might sketch the front gardens for our paintings," she said from the threshold, and I let the axe fall back against the house. Lenora clutched a small sketchbook against a hooded mohair shawl that shadowed her eyes. It lent her an aspect of deceitfulness as though she meant to disguise herself, but she was the very picture of loveliness.

"Perhaps it will help you plan how you wish to arrange it," she said.

I took her arm, and we walked down the steps into the light, blinking and smiling like idiots. The glorious sun had returned at last to remind us all that spring must come and will come if only given time enough. A great weight lifted off my shoulders, and I forgot the dead of winter that flanked us on either side.

"Where's the dog gone off to?" she asked, and then whistled, but Molly did not appear.

We carried on without her. I slipped out of my greatcoat and draped it over a tree branch, and Lenora brushed back her hood and let the shawl gather in the crook of her arms. Patches of snow melted into puddles, and the birds emerged from their winter nests to sing for us. My gloom vanished with the snow.

"The sunlight becomes you," I said, and she smiled at me.

The gardens were not in so terrible a state as I believed when I had first arrived. Tangles of weeds choked every tree and statue, but the fruit trees still stood tall. The fountains, though shadowed with lichen, remained whole and upright. They needed only to be cleaned.

Pebbles crunching underfoot, Lenora and I strolled around the house in search of a place she might sketch. She pointed to the graveyard on the hill, the stones black stains against the sun.

"Have you been to visit them?" she asked.

"I leave the dead to themselves. They've nothing to do with us here."

"Are we not here because of them?"

I thought of my mother's grave, and then of my father, whose grave was empty.

"You're a philosopher and an artist."

She laughed. "Perhaps I am."

We continued around the bend. The path led us to an ivy-draped pergola nestled in the forest, a curtain of willow branches casting strange, thin shadows on its roof. Lenora sat on a stone bench damp with moss and motioned for me to sit beside her, our arms still entwined.

"Do you hear the cardinal?" she asked.

I said that I did, though I could scarcely tell a sparrow from a pigeon.

"They say cardinals are visits from loved ones who have passed on."

"Do they?"

I cared nothing for cardinals or superstition. I could not take my eyes off her. She leaned into me, the scent of lavender in her hair. Melting snow pattered all around us like a spring rain. Far off in the distance, a train whistled as it carried visitors to the Hotel Kaaterskill. When she looked up at me, her eyes large and bright, her hand clasped around my arm, I lost myself. The birdsong fell away. Time fell away. I wanted to touch her face, to feel the silk of her hair through my fingers.

"Lenora," I said, but I do not know what I wished to say. Perhaps I'd only wanted to say her name aloud, to taste it again on my tongue. She looked away.

"The sun is deceiving," she said. "It makes me think we are safe from the ghosts."

I laughed quietly. She did not. The stillness, broken here and there by the cawing of a jay, troubled me. Lenora, perceiving the trembling of my leg as I tapped it against the bench, patted my hand and stood to brush her dress.

"Shall I make my sketches then?"

"Please," I answered. "Let's return to the porch. You may sketch and I will drive a few more nails into the boards. They groan so."

We retraced our steps along the gravel path, passing the garden shed where I collected an old box of nails, a hammer, and a rusted pair of garden shears. My mother's once magnificent roses were now little more than a thicket climbing the front stone.

"This afternoon," Lenora said, nodding to the thorns as they came into view, "if the weather holds, I will prune those."

"You seem to always know my mind," I replied. "The gardens were my mother's occupation. I think we ought to begin there." We passed her vegetable garden, and that old familiar pang pierced my heart. Lenora hesitated, and then she took my arm again.

"I've heard stories of Mrs. Garrett's lavender. Have you been to the fields yet?"

"Nothing can grow there now," I answered. I couldn't bring myself to explain the fire, and I was grateful she did not ask.

"I would like to try," she said. "If you wish it. Perhaps a plant or two here in the garden, in honor of her."

I stopped and looked down at her. "You never knew my mother. Why should you wish to honor her memory?"

Her lips tightened for an instant and I could see that my tone had offended her.

"I've no other women here," she replied. "I should like to celebrate one."

"Have you not gotten on well with my cousin?"

She released my arm to wrap the shawl around her shoulders. "Oh, Anna. She has been very cold. She is not to blame, *claro*. The townspeople have influenced her. I know what they say about me."

"What do they say?"

"Ridiculous things. Some say I'm a witch, a ghost. All lies. Every last one."

She took a few steps forward, but I grasped her hand.

"What are you, then?"

"I'm an artist. That's all."

I believed her and was sorry for the pain this place had caused her. It seems to be the chief export of late.

"Let us prove it to them, then," I said, and before I had taken the time to think, I added, "We'll have a party."

"A party?"

"Yes, we'll make an art gallery of the sitting room and display your new paintings for all our friends."

"I have no friends here. Who will we invite?"

"Everyone, all of them. They'll see they were wrong about you, about this house, about me. All of it."

Lenora considered this a moment, her eyes fixed on the house as we faced it squarely. "And you think one of them will relieve you of it?"

"It's fine idea, is it not?" I don't know what came over me, for I had no real friends here either. In fact, I largely disliked most everyone in town. My wife would have noted with a knowing smile that I simply wished to tell them all I had returned, and that Ravenswood Hall belonged to me. She would've had it turned about, however. I had not inherited this miserable pile of stone at all. It had inherited me.

Lenora sat in a creaking swing beside the marble fountain, its cherubs and parched basin black with mold, and set to sketching the house.

"When I was a boy, there was a beautiful lattice climbing this side of the house, and this oak here"—I motioned to its remains, decomposing across the lawn—"reached to my window."

One of its branches had crashed through the porch railing, splintering it. I hefted it away and tossed it into the grass, disturbing a veil of spiders' webs.

"I will try to paint it as you remember, Will," Lenora replied.

We set to work, whiling away the time with my hammer and her pencil as the sun kept pace overhead.

Peter appeared with a tray of sandwiches and tea sometime after the noon hour. I met him on the porch to carry it myself to Lenora, but before he could relinquish it to me, the sensation of the silver under my fingertips struck a memory into my brain with as much force as a bolt of lightning.

I was a young man again, with my hands on this very tray. Tears plunked onto the silver, and onto my mother's teapot. My mind revolted at this image, smearing it until only sound remained—the gentle rolling of a glass vial as I walked. An empty vial.

I released the tray as if it bore a viper, and so too did Peter. My mother's teapot slipped from the tray and fell toward the floor, its top flying off and breaking against the woodpile, slowly and strangely without sound. Time caught up to itself an instant later, and the whole lot shattered with a crash upon the boards.

Lenora dropped her brushes and hurried to my side as Peter knelt with a curse to retrieve the larger shards. Murdoch appeared in the doorway, but he only observed the chaos and then vanished into the house.

"Apologies, Will," Peter said.

"I am to blame," I said, and Murdoch returned with a broom, which I took.

"That beautiful teapot," Lenora said beside me. I looked at her as I swept up the shards, but I did not see her. My mind lingered with my mother and the empty vial on the tray. Dr. Johnston's words repeated over and over in my ears, along with the *drip, drip* of my own tears.

A tincture of laudanum for your mother.

Although I tried, and continue to do so as I write this, I can recall neither the events that preceded this memory nor those that followed. There was no nostalgia in it, nothing of the common feeling when one remembers a thing from long ago. It felt as if I experienced it for the first time instead of the second, and I don't know what to make of this. Does this memory belong to me at all, or is it an implant, a foreign body lodged in my brain by my father's hand?

Murdoch left with the remains of the teapot gathered in a dustpan, drawing my attention to the present. I was sorely grieved at the fate of that piece of china. My mother had purchased it while on a trip to Boston one summer, before the darkness folded itself into our lives. She'd seen it in a shop window and nothing my father said could persuade her from bringing it home. Over time, the delicate yellow daffodils painted all about the base and blossoming on the handle faded to a mirage. I restrained myself from following Murdoch into the house and rescuing a piece of the handle for fear that Lenora might think me childish, but a piece of my heart broke along with that old pot.

Lenora touched my forearm.

"Perhaps it can be fixed," she said. I forgot myself when her fingers met my skin, for I covered her hand with my own.

"Perhaps," was all I said, and I remained beside her until her fingers slipped from my arm and she returned to her painting.

"You ought to rest, Will," she said, looking over her canvas, her tone languid but firm, as if she were speaking to a child. I minded not—the sound of my Christian name on her lips was so sweet to me that I obeyed her immediately and sat on the steps. It was buttercream on one of my mother's cakes, or a drop of sugar from a honeysuckle blossom.

In the end, I must have spent too much of my energy, for although the porch no longer creaked, nausea obliged me to rest. This mountain air seems to have had the opposite effect as it ought. I feel somehow that my strength has slipped away.

Although night has fallen now, my heart is glad with the recounting of a day full of sunshine and good work. I will no longer languish here, declining into my father's madness, allowing ruin to seep into my bones. No, Lenora and I will restore Ravenswood Hall together. Before I close this journal for the night, I must allow myself this happiness, for I know not what tomorrow will bring.

Chapter IX

WILLIAM GARRETT'S JOURNAL

January 15, 1889

No wailing spirits or ponderous, rattling chains disturbed my slumber last night. I did not even dream. Although I woke again to ice assaulting the windows, my cheer could not be so easily trod upon. I had springtime in my heart. I dressed quickly and went downstairs, but Lenora had not yet risen.

I wandered about the house aimlessly in those early hours, straightening picture frames and running my fingers along the wood paneling, feeling the coldness of unused rooms and the welcome warmth of a dying fire in the sitting room. The clocks tolled six. I listened for her footfalls on the stairs or the gentle rustling of her dress, but she did not come.

Murdoch approached my father's chair, where I had ultimately landed to watch the sun rise, and handed me two envelopes without greeting.

"Letters for you, sir."

The first was from Dr. Johnston, the latter from my daughter. I had written the doctor yesterday for more information on my father's demise, but I did not expect so prompt a reply. Although curious, I set this aside to open Lottie's letter.

A LETTER TO DR. WILLIAM GARRETT

14 Albany Square, Baltimore, Maryland, to Ravenswood Hall Postmark Illegible

Dear Papa,

You'll likely be furious to know I had a very successful séance with the neighbors yesterday. We made contact with Mrs. Fletcher's son, Samuel, who went missing during the battle of Chancellorsville. I do hope I've given her some closure after all this time. I refused to take her money at the end of it, but she insisted, so our credit with the grocer is restored to good standing for a time. Mr. Chatterly, though, is not so easily appeased, unfortunately. I found his eviction letter nailed to the door yesterday morning. He has graciously given us until spring considering your absence, but it appears we shall be quite homeless come April.

I am resigned to leaving our home if we must, Papa. Surely Ravenswood Hall cannot be as terrible as you describe. It would do me well to breathe in such clean mountain air. All this to say, you needn't worry about me. I am wherever you are, and that is enough.

Before you ask, your remaining patients are doing well. I've paid a visit to each personally, and aside *from a* mild cough from Mr. Burns, you've nothing with which to concern yourself. I gave him Mama's recipe for chamomile tea and I expect that should set him back to rights. I was unsure how to reply when he asked about your return. With all that you've mentioned, I suspect you plan to stay well into spring? Do tell me your thoughts, and I shall relay them.

Now, I'm uncertain where to begin in reply to your letters. What is all this talk of madness? Cruel men are always predisposed to lunacy, Papa, and it really is no surprise that Grandfather succumbed to it in the end. You haven't an ounce of cruelty in your body.

So, you say the doctor confirms your visit prior to Grandmother's death. I say, what of it? You know laudanum has many uses. An errand is no indication of homicide. Grandfather's accusations are blatant lies, bent on destroying all you have built. We both know this to be fact. You must not let him succeed.

The murder case of the undead Miss Laveau is curious, but I'm sure can be explained rationally. You describe her as though she were some kind of siren, what with all that mystery and beauty woven into one person. I think she may have beguiled you, Papa. You scarcely know her and already refer to her by her Christian name? A woman must trust her instincts, after all, and mine tell me that your mysterious Miss Laveau may not be who you think she is.

I was pleased to learn that I have a cousin. Why have you not told me of Anna before? Please give her my love and tell her that she is always welcome here in the city. We have the spare room upstairs, you know, and your medical journals and all of those silly penny dreadfuls make poor tenants. Perhaps she could take a nice position as a housemaid nearby. How wonderful it would be to have family with us, and an additional income would settle Mr. Chatterly's mind. You will tell her, won't you, Papa?

I'll close for now. Mrs. Newman's son has fallen ill with fever and I'm off to play at nurse. I will write again for guidance if the condition warrants it. Do cheer up, Papa. I dislike reading all of these thoughts on darkness and death. Such things are a part of life. Like Mama always said, we have each other, after all.

All my love,

Lottie

P.S. I took your sketch of the trinket to my friend, Beatrice, who is Catholic (you met her at the Christmas party). It's really quite a terrible drawing, Papa. You would do well to take a lesson once in a while. I'm grateful to have inherited Mama's inclination for art. In any case, Beatrice believes it may be one of the patron saints of medicine. This, in the very least, solves the mystery of why it was given to you. No doubt the boy's mother recognized you—either by face or reputation—and offered the little talisman as an ode to your profession. You may set that to rest if nothing else.

WILLIAM GARRETT'S JOURNAL

January 15, 1889, continued

I read Lottie's letter with tears in my eyes. I missed her so dearly that these sensible words were like honey to me, excepting the bit about my being beguiled, which was nonsense.

Dr. Johnston's letter awaited me next. I unfolded it and read:

My journal is all I am able to offer. You must speak with Devlin.

I frowned, unsatisfied. I'd been confident the doctor could offer some kind of explanation, but here, yet again, was another mystery.

"What is it, Murdoch?" I asked, for he stood by the fireplace with his arms behind his back.

"Will you be having breakfast early today, sir?"

"Yes, I think so, and if you could have Wilson prepare the horses."

"Going into town, sir?"

"No, I need to pay a visit to the constable."

"Very well." He bowed, and then added, "If you see young Christine, do tell her to return to her duties. She's in the habit of hiding to read those novels of hers, like you when you were a boy."

"Ah, she's only a child," I said, remembering the musty scent of the linen closet, where I whiled away many hours with naught but a candle and a well-loved book. Somehow sharing this place with the rodents and moths was less frightening than my own bed when I was a lad.

"Even still, sir. She is neglecting her duties."

He turned to leave.

"Murdoch," I called after a moment's hesitation.

"Yes, sir?"

"What do you know of Lenora's disappearance?"

Murdoch frowned. "Begging your pardon, sir?"

"When she left and then returned months later. What do you know of it?"

He appeared quite grave, his gaze floating toward the window. "Nothing at all, sir, only when she returned, she was quite different."

"How do you mean?"

"My eyes aren't what they used to be, as you well know, but I hardly recognized her. Something in her manner spoke of tragedy. She came back to us in body, but her spirit stayed behind." He inhaled and lifted his bony shoulders. "But pay no mind to the musings of an old man. You asked a question, and I have answered. Will that be all?"

Puzzled by so enigmatic a reply, I could only nod, and he left to have Wilson ready the horses.

These were not the plans I wished to make today, but what choice did I have? Only the truth, as the saying goes, could set me free from this place. Until I restored the Garrett name, until I proved the tenants of Ravenswood Hall were all flesh and blood, I had no hope of selling it. If Constable Devlin could provide me with the answers, I had rather go now and be done with it.

I breakfasted but took no notice of the food. When Wilson drove the carriage to the door, he greeted me with his usual grin and a tip of his hat.

"How are you, sir?" he asked. "Perfect weather we had yesterday, aye?"

I nodded and climbed into the carriage without so much as a good morning or a thank you. The ride passed swiftly, as often happens when one does not wish to arrive, though the road was treacherous and twice I was obliged to assist Wilson in clearing mud from the wheels. This did not improve my spirits, though admittedly I was not entirely present. I spent much of the ride in a kind of hopeless reverie, lost in the charming memories of yesterday. It seems now like another life. How quickly I had been cast back into the dark wood.

By the time Wilson guided the horses down the constable's drive, all of the warmth of yesterday had gone out of me. He opened the carriage door but did not announce our arrival as usual.

"Forgive me," I said as I stepped out. "I'm in a foul mood today."

"It's no business of mine, sir," he replied. Then he brightened, saying, "We can drive into town, if you like, to see the train. That'll lift your spirits, no doubt!"

I smiled at him and patted his shoulder. "You're a good man, Wilson." He lifted his hat to me and then took my place inside the carriage to wait for my return, unfolding a newspaper to pass the time.

"I won't be long," I assured him.

The constable's home, while little more than a modest log cottage nestled into the side of the mountain, had been lovingly kept even in the dead of winter. Stacks of firewood lined both sides of the house, the right still covered in a blanket of snow as it rested in the perpetual shade of a massive oak. A hand-carved bear figurine stood guard on the porch, its paws clutching a fish of some sort, and the remains of a meager vegetable garden rested peacefully beneath the window. Through said window, I spied the constable and his wife just sitting down to breakfast. Although I did not wish to disturb them, I had come a long way, and the aroma of stewed rabbit permeated the cracks and crevices of the house, making the whole place nigh irresistible to me. When I knocked on the door, a cadaverous woman, presumably Mrs. Devlin, opened it with a drawn but cheerful smile.

"Good morning," I began, removing my hat. "I am Dr. William Garrett. Is the constable in?"

"Why, yes, he is. I've just put breakfast on the table. Won't you come in?" She swept a dull lock of silver hair from her brow and showed me into the dining room, announcing, "A Dr. Garrett for you, dear."

The constable pushed his chair away from the table and unfolded his huge frame to shake my hand. While age had withered him some, he still gave the impression of having once maintained great physical power.

"To what do I owe the pleasure, Dr. Garrett?" His dark hair had fooled me, but the accent was distinctly Irish.

"I hope you'll forgive the intrusion. I shan't keep you and your wife long from your meal—"

"Bah," he interrupted and pulled out a chair for me. "Mary,

bring Dr. Garrett a plate."

"I couldn't impose," I said.

"Nonsense. It'd be a shame not to share it. Left over from last night's supper, you won't mind?"

I bowed to him as his wife disappeared into the kitchen, humming a jovial tune a bit like a lullaby.

"Most kind, Constable," I said. As I sat at their table, watching the two of them go about the setting of my place and the serving of what seemed to me the most beautiful meal I had ever seen, a great sadness descended upon me. It was akin to loneliness, but somehow darker and more hopeless. Such a simple, happy life they had, one that I could only hope for but never again attain. Such was my lot.

"Now, what brings you about this early?" the constable asked once we had settled. Mrs. Devlin passed a plate of sliced bread and butter, which tasted wholesome and wonderful.

"I believe you were acquainted with my father. You investigated a case of a missing woman at my estate some months ago."

"Aye," he said. His head bobbed up and down as he slurped his stew, the muscles in his neck bulging. "Ravenswood Hall, is it?"

"You've a good memory, sir."

"An easy case to remember. All anyone could talk about for weeks. Quite the scandal."

"So I understand. I'd like the facts, though. I've no interest in rumors."

"Fortunately for you, we police types deal only in facts, don't we, Mary?"

"No truer words," she answered. "Dr. Garrett, how do you like your rabbit?"

"The best I've ever eaten, ma'am." She blushed at this. "Did he confess?"

"Lord, no. He was sealed up as a tomb. No, it was that young girl who reported it. What was her name, dear?"

I answered before she could speak. "Christine."

"Ah, yes, Christine. Said she saw the whole thing. Quite a tale, it was."

Mrs. Devlin clucked her tongue. "A shame is what it was, for a child to weave a story such as that, out of nothing, too! What was in her head, I wonder, to make her speak so? There's something not right with her. You'd do well to avoid her if you can."

"She has been doing her best to avoid me, I think."

"Well," the constable said, "don't take that to heart. She stopped speaking altogether after the, ah, incident. Hasn't said a word since to my knowledge."

As I pondered this, and the strangeness of Christine's only words to me, Mrs. Devlin launched into a fit of coughing that rendered communication impossible. She pressed her handkerchief to her lips and excused herself, but the frailness of her figure made more sense to me. It was a wonder I hadn't recognized the symptoms earlier.

"How long has she been ill?" I asked the constable. He looked after her as she left the room.

"It struck her just before Christmas," he answered, the smile long gone from his face. "It was a grim holiday, as you can imagine."

"I'm sorry."

"Nothing can be done. I'm sure you can see that, plain as day." He attempted to mask the hopelessness in his voice with a smile and the quick clearing of his throat. I changed the subject.

"Will you tell me what Christine Murdoch said? What did she see?"

He roused, sitting straight again in his chair. "A great many things, if she is to be believed."

"Which you do not, of course?"

"Nay, I didn't doubt the child at all when she first told her tale. The little sprite was damn convincing."

I leaned toward him and said, "I want to hear everything."

"Well, she came to the house in the middle of the night in hysterics. She grabbed ahold of my trousers crying, 'He killed her! He killed her!'"

"And she accused my father?"

He nodded as his wife returned to the table. "Are you all right, dear?"

"Yes, thank you. Pay no mind to me. Please continue." The constable squeezed Mrs. Devlin's hand, and a look of such adoration passed between the two of them that it momentarily transfixed me. I no longer felt pity for her, nor for him. I could live a thousand lives unaffected by disease and never *live* like the constable and his wife.

"The girl," Devlin continued, "claimed to have seen your father strangling Miss Laveau in some sort of mad fury. When it didn't produce the desired effect, he hoisted her over the widow's walk and hanged her with his scarf."

Christ. I closed my eyes, willing away the hideous specter of this accusation. I did not wish to believe it possible, but neither could I deny the veracity with which my mind conjured the scene. Mrs. Devlin shook her head and crossed herself.

I cleared the misery from my throat and asked, "Did you find any evidence of this?"

"None whatsoever. The nearest thing to evidence we found was a button from one of Miss Laveau's dresses, which she later claimed to have simply lost."

"Where did this *murder* occur?"

"Allegedly in your father's chambers."

"And in what state did you find my father?"

"He was just coming in from church, Miss Laveau nowhere to be found. He showed me to the room and answered my questions with perfect calm. He hadn't seen Miss Laveau all day, and no one saw her again, at least, for almost half a year. We investigated her murder for months, couldn't find a damn thing."

"And when she returned—"

"I saw her myself," Mrs. Devlin added. "In town. She was buying a set of oil paints. I inquired after her health, and she said she'd had a lovely holiday in Europe."

"And that was that." The constable took another slice of bread and dipped it into his stew. "Does that clear the matter up for you, Dr. Garrett?"

I frowned. The answers had been laid out plainly before me, but I did not feel satisfied. It was all too simple. If Lenora had only gone on holiday, what reason did my father have for believing she'd left him, never to return? And what of Christine Murdoch's claims?

"You said you believed Christine when she came to you?" I asked.

"I mean you no offense, sir," he said, wiping his moustache with a napkin. "But your father was not a well-respected man. He holed himself up after the death of his wife and became something of a pariah, a ghost in his own right. It was no great leap to believe him capable of murder."

"You're nothing like him at all," the constable's wife offered.

"Thank you," I replied. "I know well my father's failings. I hope I might restore the Garrett name to the people here. I fear the ghosts are all they see of late."

Mrs. Devlin reached across the table and patted my hand. "Never fear, dear. They'll know the truth by and by. Blood will out, as the saying goes."

Chapter X

WILLIAM GARRETT'S JOURNAL

January 15, 1889, continued

After altering course to post a hasty reply to Lottie, Wilson guided us at last toward Ravenswood Hall, the setting sun pouring molten fire down upon the mountainside. I wish now that I had lingered in town longer. I could have looked for a place to settle myself amid the protection of a great number of people, in a well-lit hotel or a warm tavern. I tarried in town only while though, for I could not well bear the strange glances and whispers that met me at the door of any place I entered.

Instead, I spent the remainder of the journey transcribing the visit with Devlin and turning this blasted silver trinket around in my fingers. I might have noted the peculiar sunset as I did so, might have taken such a violent display of nature as a portent of what awaited upon my return, but I am either too science-minded or simply too dull, for only the usual ill-ease met me as we rattled up to the doorstep.

This gruesome sunlight cast its spell across the whole of my estate, rusting over the stones and gleaming on the windows like the eye shine of owls. Shadows from the frail branches of the willow stretched like monstrous spider legs across the house, and the box elders took the forms of men. As the images of my nightmare crept about in my mind, I perceived movement in Lenora's window.

There she stood, looking down upon the garden, her face pale and disembodied against a black dress that had all but married the room's darkness. Although I was not yet near enough to see her expression, the sight of her chilled me. I scarcely recognized her.

Before the horses could rest their tired legs, Peter flew out of the house and tore open the carriage door. Lenora disappeared from the window.

"Is she with you?" he cried. "Is she here?"

"What the devil? Who?"

"My daughter! Did you take her with you?"

"Calm yourself, man," I said, setting my hands on his shoulders. "Christine is not with me. What's happened?"

"Oh, God," he sobbed and stumbled backward, his hands in his hair. "She's gone." He turned back to the house. I sat in the carriage, dumbfounded, staring after him as he strode back inside. Wilson left the horses and turned to me.

"The master of the house will be wanted," he said, and then followed Peter into the house. Stirring from my bewilderment, I abandoned the carriage and went after them to find Peter and Lenora already engaged in what appeared to be a heated argument in the sitting room. Peter rubbed his temples and shook his head. Lenora gestured violently, but they spoke in too low a tone to be heard. My boots on the wooden floor gave me up. She looked up and bade me enter. Murdoch dropped down into the chair before the fire, his shoulders shaking.

"What's happened?" I whispered as she met me beneath

the threshold of the room. Her hair had fallen down around her face and she slipped a wayward strand behind her ear, rosy with cold. Mud stained the hem of her dress, which was not black at all but plain and gray. A wool riding coat dried over a chair before the fire, still dripping onto the stones. I could not fathom how I had so mistaken her appearance, but I had little time to ponder this peculiarity, for the answer to my question came hard upon its heels.

"Little Christine's gone missing."

"What do you mean she's gone missing?" I asked.

"We've been out looking for her all day. We thought she was with you."

"I haven't seen her since yesterday at breakfast."

"Nor I," she said, but this was spoken internally, a thought said aloud.

"Perhaps she only went to see the horses?"

Lenora shook her head. "I've checked the stables twice. Molly has disappeared too."

The door opened, and Anna's voice sounded in the foyer. Peter ran to meet her.

"I searched all along the road," she breathed, her footsteps on the stone. "No sign of her."

"Please, Anna," he replied, his voice thick. "If you—"

"Has Will come?"

"In the sitting room with the others."

She rushed into the room, untying her shawl, her eyes searching each face until she came at last to mine.

"Will, what a horrible thing," she cried and threw her arms around me, as was her custom, but her heart was not in the embrace.

Murdoch shuffled up beside me, his voice trembling. "I sent Wilson to fetch the constable. What shall we do, sir? She must be found."

"You've checked the whole house, every room?"

Peter nodded. "All but the root cellar, which remains locked at all times."

"We'll find her, old friend," I assured him with a firm hand on his arm. "Just a child's game. We'll discover her hiding in a closet or a pantry in no time. Ladies, will you stay with Murdoch? I'm afraid he'll need looking after. Peter, you and I will check the cellar. It won't hurt to be thorough."

Thus employed, Peter and I left the women with Murdoch and journeyed toward the kitchen. I removed a ring of keys from the hook on the wall, selected a cruel-looking skeleton key, and inserted it into the lock. The door swung open to a stone staircase that fell down into darkness. I lit my candle and tipped the flame to the wick of another, which I passed to Peter.

I had been raised in this house. I knew every place the floorboards creaked and every room behind every locked door. I knew the earthy odor of the cellar as well as I knew the scent of lavender in my mother's dressing room. Even the scratching claws of mice scurrying to and fro in the pantries was familiar, but as I looked down the steps into the emptiness, I sensed something foreign. It prickled the hairs on my arms and tickled the back of my neck as gently as a breath. I held mine deep inside my lungs, waiting for this presence to make itself known to me, but no shadows writhed below. I heard only the dripping of water from the pump to our left.

"Shall I, then?" Peter said, and I waved him off and descended. "I've always hated this old cellar. Father used to make me fetch the potatoes when I was a boy."

"I remember. You used to trick me into coming with you. I dare say we haven't grown out of our distaste for it."

"I think you're right." He attempted laughter, but it was only the dried husk of mirth. "Will, the chances of Christine being here are nearly nothing. We found the door locked. It cannot be locked from the inside."

"Children are wily," I said by way of answer.

Our candles lit the small room dimly, but all around us were faces—my father's face in deep blues, Murdoch's in pastel,

Lenora's in grays, her likeness so exact that I felt she might smile at me at any moment. And yet, even as I stood before her very simulacrum, there was darkness about the eyes and mouth that reminded me of a corpse.

"What the hell?" Peter whispered.

"These must be Lenora's paintings," I said, but I could not imagine her painting these. It was as if she had blended putrescence into the paints, as if we stood not in a cellar but in a mausoleum. Propped up against a row of wooden shelves was a portrait of little Christine sitting quietly at the bay window with a copy of *Robinson Crusoe*. Spellbound and horrified all at once, the effect that these discarded portraits had upon us fixed us both to the earthen ground, unable to move but for our candles, which trembled in the darkness.

Anna called our names, her voice hollow as it made its way to us, the way a shovel sounds when it strikes a coffin. I knew this sound well enough to be chilled by it. A long time ago, in the mad throes of grief, I had taken it upon myself to prove that my mother's death had been a lie. I took a shovel and went to her grave, digging throughout the night until exhaustion made me haggard and half-crazed. Peter found me as I knelt atop the coffin, clawing the earth away with tears in my eyes. He pulled me away before I could open the casket. What I would have found inside, I am certain, would have haunted me for the rest of my life. I owed him dearly for saving me from it.

When Anna called again, Peter and I were already half way up the stairs. There was something unholy about this place, something veiled that should remain so, like reading a woman's journal without her consent or disturbing a grave after a century of silence.

"Christ," Peter mumbled. "Those were...were..."

"Horrible," I finished. "Don't speak of them." I said this knowing that I would, I must, ask Lenora about them.

"Are you all right?" Anna asked as we emerged from the stairwell. "What was down there?"

"And the constable?" Peter asked, in lieu of answering.

"He's not yet arrived," she answered, and the three of us walked together back into the sitting room.

"I'd like to search the rooms again," I said, addressing them all. "I cannot wait idly. Who will join me?" Although the Devlin home was but a few miles down the mountain at the edge of town, I suspected the encroaching darkness would delay them.

"They've been searched twice over," Lenora said. "She's not here."

Peter set his hand on his father's shoulder, who took no notice of it at all. "It's damn better than sitting here waiting. I'll come with you, Will."

"Very well."

"The widow's walk," Lenora said as we turned to take our leave.

"What of it?" I asked, but the dread had already coagulated in my chest, catching in my lungs so I could not draw a full breath.

"I searched your father's chamber," she answered. "Inside every wardrobe and behind every curtain, but not the widow's walk."

There was no resisting it.

"Then it must be searched," I said, and turned to the stairs before I could lose my nerve.

Peter followed I'm sure, though I don't recall his presence until I had reached the balcony door, when he lit a lamp beside me. I tore aside the curtains with such swiftness that one of the brass rungs snapped. Violet twilight had already descended over the mountain, but whether I could blame my haste on the deepening dark or my fear of it, I cannot say.

Only Peter's face and my own looked back at me, made sinister still by the glowing of the lamp. I closed my fingers around the doorknob. I did not want to open it. I did not wish to see, even in my mind, my mother's eyes, veiled by the milky cloud of death. How they had admonished me that night.

You did this.

Her voice came to me as if from another plane, a memory but darker. A nightmare.

"No," I whispered.

"Will, please," Peter said. My senses returned me. My mother's voice lingered not in my ears but in the hollow of my throat, aching. I turned the knob and stepped out into the icy air, the wind billowing the curtains behind me.

Her chair remained after all this time, moldered and darkened by moss. I turned my eyes from it, toward the woods. To my left, the Hudson carried on its course, unaffected by darkness or cold, and below me stood one of the few remaining hemlock groves in this part of the country. My father had fiercely protected his forests despite numerous offers from tanneries that required the tree for their industry. Most of these are closed now, their resources exhausted.

Large outcroppings of rock jutted between the trees, some split by streams, others washed white by centuries of unforgiving wind and rain, and beneath me directly they fell into something of a plateau. This place, I am certain, was where my father had met his end. In the falling dark, I could make out nothing but the pale swath of gray stone, though my eyes strained against my will for signs of death, for blood or fragments of clothing or scraps of flesh. I set my palms on the railing, Christine forgotten until a blur of white dashed across the plateau. I squinted in the low light, waiting with my breath in my throat. A bobcat, perhaps.

No, there it was again.

Christine. She stopped beneath me, her hair mussed with dead leaves, and then she looked up and smiled.

"Jesus Christ," I cried, stumbling backward. I shall never rid my memory of that horrible smile, gaping and toothless, her jaw hanging slack, eyes shining in the milky moonlight like those of a possum. She darted back into the trees, but they did not shudder with her passing. It was as though the forest had simply absorbed her.

"She's not here, Will," Peter said behind me. He'd been inside. He could not corroborate what I'd seen.

"Come!" I said, brushing by him and running toward the hall.

"What?"

"She's injured. Come quickly."

I ran like a madman through the house and out the kitchen door, the quickest route to the old trail I'd created as a boy. Many years ago, I had taken my father's hunting knife and hacked my way through the thickets and brambles so that I could gain the plateau. It had been the only place on our property that had been forbidden me, being simply too dangerous. Naturally, it was the only place I'd wanted to go, and so I found my way with the strength of my defiance. Until this moment, the trail had remained a secret.

Peter kept pace behind me and called out every now and again for explanation, but I had none, so I continued on in silence. We ran behind the leaning smokehouse, which smelled still of pork, and I led Peter to the path, heedless of the thorns that choked it. In only moments, the way became so steep that descending backward was the only option. My toes sought purchase amid the stones and mud, my fingers clutching roots and saplings.

"Will, what the hell has come over you?" Peter cried above me. "Where are we going?"

"I saw her!" I called back. My feet landed on flat stone at last and I turned, running across the plateau to the place where she had disappeared.

"Christine!" I yelled. My voice echoed off the mountain, disturbing a pair of ravens who flew off into the night with screeches of protest. Darkness had fallen completely, and I'd had the forethought to take neither a lamp nor my coat. I squinted into the shadows and shivered, for the wind had picked up and blew my hair into my eyes. Only once the moon peered out from behind the clouds could I see the forest floor and all of the shadow that it held within.

There! Christine slipped out from behind a shriveled bramble bush, a hair ribbon in her hand. She held her hand out, beckoned me to follow, and then shot off into the trees. When the moon slid again behind the clouds, I had only this scrap of bright fabric to guide my way. Branches scratched my face as I followed, tearing at my clothes and skin, but I paid the pain no mind.

"Will!" Peter called, but I did not hear his footfalls behind me. He'd lost sight of me.

I tripped, inevitably, on an exposed root and fell hard against a stone. Strangely, unconsciousness took on a red aspect instead of black, so thick was the darkness already. I do not know how long I lost myself, but when I woke, Peter still called out to me and the ravens had returned. My eyes struggled to focus as the moon again lent its light, and when I at last regained my vision, I thought I might still be unconscious and in the throes of a nightmare.

A human skull peered back at me.

I cried out and twisted away from the wretched thing, still aware enough of my surroundings to move carefully, lest the earth drop away beneath me.

"Will! Where are you?" Peter cried, and his voice reached me three times, but I could not answer.

I plucked the skull from the pine needles. Many creatures had feasted upon it. Only small bits of flesh clung to the nasal and lacrimal bones, and the mandible was missing entirely. Deep scratches covered every surface.

I recognized my father's remains by the absence of the second bicuspid, which had become infected when I was a boy and had been extracted. In my heart, I knew this was all I would ever find of him. I wanted to throw it off the mountain, to crush it under my boot, but I could not. How I hated him. My God, I hated him with more fire than I'd ever loved anything, but it had all been so pointless, such a waste. Was this all I would ever have to curse, these fragments of rat-gnawed bone? Tears filled my eyes as I held it, and then my thumb brushed across a small hole beneath the parietal bone.

I knew by the shape what had created it, and I knew as surely as I held his skull in my hands that my father had not in lunacy flung himself from the widow's walk.

He had been murdered.

Chapter XI

WILLIAM GARRETT'S JOURNAL

January 15, 1889, continued

These last pages in my journal seem to have written themselves, for I scarcely remember sitting down to write them. The blow my brain sustained has perhaps affected my memory. A kind of spectral fog still shrouds my recollection of recent events, but I shall recount them as coherently as possible. I swear on my mother's grave that I *did* see Christine, though Peter tells me he could find no sign of her.

I must have lost consciousness again after making my discovery. In one moment, I was cradling the remains of my dead father in the forest, and in another, I was lying on the sofa with Lenora, Anna, and Peter peering down at me. I haven't the slightest idea how Peter managed to drag my lifeless body all the way back to the house.

"Will?" Lenora said softly as I opened my eyes. "Will, thank heaven."

"Where is it?" I mumbled. "Where is it?"

"Where is what?" Peter asked.

"The skull. My father's skull." I sat up quickly and tried to stand, but three pairs of hands pushed me back down.

"You must rest," Lenora said. She pressed my hand.

"He was murdered!" I cried, brushing her away. "What have you done with it? Where is it?"

"Will, for Christ's sake," Peter said. "You hit your head. You're not making sense."

At last, I was able to stand, but a wave of vertigo struck me so violently that I dropped back down onto the cushions, my head between my knees.

"Oh, my God, it's gone. It's gone." Tears came unbidden then, and I sobbed like a child. I could no longer cope with all I had witnessed, all I had learned.

"Peter," Anna said, "call the doctor. He's not well." Peter left the room without another word while I rocked my head in my hands. "Lenora, wait here for the constable. I'll take him to bed."

I walked on foal's legs, my cousin guiding me up the steps.

"What am I to do?"

"Hush, Will. You must rest. We can talk more in the morning."

"And Christine? I saw her, Annie. I swear it."

"You hit your head," was her maddening answer.

When we at last arrived at my chamber, I sat on the bed, wringing my hands and muttering to myself like a raving madman. Anna sat beside me.

"Cousin, you must stop this," she said, and the firmness of her touch calmed me enough to at least consider reason. "It's simply impossible for you to have seen your father's skull."

"There was a wound from a bullet, Anna. I've seen enough in my profession to know it by sight, and I saw it with my own eyes, felt it with my fingers." I held up my hands, but she set them back in my lap. "I must go back down."

"Are you mad? You could have died. I thought I lost you once. I won't suffer it again."

The anguish in my expression must have moved her. In a moment, she had her arms wrapped around me and I exhausted my remaining strength in keeping the tears at bay against her shoulder.

"I am lost, Cousin," I said, and she smoothed my hair at the nape of my neck, as she had when we were children. "Who am I to believe?"

At this, Anna pulled me away and, with her hands firmly on my shoulders, said, "Me, Will. Believe *me*. I tell you that Peter found neither his daughter nor your father in those woods tonight. Now, you must rest."

I could only manage a partial nod. Anna kissed my forehead and left me.

Several hours passed before I became master of myself again. I wrote in my journal to gather my thoughts and then dozed by the fire in a sort of languishing psychogenic fugue, the silver trinket clutched tightly in my palm.

I woke again just past midnight to Devlin's voice, and I ran down to meet him before I had even time to step into my slippers. I yearned to tell him all I had witnessed and to hear what he might make of it, but Lenora stopped me at the bottom of the stairs as Peter led the constable into the sitting room. He had seen me out of the corner of his eye, I'm certain, but either did not know what to make of me in such a condition or did not wish to interrupt Peter's explanation of events. These were both reasonable reactions, but I felt slighted that he should not wish to discuss these matters with me directly.

"I need to speak with him," I said, looking beyond Lenora, but she stayed me with her hand upon my breast.

"Peter and I can manage, Will," she said. "You ought to return to bed."

"I've had a shock, that's all," I said, and she took my hand, lips pressed as though she wished to speak her mind but could not. Devlin asked his questions in the other room. Who had seen her last? When? Did she seem frightened?

"He'll be wanting to speak to the master of the house," I said. I withdrew my hand and walked into the sitting room. The Murdochs stood before the fireplace, each merely a double of the other. Peter's shoulders drooped nearly as much as his father's.

"Ah!" Devlin exclaimed at the sight of me. And quite a sight I must have been too, for I stood before them barefoot with my hair hanging down into my eyes, still wearing the wrinkled, mud-caked clothing from earlier. This was the only physical evidence I had to prove it had happened at all.

"A pleasure to see you again, Dr. Garrett," he said, shaking my hand vigorously. "Though the circumstances are unpleasant. I am sorry for that."

"As am I," I answered. "Thank you for coming."

"It took a great deal longer than I'd hoped, it did. My wife is not well tonight."

"I'm sorry to hear that," I replied, and uncertain what else I ought to say on the matter, I moved on. "Peter has apprised you of the situation?"

"An odd thing, it is," he mused. "Is there anyone else in the house?"

"Only my cousin, Anna," I answered. "I presume she's gone to bed. Shall I wake her?"

"Certainly not. I'm sure you and the others can answer my questions."

He asked a great number of things, nodding all the while and writing notes in a little black book as if every detail were of the utmost importance, though I couldn't see what he intended to make of it all. Peter dropped down into my father's chair when these questions dwindled, leaving the elder Murdoch alone and wavering by the fire. He rubbed his eyes, his countenance the very picture of misery.

"I will put every effort into this case to ensure the safe return of your daughter," Devlin assured him. "In most cases like this, the child's only run off. Is there any chance she might have wandered out into the forest?"

"No," Peter said quickly. "She knows never to go there. She's a good girl, Constable."

"Aye, of course she is. Of course, she is." He pressed his hat down onto his head. "Right then, I had better get to it. Keep your hopes up, friends. I'll show myself out."

"Constable," I called after him. "Might I have a word with you in private?"

We paused at the door and he listened intently as I described everything I had seen in the forest, nodding and frowning occasionally with his arms folded across his chest. It was a relief to tell it all, and I felt better for it once it was done, even if he had no more answers than I.

"I'll return tomorrow then, shall I? We'll have a look down there for ourselves."

"I'd be obliged to you, Constable. I'm afraid the others believe me a bit of a lunatic, though I can't say I blame them." I said this with a laugh I did not feel, and he offered none in reply. I suggested he might remain here for the night, put up in one of the guest rooms.

"Very kind of you, sir, but I must return to my wife. I hate leaving her in her condition, you understand."

"Yes, of course."

When he had gone, I returned to the sitting room and set my hand on Peter's shoulder.

"We will find her, old friend," I said, but he shook his head.

"Friend?" he muttered without looking at me. "You ought to admit you'd forgotten me until you returned for your father's money."

I could only look at him, stunned.

"You're under a great deal of stress. Your opinion of me can't be so low as that?" When he said nothing, I pressed, "We were schoolboys together. Surely not so much has changed."

"Everything has changed," he whispered. "You're no better

than him."

This barb hit me squarely, and although I knew he wasn't in his right mind, I repaid it in full.

"You forget your place," I said, stepping around the chair to face him. Indeed, we had been playmates as children, but I was the master of this house and I should have liked him to remember it. "You will stand when you address me."

He cocked his jaw and then rose.

"My father needs me," he said through his teeth. "I won't turn my back on him."

He brushed past me and collected his father so they could retire for the evening. A glance passed between him and Lenora, and then she dropped onto the sofa, exhausted.

"I am sorry for all of this," I said. She placed her fingers on her lower lip, her eyes far away. I added, "Peter is cross with me. I'm afraid I've treated him unfairly."

"Hmm?" she hummed, and then looked at me as if she'd forgotten I was there. "Oh, yes, he's cross with everyone."

"I saw him arguing with you."

"That poor child," she said absently. "How frightened she must be."

I seated myself beside her and covered her hand with mine, saying, "We'll go out again at first light to search for her."

"It's too cold, Will." When she met my eyes, the depth of sorrow in them made my heart ache. I'd clearly misunderstood her relationship with the girl. She leaned into me and rested her head against my chest. She must have been searching for hours. I could feel the tension in her body, and her hair smelled of the forest.

"She won't survive," she whispered.

"Don't say such things." I shushed her, folding my arms around her and holding her against me, my chin atop her head. In a moment, she roused herself and sat up.

"Forgive me," she said, "I should like to bathe and go to bed. I am tired."

"You'll be needing water, then."

"Don't trouble Peter. I can bring it myself."

"You've done enough today. Let me, please."

Lenora hesitated but then agreed with a weary sigh. That she would exhaust herself so utterly for a child of no relation to her spoke volumes. She rose and walked toward the staircase, ruined dress dragging behind. She seemed to me the most beautiful creature in the world.

Within a quarter of an hour, I found myself again in my old washroom, steam from the bath both threatening the candle flame and clouding the mirror so my reflection appeared spectral. Lenora's hairbrush, with its ornate mother-of-pearl handle, sat on the pedestal beside the water basin, and I ran my fingers across the smooth surface. I could hear her undressing in the room, but I daren't look.

"It was my mother's," she said a moment later, stepping into the washroom in her dressing gown, her hair loose and falling to her waist. I averted my gaze and caught the reflection of her fogged smile in the glass.

"It's beautiful," I answered.

"You are the strangest man," she whispered, and then turned my face so I was forced to look upon her. The depths of her dark eyes, as unfathomable as the sea, called forth a demon from my heart, but she held no power to exorcise it. It wished to possess her. *I* wished to possess her, to enter her body and take it as my own.

I drew nearer, a breath from her lips, resisting. I had inherited this monster inside me from my father, and I knew in my heart that once I released it, I would not be able to leash it again. She traced the lines of my mouth with her delicate finger as if I were only a canvas, ready to be remade into another image.

Unable to breathe, I could do nothing but stand before her, at her mercy.

She whispered, "A man of pure heart would not look at me so."

"Did some fool tell you I was pure of heart?"

I kissed her then, God help me.

She slipped her hands into my hair, a delicious little sound of surprise passing between us, and I was lost. My arm banded around her waist, drawing the length of her against me. I watched in the mirror as I devoured her, scarcely knowing my own reflection.

I did not become master of myself until the candlelight struck my ring and shone it back to me in the glass.

"My God," I breathed, pushing her away. "Forgive me."

Her fingers flew to her lips, her wide eyes afire. I fled before she could speak, out to the bitter hall and into my own chamber, my chest heaving.

I collapsed onto the edge of the bed, my wedding band burning as I twisted it.

"Charlotte," I whispered. I turned my eyes to the heavens, but found I hadn't strength to look toward her, and so I let my head fall into my hands. "Charlotte, my love."

My hands trembled as I raked them into my hair, a terrible ache pulsing in my throat. I felt I might split apart, ripping along the scars and jagged seams.

"Forgive me," I said, and then I wept.

Chapter XII

A LETTER TO MISS CHARLOTTE GARRETT

Ravenswood Hall to 14 Albany Square, Baltimore, Maryland
Postmarked January 16, 1889

Dear Lottie,

This place is diseased. Though the doors close tightly and the floor is sturdy beneath me, I feel unstable and isolated, as if within these halls lurks some darkness waiting to wrap its creeping vines around me. I have been exposed to madness here as if it were consumption, infected by it so that I doubt my own senses, my own memory. Something unholy is going on here, my girl, and I am affected as much by superstition now as I am suspicion. Old friends are strangers. Shadows are monsters. God help me.

A peculiar thing occurred this morning, which I shall

describe here in the hope that you can offer some explanation, logical or otherwise. I am open now to both prospects. But first I must inform you of some other ill news. My old friend Peter's daughter, Christine, went missing yesterday, and we have been unable to discover her whereabouts.

As such, I had given Murdoch and Peter leave to gather a search party for the missing child. Lenora and Anna had not yet risen, so I took it upon myself to prepare a small breakfast for us. Certain events, of which I will not go into detail, have transpired recently that kept me from sleep, so I prepared toast and jam in a fog, feeling generally out of sorts and only mildly aware of a distant ringing in my ears.

This sound, clear after a moment as the tolling of a small bell, grew louder until I realized that it was not my ears at all but one of the servant bells at Murdoch's station in the corner of the kitchen. It rang with so much urgency that it might have detached itself from the wall. At first, I thought perhaps Lenora was signaling some emergency upstairs, but it was not her bell that rang.

It was my father's.

One by one the others chimed, rising to such a pitch that it filled the whole house, filled my whole head. I dropped one of the saucers on the floor as Lenora ran into the room.

"What on earth are you—" she cried, but the sentence died in her throat when she saw that I did not control the horrible little devices. All at once, the bells fell silent, leaving only their ghosts still ringing in my ears. Lenora clutched her dressing gown around her neck, looking at me wide-eyed and humming a question mark, but I could offer her no explanation.

"Your father is displeased again," she whispered.

"Why do you say things like that? A rat got hold of the cord, that's all."

It left my mouth a bit pricklier than I had intended, but all of this nonsense about my father's ghost haunting Ravenswood is as ridiculous as the idea of Lenora haunting him. Still, I can think of no other explanation for these blasted bells.

"Have you not heard him with your own ears?" she answered.

I could not deny it, Lottie. I had heard him, hadn't I? I'd heard the bells. I'd held his skull in my hands. What do I do? Tell me, what shall I do?

WILLIAM GARRETT'S JOURNAL

January 16, 1889

My God, where do I begin?

I write now by candlelight as has become my custom of late, but I cannot close my eyes for fear of what dreams await me. How much more terrible will the nightmares be when inspired by a day such as this? 'Tis now the very witching time of night and the churchyard has coughed up its dead.

Until the cock crows thrice, I must remain alert. I shall begin with the morning, and in doing so hope to dispel some of the horror that plagues me.

After the incident with the bells, Lenora and I sat beside each other to take our meager breakfast, but we were not together. Her thoughts, I presume, were with Christine, and mine were fixed upon the writing of a hasty letter to Lottie, who I thought might offer me some advice. I'd not had the courage to speak to Lenora about the events of the previous night. I wished she would smile at me or take my hand or offer me some kind of glance to show that our kiss had affected her, but she drank her tea in silence until I could bear it no longer.

"Lenora," I said, laying down my pen. "Last night...I owe you—"

"You owe me nothing," she interrupted. Her expression softened, and she sent me an affectionate smile. "It has been a long time since I have felt alive, Mr. Garrett. I am not sorry."

"Nor I," I said, but I think it was a lie, for I felt ill even as the words left my lips. I had known this woman but a few days, and with each day that passed, I knew myself a little less.

"I've found one of my old sketches of Christine," she said, removing a small leather-bound notebook from the folds of her dress. "Will you come to town with me to show it? I cannot sit here and wait all day."

She opened the pages to a lovely pencil drawing, all soft lines and gentle shades, with absolutely none of the darkness that tainted the portraits in the basement. I could not bring myself to mention them.

"A fine idea," I answered, grateful for the change of subject. "I should like to visit Dr. Johnston as well to further discuss the matter of my father's death. Has Anna made any progress with the journal?"

"She does not keep me informed on your interests," she replied and rose, returning the sketchbook to its hiding place. "Wilson drove her home early this morning with the idea that Christine may have sought shelter there overnight."

"We shall collect her on the way, then," I said, noting the bitterness in her tone but lacking the courage to draw attention to it. Lenora nodded and left the room to ready herself. As her footsteps vanished up the staircase, the wheels of a carriage sounded outside on the drive. I rose and drew the curtain aside, frowning. Perhaps the attorney had discovered some loophole in my father's will.

A hansom cab pulled up to the house, and a woman stepped out before the driver had time even to climb down from his perch. I knew her before she lifted her black veil to gaze up at the hideous face of Ravenswood Hall and before she spied me and called out my name.

"Hello, Papa!"

"Lottie!" I cried, beaming. I ran to the door and wrenched it open. The damp, biting cold held me back but a moment, and then my daughter dropped her carpetbag onto the porch steps and flung herself into my arms. Some dark piece of me believed I might never see her again, that this place would finish me. To have my arms around her once more sent tears stinging in my eyes. There was hope yet.

"Papa, you're squeezing me to death," Lottie said against my shoulder. I laughed and released her, but only at arm's length so I might look at her. Her mother's wild strawberry hair peeked out from beneath the veil as she grinned at me.

"It's good to see you, my girl," I said. The sound of her laughter poured sunshine into my heart, and I embraced her again.

"Come now, it hasn't been but a week!"

A *week*? I might have been trapped in this house for months, decades even. Time means nothing here. Even as the sun rises and sets, Ravenswood reforms the days according to its own will.

I was forced, at length, to let her retrieve her carpetbag and went down to aid the driver in collecting her trunk. I settled the debt for the fare, which was far too much, but this man had brought me my daughter and I would have paid him in gold if I'd had any.

"Are you in mourning?" I asked, restored to the porch with her trunk. The driver whipped his horse, and it took off, eager to escape this place. Lottie touched her veil and looked down at the tweed day dress and shawl, which did not match the hat but had been her mother's.

"I don't know. Are we in mourning? I thought it best to come prepared, just in case."

"We are not. There isn't time."

"I hope there's time to mourn when I die," she said, and then tucked the hat under her arm. Her presence meant she'd likely not received my letter about the bells, which was for the best. The clear explanation was that some rodent had been gnawing the wire that connected the bell, and it wouldn't do to have her questioning my position on matters of the supernatural sort.

"What are you doing here, Lottie?" I asked. As pleased as I was, she was not but seventeen and the idea of her making such a journey alone troubled me greatly.

"Cousin Anna wrote me. She's terribly worried about you."

"About me?"

"Is she here? The painter?" Lottie looked over my shoulder, standing on tiptoe. "Anna's told me a great deal about her, and frankly, Papa, it's made me quite nervous. I came straight away on the next train."

"What the devil has she told you?"

She waved her hand, dismissing the topic. "I've had a trip, Papa! You wouldn't believe. We were waylaid by a lame horse near that grand hotel, and I couldn't find a soul who would take me the rest of the way."

"I wish you'd told me you were coming. I would have liked to meet you at the train station." Then I added, "And saved quite a bit of expense."

"But then it wouldn't have been a surprise."

I shook my head with a smile that warmed me despite the bitter air.

"Come in out of the cold," I said. "I'll have a room prepared for you."

I hesitated with her at the threshold. Would this place consume her as it had me? Would it leave her stained, darkened like the moldy stones? These were foolish questions, but I'd been so affected by it all that I couldn't bear the thought of her stepping inside.

Lenora saved us from the decision. She appeared at the door in a violet riding dress, woolen shawl wrapped over her hair.

"You must be Lenora," Lottie said, and politely extended her gloved hand. Lenora took it and drew her into the house. A current of panic shot through my blood, but I suppressed it.

"And you are Lottie, *claro*. You have your father's eyes."

"I've heard so much about you," Lottie answered, pressing her hand.

"And I, you."

I do not know how to write the feeling this meeting inspired in me. It was akin to shame, as if I'd shown Lottie my darkest secret, as if it would somehow taint her image of me. I could only clear my throat.

"Perhaps we could go into town this afternoon," I said to Lenora. "I'd like to get my daughter settled, and I'm sure she wishes to rest."

"I didn't come here to rest," Lottie said. "Shall we go into town together?"

"I'm afraid we've some unpleasant business to attend to," I answered, meeting Lenora's heavy gaze. Lottie had not received my letter in travel, so she was unaware of the child's disappearance. I explained as succinctly as possible, and come the end of it, my girl's enthusiasm had all drained away, drawing her shoulders forward.

"How horrible," she muttered, and after a moment's pause, she lifted her chin and said, "Well, have your carriage brought 'round then."

Lenora touched my hand. "Wilson has not yet returned from Anna's."

"Is it near enough to walk?" Lottie asked. "I'm tired of train cars and carriages and their hard seats."

"We could make it to Anna's on foot," I answered, shivering. "But I won't hear of it. It's much too cold."

"Have you riding horses, then?" She turned the Lenora. "Do you know how to ride?"

Lenora's lips stretched into a stunning smile, and I had the distinct impression that it was the first genuine expression of happiness I'd seen on her face.

"My father was a jockey before he met my mother. He had a fondness for horses that I share."

"It's settled then." Lottie drew her shawl around her shoulders and looked to the sky. "The air smells of snow. We mustn't tarry."

The three of us walked to the stables, and having no Murdochs to assist, we saddled our own steeds. Somehow, I'd been left with the old mare again, but I minded not. I had my daughter with me now and little could trod on my spirits, despite our dismal mission.

I lagged behind, of course, watching Lenora's shawl wave behind her like a battle flag in the rising wind, her hair flying loose from its pins. The etchings of Artemis in my mother's book on Greek mythology came to mind—a fiercely beautiful woman on the trail of a clever fox, her pack of hounds marking the way. Lottie kept pace beside her. Neither was sidesaddle. They rode like men, and likely better, their skirts draping the rears of the horses and the fog of their breath trailing behind.

"You're running those poor horses to death," I called after them. Sodden earth flung from the horses' hooves, so I was obliged to lag back even farther.

"And *you're* falling behind!" Lottie called back. "Come, Papa. We've little time to lose."

My horse snorted at me when I spurred her, so I was obliged to merely trot while Lenora and Lottie raced to Anna's house.

My carriage waited in her drive, Wilson upon his perch. Although only his profile was in view as we approached, the rigidness in his shoulders spoke of distress. Peter, who I was surprised to see there, stepped into the carriage and shut the door with such force that the horses pawed the gravel. His silhouette joined another behind the darkened glass, whom I presumed to be Murdoch. The poor man slumped against the seat as lifeless as a corpse.

Anna saw them off and then hooded herself with a woolen shawl. She'd not yet seen us. Large, wet snowflakes fell into our hair and clung to our horses before melting on their steaming skin. Lottie brought her horse up around the carriage as Wilson flicked the whip.

"Cousin!" she called as they drove past. Anna raised her hand to her heart.

"You gave me a fright," she said, but then her usual warm smile swept away any remnant of alarm. "You must be Lottie, then! You arrived quickly."

"Thank you for writing me," she said, bringing her horse to a halt. "My father is lost without me, you know."

Anna chuckled. "I gathered as much. I'm so glad you've come." She appeared ready to speak further on the matter, but Lenora and I rode up beside Lottie.

"Have you found Christine?" I asked. "Why were the Murdochs here?"

"The Murdochs?" she repeated. "Oh, I had Wilson take me into town to take care of some personal matters. We passed them in the square. They looked so downtrodden, I insisted they come here to rest a spell." She shivered, drawing her shawl around her throat and stepping back beneath the shelter of the porch. "I'm sorry to have left you without a carriage, Will, but it's just awful. There isn't a search party."

"What do you mean there's no search party?"

"No one will help," Lenora replied for her, knowingly. "They are too afraid."

"Afraid of what?" Lottie asked.

Lenora looked at me and lifted her brow as if to ask, *has no one told her?*

"You'll come to know by the by," I answered.

Lottie shot a glance toward Lenora, as quick and sharp as

a dart.

"They're afraid of *you*," she said to her.

"Lottie," I began, ready to chide her, but Lenora brought her horse around until she and my daughter faced one another. The horses knickered and snorted as the snow fell upon their backs.

"As your father's daughter," Lenora began, "you must be too intelligent to judge a matter before you fully know of it. Is this not true?"

Lottie pressed her lips silently, Lenora's remark more effective than any lesson I might have bestowed upon her.

Lenora turned to Anna. "We are going to town to show Christine's portrait. Will you come?"

"I haven't a horse, and Wilson's just driven off with the carriage," Anna answered. "You are wasting your time. No one will help you."

Lottie roused herself, her fingers tightening on the reins. "You can ride with me, Cousin. We mustn't give up so easily."

Chapter XIII

WILLIAM GARRETT'S JOURNAL

January 16, 1889, continued

We continued on toward town in this inexplicable manner, with Lottie's foolish hope driving us all. The shadow that had descended upon the whole of Ravenswood trailed behind us as we plodded alongside the railroad track, each of us feigning ignorance but knowing all along the entity at our heels.

The town, unchanged these many years, had been a place of joy for Anna and I in childhood. We passed Selleck and Brown's Bakery, where we'd spend our coins on sugar candy, and then the cigar shop, which still bore the same tobacco sign, though the elements had faded it nearly beyond legibility. Old Tom Tynan, the farrier, raised a hand to us as he shod a palomino mare, and all the while Catskill Creek carried steamboats along beside us, its dark water smearing into the gray sky. Carriages sloshed through filthy, sodden snow and children threw snowballs at one another with their pockets full of candies from the general store, the atmosphere reminding me, on the whole, that a world existed outside my own.

We tied our horses to a hitching post outside Shaler's General Grocery. The same bell heralded our entry as in the old days. While I recognized neither the group of women gawking at me from the spice shelves nor the pair of men who whispered among themselves beside the pipe tobacco, I'd become accustomed to this reaction to my presence and paid it little mind.

"William Garrett," the old shopkeeper called, his hand halfway into a jar of flour. The patrons, who had not initially noticed me, did so now. Heat bloomed across my cheeks and ears and I avoided their eyes by removing my hat to brush away the snow. The old man dusted his hands on his apron and rounded the counter to greet me. He had gained a few pounds each year I had been away, and his coal-dark hair had turned the color of ash, but he otherwise remained unchanged.

"Mr. Shaler," I said, with as grand a smile as I could manage.

"I was wondering when you'd come 'round," he said, shaking my hand enthusiastically. "You look just the same. Here now, let me find some of those peppermint sticks you liked so much. They're not as good as before, when the missus made them, but I carry on as best I can."

"Mrs. Shaler?" I asked as he rifled through a jar of candy.

"She's gone on, left me with the lot of it." He said this as if his late wife had only gone to visit her cousin in Virginia, and so I did not offer him my sympathies. "Aha!" he exclaimed, holding the candies to the light and then noticing for the first time the three women who had entered behind me.

"Ah, ladies," he said, dropping the candies back into the jar and scurrying back around the counter to kiss each of their hands. "Are you keeping young Will company these days? A lucky man, you are," he said to me. "A lucky man indeed."

"You'll have no argument from me there," I said.

"Mr. Shaler," Anna said, greeting him with as lovely a smile as ever. "Always a pleasure, though, I'm afraid we've come with some ugly business. Young Christine, Peter Murdoch's daughter, has gone missing."

"Yes, I saw the Murdochs earlier today," he said, his cheerful countenance falling away. "She came in just the other day for some licorice. Such a gentle thing."

"And," Anna said, "if anyone should see her, you know where to find us?"

"Ravenswood Hall," he answered in a low voice, leaning toward us. "But you can be sure no one'll venture there even if she is spotted. That old place is as cursed as a witch's cat, it is. And haunted to boot, but I don't need to be telling you, what with living there yourself."

When I first arrived here, I might have thought the old man was off his head, but I know better now.

"A curse and a haunting," Lottie replied, doing little to stifle her intrigue. She is but a child and does not understand.

"You've got my sympathies in any case," Mr. Shaler said as he shrugged. "I wouldn't want to spend one night there, no sir."

We left him with our pockets full of peppermint as in the days of old, but there was no joy in it. Anna and Lottie rode off together to become better acquainted, taking a turn around the wharf so Lottie could admire Catskill Creek. Lenora and I walked arm in arm to the church and attempted conversation. There were eyes upon us all the while, the wives with their bolts of cloth and loaves of bread, the men outside the cigar shop, even the children looked at us as though we had walked out of one of their bedtime stories, the kind that keep them out of the forest at night. Their whispers trailed behind us like coattails.

Deacon Barnes opened the great wooden door of the one-room church and bowed to me. I had not stepped inside a church since my mother died, for it was her faith alone that drove us here each Sunday. The deacon did not admonish me for this. Instead, he smiled and took my hand. The years had aged him more than I'd expected. The flesh clinging to his face appeared as melted as a candle on the fireplace mantel and he moved with great difficulty, as one of five and eighty. Only a few tufts of gray hair remained on his scalp, gathering about his large ears. He looked like a proper monk now, though I guessed it was age and not piety that gave him his tonsure.

"Welcome home, Dr. Garrett," he said.

Lenora offered her hand and introduced herself, but he did not take it.

"We know who you are," he said, and then looked again to me. "If you wish to enter, Dr. Garrett, you must do so without her."

"What? Why?"

Lenora smiled ruefully, slid her arm into mine, and leaned in close, her eyes on the deacon.

"Haven't you heard, Will?" she said in my ear. "I'm a witch."

I laughed. The deacon did not.

"You can't be serious."

Lenora set her hand over her heart. "By the pricking of my thumbs."

"Barnes, what the devil is the meaning of this?" I asked. I'd heard the rumors, but I'd not yet met anyone who truly believed them. Barnes had always seemed like a reasonable man and such superstitious nonsense, even at the church, surprised me.

"Forgive me, but I can say no more in the presence of Miss Laveau. She has no business walking about with the living."

"Are you mad?" I asked, incredulous, and Lenora's fingers tightened around my arm.

"Enough," Lenora said. She removed the drawing of Christine from her dress and showed it to the deacon. "A little girl is missing. Have you seen her?" And when he did not reply, she repeated, "For her sake, not mine. Have you seen her?"

He answered that he had not, crossed himself, and then retreated inside, the door closing heavily behind him.

"It seems we've been excommunicated," I muttered.

"On my account. You need not defend me here. I am fully

aware of what people presume of me." She did not give me time to answer, but instead she hastened ahead, showing the sketch to anyone she passed. I followed at my own pace, hope waning, as the cold seeped beneath my bloodless skin.

Behind me, a woman's voice asked, "Do you still have it, sir?"

I turned.

The woman from the tavern stood before me. I knew her immediately, for I could not soon forget the one who had offered me at once such comfort and such trepidation. She wore the same threadbare shawl, layered upon a great quantity of old clothing. It did not keep her warm it seemed, for she trembled as she approached.

"The trinket?" I asked, and upon her gentle nod, I removed it from my pocket to show her. She plucked it from my palm, and I feared she meant to take it back. I had the irrational conviction that, should I allow this object to be removed from my possession, some great misfortune would befall me.

"Very good," she whispered.

I asked her the question I'd had on my lips since her son first brought it to me. "Who is it?"

"Saint Cosmas," she answered, a fond but fleeting smile on her lips. "The patron saint of pharmacy and medicine."

That was plain enough and set my mind at ease, but an expression of mourning clouded her eyes as she caressed the trinket with the pad of her thumb.

"One of a pair," she added.

"There is another?"

"Yes. Saint Damian. They're twins." She lifted her eyes over my shoulder. Lenora stood in the road, watching. "I gave the other to a friend."

Lenora lifted her hand to wave at me, the wrinkled, damp portrait of Christine fluttering in the wind.

"Never mind that, though," the woman continued, taking my hand and placing the trinket in my palm. I closed my fingers around it instinctively. "They'll be reunited in the end."

And then she turned and slipped away into a dress shop, where her son danced gaily around a wicker mannequin.

"Who was that?" Lenora asked, walking up beside me. I dropped the trinket into my pocket.

"A woman I met once." I found I could explain neither the trinket's significance nor the woman who had offered it to me, so I said no more.

The sun climbed higher in the sky, and we rendezvoused with Lottie and Anna at the hitching post. After a mediocre lunch of roast beef and onions, we set off toward home. No one in town had seen young Christine, but our journey had not been in vain. I, for my own part, managed to secure some credit at the hardware store and found a boy willing to deliver my purchases on his cart first thing tomorrow, including a good bit of lumber, wallpaper, and an acceptable rug for the sitting room. Fungus had sprung up beneath the window there, and the perpetually damp rug filled the room with stifling mustiness.

Anna and Lottie had got along splendidly all morning, and it warmed my heart to see my daughter with her kin. She has few friends at home—a consequence, I believe, of her interest in the supernatural. Perhaps my cousin can talk some sense into her on that front, though I suspect Ravenswood may have tarnished Anna's views.

"I'd like to pass by Dr. Johnston's," I said, as we came to the crossroads at the end of Main Street. To the left, the road narrowed into treachery and climbed into the forest toward Ravenswood. We continued forward, where rolling, blanketed farmland stretched to the icy Hudson. "There's a matter I still need to discuss with him."

"We ought to head back, Will," Anna called. "The horses are struggling already."

The howling wind whipped snow into monstrous forms. We tucked our heads beneath our hoods and rode on, storm be damned. I sensed something odd as we came around the bend leading to Dr. Johnston's house, something off-putting, but I could not set my finger on the pulse of it. Lottie and Anna rode up beside me as we neared. The doctor's door stood open, a drift of snow gathering on the rug.

"I don't want to go in there, Papa," Lottie called above the wind. "Something bad has happened."

I dismounted, instructing her to stay on her horse, and approached the house.

Silence reigned inside, and beneath the scent of musty upholstery and the flint-sharp winter was the bitter suggestion of blood. I crept into his office but found no sign of him. His case of antique surgical instruments had been shattered, but this was the only sign of violence. A quick inventory of the instruments, as I'd regarded them so often as a boy, revealed a single missing item—the ivory-handled scalpel.

I called for him still, but in my heart I suspected a grim truth. The other chambers had not been disturbed. Dr. Johnston was gone.

Lottie peeked her head inside.

"Get back on your horse," I commanded, and when she hesitated, I added, "Do not disobey me again."

"He's dead," she said.

"We can't know that for certain. We must fetch the constable."

Lottie lifted her eyes to the ceiling and looked about, as if listening, and then she backed slowly out of the house.

"No, Papa," she whispered. "He's dead. I'm sure of it."

Devlin was not at home when we all arrived. His wife answered the door with a cloth over her mouth, looking paler and more wasted than before.

"He's gone up to Ravenswood Hall," she said. "Something about a skull? Forgive me, Dr. Garrett, I can't remember."

He had apparently, per my request of last evening, come to the house in search of my father's remains. I had entirely forgotten this appointment and do not believe I actually thought he would discover anything. Even as I think on it now, it all seems like some sort of fever dream.

The lot of us hastened up the mountain as quickly as we could manage, though the horses sank in sucking mud and lost their footing on the gathering ice. My mare nearly threw me when the wind tossed a yew branch into the road before us. I hardly felt the presence of the others in my company, and indeed, I could scarcely see them as the snow swirled around us.

"Papa!" Lottie cried. We had traveled a good distance at last, nearly to the tangled thicket of lilac bushes my mother had planted after I was born. "Papa, do you hear that?"

I stilled my horse, listening. A dog howled up ahead, and then Molly burst out from the thicket, barking wildly and running toward us.

"What is the matter with her?" Lenora asked. I had never seen the sweet little dog act in so violent a manner. Blood matted her fur and leaves clung to the tangled feathering on her legs. One of her ears had been torn clean off, leaving only a mangled stump. When she reached our horses, she turned and ran back into the thicket, her hind leg dragging behind her. I spurred the mare to follow, dismounted, and plunged into the thorns, heedless to the others calling out behind me. The snarled vines sheltered me from the storm.

I followed the sound of Molly's barking and found her in a small clearing, a murder of crows hopping about and screeching. She barked at me once more and then laid down, shivering, across a mound of leaves and tattered fabric all shrouded with snow.

"Will, what has become of you?" Anna called from the road, but I could not answer, for I saw what Molly protected. For a moment, neither man nor beast moved. The crows, having seen me, had ceased moving all but their twitching black eyes, gazes bouncing off of me like pellets of ice. Lenora arrived then, breaking the spell.

"*Dios*," she breathed. "Is that—"

The birds dispersed with wretched cries as I approached, and Molly whimpered and stumbled aside, leaving the child's tiny body exposed to the elements. I recognized Christine's blonde ringlets and the pink ribbon that held them together, now frayed. Scavengers had torn open the flesh on her bare arms, tinged blue as much from death as from the ice that had seeped from the earth and into her veins. Something like a fox, based upon the marks left by the teeth, had veritably chewed off her left hand, leaving only a portion of the thumb.

"Don't look," I warned, but Lenora was beside me in a moment, and in another kneeling before the girl's body.

"What have you done?" she whispered, apparently to the girl, though I could not be certain. It did seem likely that Christine had wandered off and frozen to death, but Lenora, like me, must have suspected something darker afoot. It was not ill luck that gathered in the edges and corners of Ravenswood, but ill will. So, at least, I was beginning to learn.

Although we both knew the identity of the poor little girl, I took her frozen shoulder and rolled her onto her back so that we could be certain.

"Good God," I cried, releasing her. A grotesque smile stretched her cheeks and displayed her small teeth, like a horrible doll painted the color of ice and not of flesh. White film clouded eyes fixed on the sky, beyond us all. I shall be haunted by this face all of my life.

"We must tell Peter," I whispered.

"How will we get her back?"

"We aren't far from the house." I did not wish to offer the answer that came to my mind, but it came anyway. "I must carry her."

"Will…"

"Ride ahead with the others and gather the Murdochs. I will bring her home."

Lenora heaved a great, shuddering breath and disappeared

through the thicket, leaving me alone with the dead. Doctors do not have weak stomachs or weak wills, but both of mine failed me as I prepared to slide my arms beneath the little corpse. Instead, I wretched into the withered lilac bushes, the contents of my breakfast steaming on the snow. Disgusted as much with myself as with the course of events that had unfolded here, I sat on the frigid earth and closed my eyes. A full five minutes I gathered myself, grateful that Lenora had gone. This child did not deserve such a cruel end. Ravenswood had repaid her innocence with horror, and I had no recourse for it.

I opened my eyes to find Molly only inches from my own, sniffing me and wagging her tail. Her soulful eyes brought me to tears. Men do not deserve dogs. We have done nothing to warrant their unadulterated compassion, but it gave me courage. At last steeling my nerve and unheeding the cold, I removed my greatcoat and wrapped it around the child, covering her face for my own sake. With Molly close behind, I carried Christine's stiffened body out of the forest. Lottie had stayed behind and waited for me, Anna having gone on with her horse.

"Walk ahead, my girl," I said. I did not wish her to see. Instead, she took a blanket from the saddlebag on my mare and draped it around my shoulders.

We tramped along silently perhaps a quarter of an hour, my mind emptied of all but the sound of the crunching snow beneath my feet and the whimpering of poor Molly as she struggled to keep pace against the wind. A crow called after us, angry that I had stolen its supper. My arms ached under the child's weight, but I was grateful for this pain. It offered me a distraction from the golden curls that draped the crook of my arm and the tiny shoes peeking out from under my coat.

We gained Ravenswood Hall at last. Peter greeted me at the gate and relieved me of my gruesome parcel, his face displaying none of the grief I knew must be suffocating him.

"Thank you," he said, as if I had brought home a loaf of bread or a basket of fruit. He carried the child into the house, and Lottie led my horse to the stables as I walked into the hall with the dog. Anna was nowhere to be seen, and I suspected she'd gone out to search the grounds for Devlin.

Lenora set her hands on Peter's face as if to steady him, but he was turned from me, so I could not see his expression. I caught only a few of her words.

"...left her on the road...for the animals."

Chapter XIV

WILLIAM GARRETT'S JOURNAL

January 16, 1889, continued

I tended to Molly's wounds, which I suspect to be the consequence of a battle with a fox, given the indications on Christine's body. The poor creature had no doubt remained loyally by her girl's side for days, doing her utmost to guard the body. The cuts are deep and I fear she may never regain the use of her hind leg. I have never met such a courageous dog in all of my life. She gives me courage to continue with this narrative when I wish nothing more than to cast this wretched book into the fire.

Even when we laid the child down in the parlor, wrapped all in white to hide the decay that pulled her lips back from her teeth and clouded her eyes, the dog laid down beside her. Lenora picked the leaves from Molly's tail with tears in her eyes, speaking sweetly in Spanish. Murdoch and Peter stood together before the window, awaiting Constable Devlin.

The clock ticked and ticked, but never chimed the hour. No one spoke. Perhaps we all feared waking the child.

Lottie stood beside me with her arms wrapped tight around herself, and after a while whispered, "Who could have done this?"

I had neither answers nor comfort to give her.

"You should not have come here," I said instead.

At last, Devlin entered our death house without a word, Anna close behind. Both were shivering and soaked with snow. Only I greeted him, and even then, I could manage but a nod in his direction, which he returned. He stood over the child with his hands in his pockets for a long while until Peter turned to him.

"May we bury her, Constable?" he asked, his voice so low it seemed his very soul had left him. He was a shell of himself.

"I'm sorry," he said. "I am, truly, but I cannot allow it. There must be an autopsy."

"You can't—" His voice failed him then. Anna set her hand on his arm, but he wrenched it away.

"There must be an investigation, Peter," she whispered to him.

"Do not speak to me of what must be," he said, his voice like sand through his teeth, but he did not complete the thought. Lenora rose from her place on the floor.

"*Déjalo en paz*," she said to my cousin, but Anna turned on her as savagely as a wild dog.

"Do not speak your Spanish at me," she cried. "None of this would have happened if you'd stayed in Spain where you belong."

This comment, and the violence with which it had been spoken, shocked me.

"How dare you," Lenora whispered.

"What is the meaning of this?" I asked, motioning for their silence with a wave of my hand. The three of them fixed a collective glare upon me that might have turned me to stone. Peter finally closed his eyes, and let his shoulders slump. He turned back to the constable.

"You insist upon an autopsy, then?"

"I do."

"But," Lottie began, biting down on her lip. "Something awful has happened to the doctor. How can there be an autopsy?"

Devlin raised his brow at this, and I explained what we discovered at Dr. Johnston's house. He rubbed his chin, listening and frowning all the while.

"This is far and away more than I can rightfully handle myself," he said. "I'll send word to New York's finest. Their captain is a personal friend of mine. Maybe he can spare his coroner and send me a man to help search for the doctor."

"It will be days before anyone arrives, Constable," Peter said. "Please, I want to lay her to rest."

Then, as if guided by some kind of supernatural force, everyone in the room turned and looked at me, even old Murdoch. They fixed their gazes upon me so strongly that I stepped backward.

"I cannot," I stammered. Lenora rose from her place on the floor and walked to me.

"Will," she whispered. "Are you trained in pathology?"

I could only nod, but it sealed my fate.

"You mustn't, Papa," Lottie said, taking my hand. "It's too horrible."

"We have no one else," Lenora retorted, and then returned her steady gaze to me. "You *must*."

"Jesus Christ," Peter cried. "Is there no end to this?"

"Mr. Garrett only wishes to help," Lenora said. There, at least, she remained by my side, but the look Peter shot her, as if she had wounded him to his soul, gave me pause. There was something unspoken between them, something that nurtured the ugly seed of jealousy inside my heart.

"It may be our only option," Devlin said. I'd momentarily

forgotten his presence. "I will supervise to ensure due process. Are you quite certain, Dr. Garrett?"

"Well, I don't see any other course of action," I answered. Lottie withdrew her hand from mine and sat on the sofa where Anna had fallen back. The elder Murdoch remained silent throughout these proceedings, but then he turned from the window and made his way slowly to me.

"I will call off the search party," he said. This comment puzzled me, as Anna had led me to believe there'd been no search at all. I hadn't time to examine it, however, for he took my hands in his and said, "You will find out what happened to our girl, sir? You will?"

"I will do all I can." I could make no further promise. Although I had trained in pathology at university, I had no professional experience with corpses. All of my patients had been ailing but alive.

"Bless you," he whispered, and then released my hand. "Excuse me. I am tired."

"He needs rest," Peter said, guiding him toward the doorway. "I'm taking him to bed. I can't bear this."

I sent a glance to Lottie as they took their leave, but she wouldn't look at me.

"I will look after her," Lenora said, setting her hand on my arm.

"I haven't the time to prepare a room for her. A fine welcome she's received."

"Leave it to me."

I nodded, and then turned to Devlin, my heart heavy.

"Where shall we do it?" I asked him, though I already knew where the dreadful thing ought to be done. I was loathe even to think of performing such a ritual in so dismal a room, but there was nothing for it. It was colder down below.

"The cellar," he confirmed, and acid rose into my chest.

"Let me bring the candles," Lottie offered, rising.

"You'll do no such thing, miss," Devlin said before I could

raise my voice. "I will not have a woman anywhere near such gruesome proceedings." Heretofore, I hadn't believed him capable of so forceful a tone, but he said this with such authority that Lottie pinched her lips together, curtsied, and sat back down, leaving the two of us to carry out our morbid plan.

We carried Christine between us, Molly limping behind with her tail hanging low. I clicked my tongue.

"Go on now," I cooed, my hands under Christine's cold arms as we maneuvered her into the kitchen. The dog whimpered and sat, neither obeying nor advancing. I know not if dogs can mourn their masters, but she appeared at once the most loyal and the gloomiest of all of us.

The cellar stairs groaned as we descended into the bowels of the house, and the darkness swallowed us up.

"There's a table in the center," I guided. "We can work there."

The toe of my boot met the table leg loudly, and Devlin grunted as we struggled to balance the child's small body in the inky black.

"Set her head down now," Devlin said as he shifted her legs onto the heavy wooden table, once used for preparing preserves. I knew the dark stains in the wood were blackberry juices, but they did not appear so now.

We left the child to collect as many lamps as we could find, and then set them all around her, the flames shining ghastly and bright on her corpse as though we prepared her for some unholy rite. With my medical supplies organized on a barrel nearby, and the faces of Lenora's macabre paintings looking on, I prepared myself as best as I could.

"God Almighty," Devlin whispered, rubbing his eyes. "Never in my life…" but the sentence fell away as I pulled the sheet from Christine's face. She smiled at us still, and I looked away. We examined her dress first. Turning out the pockets, we discovered nothing but peppermints and a few crumbled teacakes wrapped in a handkerchief. Devlin handed me a pair of scissors and assisted me as we removed her clothing. The vulgarity of the violation we meant to perform upon this child made me ill.

"You must distance yourself from this, Dr. Garrett," Devlin said, and when I did not answer, he added, "Procedure, man! What first?"

"An external examination," I answered, my voice weak.

"Talk us through it, then."

I examined the girl's arms and legs, still stiff as if frozen, though rigor mortis should have faded some time ago based upon the milky aspect of her eyes. This body had been exposed to the elements for, I estimated, nearly the entirety of the time she'd been missing.

"I see no bruising," I began, "no signs of struggle or adhesions inconsistent with predatory scavenging. All seem to be post mortem. The toes are curled inward, as are the fingers. Some manner of convulsion, perhaps." I attempted to move the flexed digits but could not.

"What's that there on her mouth?"

I bent to examine her face. A foamy coating of diluted blood stained her lips and chin.

"She seems to have had some kind of seizure before she died," I noted.

I needed to look inside her mouth, but I could not pry it open. So contracted were her muscles that I had to break her jaw. The mandible and temporal bones separated with a quick *pop*, as fragile as a bird's wing. Devlin cursed. Sweat gathered on my forehead and stung my eyes.

"Look here, she's bitten her tongue." A large piece of the shriveled tissue had been bitten off entirely, perhaps swallowed, and the tongue was coated in the same sickly foam.

"Was she prone to seizure?" Devlin asked, stepping back.

"Not to my knowledge. We will need to ask Peter."

This, and the strange rigor of the body, called to mind a course I had taken at university, but it was too early for conjecture.

"Constable, I'm going to begin the autopsy," I warned him. He did not reply. I don't believe he had ever borne witness to so gruesome an event. "I'll be needing the light again."

"Yes...of course," he stammered, and then stepped up beside me, holding the light high. I cut into the girl with a trembling hand. Had I known that my return to this place would bring me here, to this very moment, I'd have surely remained in Baltimore for the rest of my days. Let Ravenswood rot.

"Strange," I murmured.

"What?" His light had been quivering all the while and veering off course, and I did not realize until then that he had been looking away from the gaping hole in the girl's chest, made all the more horrible by her stiffened, arched posture. "Christ."

"The skeletal muscle tissue..." I could not immediately think of the words to complete the thought, and then I remembered a man I'd treated in Virginia who had stepped on a railroad spike. "Tetanus," I determined at last.

"Lockjaw?"

"That would explain the grin."

"But how did she come to contract it?"

"I've not the slightest idea. All of her lacerations are post mortem. And there's clotting here in the small blood vessels. In all of them."

"What does that mean?" he asked.

"I don't know."

"Could it be the cold?"

"Perhaps." I had negligible experience with hypothermia and related disease, save for what little I had read on treatments. I did not know how to look for evidence of it after death. I was woefully underqualified for a task such as this.

"Perhaps the wound healed," Devlin offered.

"I don't see any scars at all," I answered, though his hypothesis was the best we had thus far.

I continued the examination of the internal organs, the stomach contents, the liver, the bladder. The liquid therein was of a strange color resembling iron oxide. I completed the remaining examinations and the autopsy, the details of which too horrible to record here, but Devlin had the foresight to inscribe our notes in his casebook.

"What should I write for cause of death?"

I scrubbed my hands in the cracked basin beside the stairs, the water thick with blood. I did not want to answer him. I needed to review my books and journals to be certain.

"Tentatively?" I asked, drying my hands on a towel that I would have to burn.

"At this point, Dr. Garrett, a guess would do."

"I will have to research further."

"Very well, but I must write something."

I took a breath and covered the corpse again with the linen. I could no longer bear her gaping mouth, screaming silently at me for justice I knew not how to provide.

"Constable," I said finally, "Christine Murdoch was poisoned."

January 17, 1889

I am beginning to detest the feel of this pen in my hand, for each evening I write, I am more plagued by uncertainty— and by horror. I no longer trust myself. I can only inscribe my perceptions, however intensely I doubt them.

I slept very little last night, so burdened I was by memories of young Christine's autopsy. It was the suspicion of her poisoning that drove me back to Dr. Johnston's after breakfast. All of my medical books remained in Baltimore. I thought I might discover a few suitable texts on what is now termed toxicology in his office.

The snowstorm had left its slick shroud upon the road, but I had no time to delay. Thank God for the skill of my driver and the fortitude of my horses, for the journey, while treacherous, took the whole of a few hours with Wilson at the reins.

Lottie has not left my side since I returned with the books.

Her presence is at once a comfort and a worry. I fear the effect these horrors might have on her. She knows enough of mourning already and does not have the stomach for investigations into murder.

We spent the afternoon in the dining room pouring over Dr. Johnston's books, running our fingers down the indexes of known toxins and diseases. We paused only for a hasty supper of cold meats, and then pressed on. Lenora was kind enough to offer her eye as well, along with the much-wanted draught of hot coffee or whiskey, since I'd given Peter and Murdoch leave to sit vigil with Christine in the cellar.

When the clock on the mantel tolled eight above our heads, Lottie dropped her chin into her hand and frowned.

"Is something the matter?" I asked, pulling my eyes from a page in Orfila's *A Popular Treatise on Poisons*.

"Anna has been in her room all day," Lottie answered. "Do you think I've offended her somehow?"

"I am to blame, Miss Lottie," Lenora said. "She holds me responsible for a great number of things that have occurred in this house. I imagine she cannot bear my company after all that has happened. She and her mother believed I was, ah, how did she call it? A *hateful influence*. I have never been able to convince her otherwise."

"Nonsense, Lenora," I said, not wishing to believe my cousin capable of such prejudice. "This house holds bitter memories for her. If given the choice, I would stay up in my room as well, but my father has bound me to this."

"You are bound by more than your father now, Will." Lenora said, returning to her seat at my right side after setting down a tray of yesterday's cakes.

As I read each and every hideous manner in which this little child might have died, I understood her meaning. I knew not how, but my father had played a hand in her murder. If I was master of Ravenswood as I claimed to be, it was my duty now to untangle the skein.

I took her hand in my own, forgetting my daughter.

"We are bound together," I said to her. "A misfortune for you, but I am grateful to not be alone in it."

Lottie stood so abruptly that her chair nearly tipped. Lenora withdrew her hand from mine.

"I must speak with you," Lottie said.

"Very well," I answered, waiting. She sent a glance toward Lenora that bordered on disdain.

"Privately," she replied, and then she fled to the kitchen.

"Lottie," I called after her, but she did not heed me, so I followed, gaining her by the woodstove. She turned to me, her anxious expression so like her mother's that I forgot the words I meant to speak.

"We haven't had a moment to speak privately since I arrived," she said.

"Forgive me, Lottie," I replied. "It's been a trying few days."

"She's lying to you, Papa."

"What the devil do you mean?" The question left my lips, but my daughter had spoken aloud my own sinking suspicion.

"You wrote me that she went to Spain during the time of her disappearance. I searched the passenger lists, and the only Laveau I found was a woman named Catarina, arriving in Baltimore from Spain around the supposed time of her return. I hadn't time to search further, but the fact of the matter is that she has lied to you."

"You've made a mistake. She's given me no reason to doubt her."

"Papa, no one named Lenora Laveau arrived here."

"These are not your matters to meddle in."

"You asked me for help, and I am here to give it. Whether you wish to hear my findings or not is of no consequence to me."

"Watch your tongue, child."

"You've let her blind you," she retorted, raising her voice. "You're beguiled." Blotches of rose blossomed across her chest and neck, revealing her distress. It had been the same with her mother.

"I am not *beguiled*," I replied, but before I could articulate this fact further, a knock sounded at the door. I heard Lenora's shoes on the stone in the foyer and then the creaking of the heavy door. A moment later, she stepped into the kitchen to announce that the boy from town had arrived with my supplies, so I went out to meet him.

He stood on the porch, shivering and looking comically small beneath the eaves of the house. His mule pawed at the snow, jarring the cart that contained my purchases.

"Begging your pardon for the delay, sir," he said, tugging a newsboy cap down over his eyes. "Couldn't make it up the mountain what with all the snow. I've got them to you now at least, and a letter from Mr. Hawkins."

I snatched up the envelope from his soot-smudged fingers and tore it open.

A LETTER TO DR. WILLIAM GARRETT

112 Main, Catskill, New York, to Ravenswood Hall
No Postmark

Dear Dr. Garrett,

I have consulted my law texts as well as esteemed colleagues, and I am sorry to report that no loophole exists to free you from the elder Garrett's conditions. The bank is bound by the articles in the last will and testament, as am I, and they will be unable to release his funds to you until the time indicated therein.

However, as we discussed previously, there are no articles preventing the sale of the estate. As such, I believe I may have a line on an interested party. An acquaintance of mine from Boston has developed a keen interest in Catskill, likely as a result of the great success of the Hotel Kaaterskill, and is of a mind to cash in, so to speak, on the sudden popularity of the mountain air. I've spoken about Ravenswood Hall at length, excepting the rumors of course, and I say, you've got a potential buyer. That is, if you can bear the thought of your ancestral home being demolished to make way for a hotel.

This party, Anderton by name, will be in Albany on business a fortnight hence, and I shall write to make an appointment to view the property if it be agreeable to you.

Your humble servant,

J. Hawkins, Esquire, Attorney at Law

WILLIAM GARRETT'S JOURNAL

January 17, 1889, continued

There! A single morsel of good news amid all of this horror. Praise be to Mr. Hawkins, God bless him. After helping the boy unload the cart, and sending him off with likely the last coin in my pocket, I returned to the dining room without the heart to continue our morbid quest. Only Lenora awaited me.

"Enough for tonight," I said, stuffing the joyous letter in my pocket. "We'll begin again in the morning, if you've the stomach for it."

She nodded, rising to take her leave.

"Lenora," I said, splaying my fingers open on the table. Perhaps I was trying to draw some fortitude out of the sturdy oak. "Who is Catarina?"

She stilled, but I could not see her face as she had turned her back to me.

"Where did you hear that name?"

"My daughter is meddlesome," I answered. "She discovered the name on a passenger list."

"That is me," she answered. Her shoulders relaxed some, and she faced me with what seemed a practiced smile. "I often travel under the name Catarina. It was my mother's name."

"Why do you not use your real name?"

"Surely you can understand the desire to feel close to your mother."

"I do," I admitted. "I'm sorry to have troubled you with this. I will tell my daughter she is not to worry."

"She will likely worry anyway, will she not?"

"Yes," I laughed. "Perhaps so."

Chapter XV

WILLIAM GARRETT'S JOURNAL

January 18, 1889

The clock in my chamber tolled one with a single, reverberating peal. I sat cross-legged on the floor with Dr. Johnston's volumes and notes scattered all around me, candlesticks positioned about like a pagan faerie circle. Once I'd determined the cause of death, all that remained was to discover the vehicle for it—that is, the poison that had so violently taken little Christine's life.

A compendium of snake and insect bites sat open at my right side, and on my lap I flipped through an encyclopedia of poisons. This book showed more promise, as I had found no indication of animal bites or the like. I eliminated arsenic, though it was surely readily available to anyone who desired it. Her death did not align with its singular effects. Overdoses of chloroform, opium, cocaine, and cyanide were also improbable.

I could not, and cannot still, presume to know or even suppose who had done this or what had driven him to it.

One by one my candles burned to stumps, leaving me to work by the light of only one. At two o'clock, the last guttered and went out, and I was obliged to fiddle around in the darkness for the candle box that I'd fortunately brought with me onto the floor. An old familiar fear grabbed ahold of me as I felt for the matches, the kind that compels a child to lift his feet off the floor and hide beneath the blankets. Vulnerable as I was to any monstrous hand that might reach out to grab my ankles, I remained in my position until my medical mind regained control. I unsuccessfully attempted to lower my heart rate as my fingers landed on the matchbook.

"Will?" Lenora called from the hall, her knuckles rapping on the door.

"Yes? Come in."

She entered with a candle lighting her face, dark crescent moons like bruises beneath her eyes and her lips unsmiling even after I greeted her. Molly followed meekly behind, whining quietly. She had lost her spirit. That she had even the will to drag her lame leg around the house surprised me.

By Lenora's light, I was able to relight my candles. The dog found a suitable place before the dwindling fire and was snoring soundly a minute later. Such a sound, while largely unimportant, was such a comfort to me that it stung my eyes.

"Are you all right?" I asked Lenora once the larger shadows had fled the room.

"It has been a taxing day," she said. "I cannot sleep."

I turned back to my books. "I could do with another opinion. I'm at a loss."

Lenora sat on the floor beside me, her nightgown billowing around her legs.

"Peter is beside himself with grief," she said. "I'm afraid he might've had some sort of nervous episode."

I had been so consumed with the mystery of all this that I

had forgotten the effect such a thing would have on the poor child's family.

"I ought to have thought to stay with him," I said, but I did not share her inclination toward compassion, at least, not anymore. Not here.

"I am not a good nurse," Lenora said. "I could only hold the cloth to his forehead. Women are supposed to have an instinct for these sorts of things." As she said this, she picked at the wax on her candlestick until it crumbled onto the carpet.

"I will look in on him shortly," I offered, and she nodded.

I looked at her over all of those books, over all of the gruesome anatomical sketches and descriptions of death, and all of the day's horror fell onto me. It dropped onto my shoulders and grabbed hold of my throat.

"Will, there is something I must tell you," Lenora said, her tone both grave and hesitant, tightening the grip. She withdrew a pair of moonstone earrings from the pocket of her nightgown. The iridescent stones twinkled in her palm, catching the candlelight as they had each time my mother wore them.

"Where did you find those?" I whispered.

She hesitated once more, lowering her gaze to her lap.

"Anna," she whispered. "I came to her quarters to ask if she could spare a glass of water from her basin. Mine was empty. She was not inside, but I found these on the bureau." She dropped them into my hand and met my gaze, but I could not divine what true feeling lurked there. Innocuous disappointment lingered upon the surface, but something darker thrashed below, in the depths. "I knew they could not belong to her. Will, I'm afraid she meant to sell them."

"Sell them? You're mistaken."

"She has no income," Lenora answered. "And no inheritance."

"I will speak with her." I closed my hand around the jewelry and tucked it safely in my pocket beside the trinket.

"No, you mustn't." Lenora rose as she said this, and I recognized the entity behind her eyes, for it had become an old friend to me of late. It was fear.

"You must work," she said, and turned to leave, but I took her arm.

"Do not leave me. I cannot bear it."

I felt her gaze upon me but I could not meet her eyes.

"Are you unwell, Will?" she whispered, and I could not answer. "You are very pale." Her hand closed around mine briefly, and then she walked over to my unmade bed and sat. "If you are set on this task," she said, "you must return to it. I shall try to sleep."

"Here?" was all I could manage.

"You have lit another set of candles, so it appears you won't be using your bed. Have I misjudged?"

"No, no, quite right," I replied in a low voice. I can't imagine that I said it loud enough to be heard, but she did not ask me to repeat myself. Before I could comment further, she pulled the curtains closed and did not speak another word.

So, per her behest, I returned to my morbid task, the earrings in my pocket heavy. I could no more suspect Anna of thievery than I could Lottie, but the accusation disturbed me on numerous levels, namely that the sale of heirlooms was strictly forbidden in my father's will. Bah, no doubt my cousin would clear it up tomorrow with a simple explanation.

Before long, as I studied those miserable books, my eyes grew heavy. Lenora's rhythmic breathing lulled me into a daze and I did not hear the clock chime three.

I don't know how much time passed before I opened my eyes again. I'd heard a sound by the window as coolness crept along my spine. The window must have come open in the night. Only when my weary eyes at last focused on the dark glass did I see that it remained sealed tight, the candlelight shimmering on the pane.

"Will," someone said. I knew the voice. It belonged neither to Lenora nor to my father. It was my mother who called out for me this time. "Will, darling."

"I'm here," I said. "Mother, I'm here." Icy wind blew across my books, extinguishing the candles and scattering my notes across the floor. In a moment it was over, and the hideous silence fell over me again.

Suddenly, the candle at my side sprung back to life, and I stared with bated breath at the medical books upon the floor. All remained exactly as before I drifted off to sleep, undisturbed by wind or draft. All, that is, except the manual on poisons that I had closed and set aside. It now sat inexplicably open before me. My eyes fell to the heading:

Strychnine toxicity in mammals; presentation in humans

"Christ," I muttered, and then again, louder. What a fool I'd been to miss it.

"Will?" The curtain flung open and Lenora stepped out of the bed, bleary-eyed and lovely. I ignored her.

"Yes, yes," I said over and over, reading the terrible symptoms—the muscle spasms and arching of the back, the convulsions worsened by external stimuli, and finally, death by asphyxiation. I could not imagine a more horrible way to die. But how had she consumed it? This poison was so bitter on the tongue that surely she would have tasted it, unless cleverly masked by sweetness. I stilled.

Lenora knelt beside me and grabbed my hand to focus my attention.

"What's happened?" she asked.

"The teacakes…" I stammered. "I must go to Devlin." I tried to stand, but my feet were numb from sitting upon them, and so I fell.

"Will," Lenora cried. "It is the middle of the night. What did you find that can't wait until morning?"

"Cause of death."

I stumbled out of the room with fire in my legs, and as I clutched my candle, the cawing of a crow sounded from the darkness at the end of the hall.

At first, only the faint impression of a shadow stirred there.

When at last the form materialized, it was no bird at all, but the hideous and malformed figure of Christine Murdoch. Her head, perched atop asymmetrical shoulders, lolled toward me, the cords in her neck stretching as a single sharp spasm bent her backward.

My candle lit her face. She had no features at all, only sunken, mottled flesh. Even in the absence of eyes, I felt her gaze upon me. Her fingers closed around the doorknob to the attic and rattled it. The sound struck my ears as a death knell, and I flew down the hall with all of her anguish in my own heart.

"What are you doing?" Lenora called behind me. Christine's specter vanished.

My courage would not fail me this time. I threw open the attic door and climbed stairs as dark as pitch. My candlelight flickered on the old wardrobe, and I knew it must be opened. I set my candle on a nearby table, retrieved a discarded iron ash shovel from the floor, and set to obliterating the lock. Lenora's breath upon my neck chilled me, for I had not heard her enter the room.

Rust crumbled in my palms as my assaults made quick work of the old brass knobs. In a moment, they clattered to the floor, and I swung the doors open wide, releasing a cluster of powdery moths. I pushed aside rat-chewed greatcoats and one of my mother's dresses, now yellow and frayed.

My father's oriental rug, rolled tightly, leaned against the back panel.

Why the deuce would he keep it hidden away up here? I heaved it out and, clutching the edges, flung it open across the floor. An ungodly stain marred the fibers, and I knew immediately that it was blood, more blood than I'd ever seen in my life, and to whom it belonged.

My father had been murdered on this very carpet, and it had been hidden away like an out-of-fashion pair of curtains.

A sound that can only be described as the wriggling of a great many worms drew my attention from the rug. I lifted my eyes to where I'd presumed Lenora to be, but she had not yet entered the room. I lifted my candle, and by this light, I saw it.

God, I saw it.

The apparition, for it could be nothing else, swung from the ceiling like a pendulum, its wrists bound with what appeared to be a silk ribbon. I could see the rafters behind the being as clearly as if looking at them through frosted glass. Its head rolled around unnaturally toward me, the angle inhuman. The long hair, dark obsidian eyes, and pale fingers...no, there was no mistaking it.

It was Lenora.

But it wasn't. Lenora's footsteps sounded on the stairs. The spirit moaned, struggling against it bonds. The sound, human and somehow *not*, shook me to my bones as if I'd been struck by a tuning fork, and the vibration that it produced inside my brain triggered such a bleakness in my heart that I scarcely kept my feet. This creature had pulled back the veil from my eyes and there was only black. Only great, cavernous darkness. *Oh, God.*

"Lenora?" I whispered, tears spilling over my cheeks.

A black, putrid substance seeped between the panels of the wall and dripped phlegmatically to the floor. The metallic tang of blood scented the air, along with something earthy, like lichen upon stone. But when I looked back to the specter, she was gone. Vanished, and the mystery substance along with her! I stared at the place she had occupied on the ceiling, unmoving, unbelieving. Each explanation that presented itself to me failed.

Lenora rushed into the room, her hand upon her chest, followed closely by Lottie and Anna. My daughter's voice broke through the heavy gauze of shock that dulled my senses.

"Papa?" she asked, her face drawn with sleep and worry. "I heard you cry out."

"I think he must be ill," Lenora whispered to them. Lottie ran to me.

"I'll fetch some water," Anna said, and then disappeared down the stairs.

Lenora offered me her handkerchief, which I used to dab sweat and tears alike from my face. Never in all my life had I experienced the paranormal so plainly as this, and with such a horrible display of absolute human misery.

"Is this what you see, Lottie?" I asked, my voice weak. I could not be certain if I trembled or shivered, only that I had frost in my blood. "When you speak with the dead, do they come to you like this?"

"What?" she asked. "What did you see?"

"Forgive me, child, I beg you. I didn't know. I didn't understand."

As the words left my lips, it occurred to me that no one had witnessed this hideous apparition. I was left, then, with but two explanations—either I had been utterly wrong to forbid Lottie from spiritualism, or I had finally succumbed to the latent lunacy in my blood.

Suddenly belief in the supernatural did not seem so irrational.

"Who did you see?" she asked.

I lifted my eyes to Lenora, my heart galloping in my chest.

"You," I whispered. "I saw you."

Her eyes widened, and goosebumps rose upon her chest.

"I've no stomach for this quest of yours, Mr. Garrett." She turned and trod down the stairs, leaving me alone with Lottie and the stain of my father's blood.

"How can I account for this, Lottie?" I whispered. "How could I have seen her?"

Lottie led me out of the room, for I felt faint and could not control my throbbing heart. I described every horrific detail of what I'd seen, and when we reached my chamber, she took my arm and patted it lovingly.

"Papa, you fear madness as if it were the plague. You must accept that the supernatural world exists alongside our own. I've no doubt a spirit tried to communicate with you, but it simply could not have been Lenora."

"What explanation can you offer me, then?"

"The mind has a tendency to imprint the familiar over the uncanny, I think. Perhaps this spirit bore some resemblances you recognized."

I could only shake my head. She handed me her candle and sent me off to bed. I spent my remaining strength fetching myself a glass of water from the pitcher beside the window, for Anna had not returned, and then I collapsed onto my bed. With Lenora's handkerchief clutched tightly in my hand and the trinket keeping watch beside me on the night table, I plunged into the darkness of sleep.

Chapter XVI

WILLIAM GARRETT'S JOURNAL

January 18, 1889, continued

It was ten o'clock before I summoned the will to rise from my bed this morning. I lay there for hours, entirely still but for the running of my finger over the embroidery on Lenora's handkerchief. The letters "C. L." had been delicately woven in the corner, alongside a beautiful rendering of an iris. Perhaps it had belonged to her mother.

I pondered my lot as the rain lashed against the window. I maintained the belief that I had found my father's skull in the forest, despite its disappearance and the possibility that I was occasionally not in my right mind. This matter weighed heavily upon me, but turn it about as I might, I could not resolve it. If I could perhaps find the weapon used against him, or any further evidence of violence, I may be able to approach Devlin with it and the blood-soaked carpet.

It was this that drove me from my warm bed to dress and enter again the bitter rooms of my father's quarters. He kept a small night table beside his bed, and inside, a revolver. I wished to examine it.

No one disturbed me as I strode down the hall, though I thought I heard Anna's voice from her quarters, humming the tune of the old Irish song I'd learned from my mother.

How strange that she should know this song. It was no great mystery, though. It would have been easy enough for her to have overheard it, so interwoven our childhoods were. Still, the sound of it troubled me, and it brought my dear mother to the forefront of my mind, where her absence still ached.

I knocked on Anna's door as she sang, remembering Lenora's accusation. She answered with a smile that spoke of sweet sympathy, the way one regards the ailing or aged.

"Are you well?" she asked. "You didn't come to breakfast."

"Last night, I, ah…" I could not find the words. "I thought I—"

She saved me the trouble of explaining that Christine's gruesome spirit had led me to an even more horrible entity, one I could not name. It was unlikely she would believe me. I scarcely believed it myself.

"You've had a bad go of it, haven't you?" she said with a knowing grin. "I'm sorry about your water last night. You were already asleep when I brought it, and I didn't wish to disturb you."

"No matter," I said, shaking my head. "Anna, I must ask you something."

"Yes?"

I drew the earrings out of my pocket and showed them to her, but her face did not change.

"These were discovered in your room," I said, pausing to gauge her reaction, but still she made none.

"By whom?" she asked at last.

"That's not important. These were my mother's. What had

you intended to do with them?"

She looked up at me, offense pulling at her lip and narrowing her eyes. "What are you suggesting?"

"Only you've been shut up in your room and I can't find a way to explain why you would have these. What is it you've been doing?"

"You may have forgotten, but it is very trying for me to be here in this place that killed my mother. This room is quiet, removed from death. I can smell her, you know. Christine, in the cellar. You must bury her soon."

"Y-yes..." I stammered, momentarily forgetting my aim. "The earrings," I added.

"If someone found them in my room," she answered, "they were already there. What use are they to me?"

"You had no intention of selling them? If you require money, Cousin, I shall find some for you in some other way. The sale of items from the estate is forbidden."

Anna regarded me, the subtle shaking of her head revealing I had crossed a line.

"You may deny it all you wish, Cousin," she said with acid in her voice. "But you are your father's son."

She shut the door in my face, and locked it.

I drew a breath and pressed my fingers into my eyes. I had so few allies in this world, perhaps because I am so skilled at offending those who care for me. Without lifting my hand to knock again, I carried on to my father's room and opened the door.

The table stood in its usual place near the bed, a fine layer of dust matting its edges. I knew I would find the drawer locked. This table, housing such a murderous weapon, had been strictly forbidden during my childhood, but those days are gone now. I wrapped my fingers around the brass knob.

The drawer was not locked. And the gun was gone.

Gone!

Well, much could have occurred in the time I'd been away.

Father could have sold it, it may have rusted in neglect and been thrown away, or he could simply have relocated it, but none of these logical explanations consoled me. In that moment, I directly correlated this missing weapon with my father's remains, which had also mysteriously vanished. I became convinced that I was involved in some great conspiracy, and I am not entirely persuaded now of the contrary.

I searched the room like a madman, dumping the contents of drawers onto the floor, tearing books from the dusty shelves. When I arrived at a small dresser near the washroom, I found the top drawer locked. Here! Surely this was where he had hidden away the revolver. A letter opener made quick work of the lock, and though I found no gun, a letter sat in the otherwise empty drawer, addressed to me in my father's hand. The pages had been stuffed inside in haste, for they were wrinkled and bent. I sat on the bed and read.

A LETTER TO DR. WILLIAM GARRETT

No Postmark

Dear William,

It has been many years now since I have heard your voice, since I have looked into your eyes and seen your dear mother. I cling to these distant memories now as a lifeline, for they are all that is real.

How I wish you might return to me now and take me from here! I can ask no such thing of you, for it was my own damnable sins that drove you away. It is too late. I am undone.

I've done a terrible thing, William, a thing for which no man can find redemption. I should have known that a woman hired to paint a man's face instead paints his soul. She knows everything, all of my transgressions laid out on a single stretched canvas, like the poor bastard in that story. What was it called?

It doesn't matter. I had no choice, do you understand? And now she has returned to seek vengeance, to haunt me until the end of days. Even now I can hear her brushes scraping against the canvas. The scent of her lingers all about me. Oh, God, I am lost!

They're all in on it, the whole lot of them. Is there no one I can turn to? I cannot ask your forgiveness. I only ask for mercy. Come home, son. For the love of all that is good in this life, come home!

I haven't much time. Before my hour on this earth is through, I need you to know that I forgive you for what you did to your mother. It was a thing done out of mercy, I believe, and although it set us down this road into hell, I laid the stones as surely as you did. I have made an appointment with our family attorney to set things right. Forgive me, son.

Your reading of this now suggests I am dead, for I know nothing else but my absence will bring you back. I tried for many years to contact you so I might give you this, the last words of your mother. Enclosed with this letter you will find another. Now you will know all.

Dear Willie,

I asked you for a cruel, wretched thing. It will burden you for the remainder of your life, I know. I need to you understand why I would ask such thing of you.

You, my sweet boy, are the hero of my story.

A mother is meant to be her child's guardian, his place of warmth and safety. I have failed this sacred task, not once, but twice. I could not protect my baby from your father, just as I cannot protect you. The scars on your back and in your heart were meant for me. You have stepped between us for the last time.

I told you what I meant to do with the tincture I requested. I told you it was the only thing I could do to save you from him. I will no longer tether you here to this horrible old house. You need not protect me any longer. So, you see, just as you have saved me from this wretched life, I have saved you. It is my last act as a mother.

I love you, my beautiful son. Don't let my long absence be a bother to you, dear.

Mother

WILLIAM GARRETT'S JOURNAL

January 18, 1889, continued

I do not know how much time passed before I became master of myself again, only that when I at last roused, I was standing out on the widow's walk. The forest stretched before me, the hemlocks groaning and creaking in the wind. My mother's chair rocked to and fro in rhythm with the gusts. Clutching the letter in my hand, my eyes blurred with tears, I dropped down into the chair where my mother had taken her life.

The chair where I had set the tray—and the laudanum. I remembered all now. The moment of sanity that passed across her eyes when she made this horrible request. The way she squeezed my hand when I, bloodied and swollen from my father's assaults, at last agreed. The lie I told Dr. Johnston, and the way she kissed my cheek when I set that fateful tray on her lap.

She was wrong. I was not the hero in her story.

I was the villain.

I ought to have taken her away, stolen her from him. As I rocked in her chair, I thought of the countless ways I might have done it, but it was too late. My mother was dead, and I had killed her. My father's slanderous letter was nothing of the sort, after all. It was the truth.

I buried my face in my hands, but I could not weep. In that moment, I was nothing more than a trivial wisp of steam, dissipated by the wind.

"Will?" Lenora said, and when I lifted my eyes to the sound of her voice, the sun was shining high overhead, skirting behind gathering storm clouds. I stuffed the letter in my pocket as she stood at the door, smelling of turpentine.

"You've been painting," I said. I did not turn my eyes from the hemlocks.

"All morning," she answered, but did not step outside. "You have discovered something, then?"

"Yes," I said, but I could not tell her.

"Your daughter has rallied us," she said, and the warmth in her voice somehow gathered me from the moving wind, like seeds brought back to the weed. "Come downstairs."

"It's no use, Lenora," I said. "I am ruined."

"You sound like your father."

"I can't make sense of anything," I said, turning to her at last. She wore a plain black dress, buttoned to the neck, in mourning no doubt for Christine.

She replied, "Nor I."

"I've seen things I can't explain." I reached into my pocket and withdrew the trinket, turning it over my knuckles like a lucky coin. "I fear I've lost my ability to discern the truth from fancy."

"You must not speak this way," she said, and I closed my eyes. "You cannot prove to everyone that your father's madness runs in your veins. You *cannot*."

The gravity she poured into this warning alarmed me, as if the whole world depended on my sanity. She had touched on a fear I kept close to my heart and my face must have revealed as much, for she crossed the threshold at last and kissed my forehead. Her lips were ice.

"You're cold," I said quietly. I could not prevent myself from reaching up and taking her face in my hands. We tarried there together, our faces mere inches apart as the sun warmed the frozen earth beyond, but I could not kiss her. I could not rid my heart of the gruesome images of all that had come before us. She straightened after a moment and turned toward the door.

"You will be wanted shortly," she said. "Peter has come up from his vigil, but I cannot convince him to eat."

"Have they chosen a plot for her? They're welcome to any place they wish."

"I'm afraid the ground is still frozen. Peter thought they might lay her in your family crypt until spring?"

"I've no qualm against that. We shall do it at first light tomorrow."

The crypt had not housed the recently deceased in many generations, owing simply to the fact that we'd run out of space sometime in the late 1700s. My ancestors must have been unable to fathom our line persevering so long. All of my known kin were buried in the cemetery atop the hill.

She said again, "You will be wanted," and then walked inside. I rose to follow her, my mind drained of every thought, of every sensation but the wind in my hair. I walked behind her, through the room, and down the stairs like a ghost, neither seeing nor feeling.

"Papa?" Lottie said as I ambled into the sitting room. Her voice startled me. "Are you all right?"

I drew my eyes from the floor to find the room in disarray. Lenora slipped her hand in mine. I squeezed it instinctively and did not let go.

All of the furniture had been pulled from the walls and stood in the center of the room. Rolls of wallpaper leaned against the windows and existing paper hung in strips from the wall, revealing the paneled wall I had known in my youth.

"I hope you don't mind, Papa," Lottie said. Her eyes fell to Lenora's hand in mine, and her voice wavered. "We didn't wish to disturb you, but I saw no reason to wait."

The whole lot of regulars had gathered here to help. Peter, despite his qualms with the sale of this place and the recent death of his daughter, had hoisted himself onto a ladder and was scraping away at a stubborn patch of paper. Anna prepared glue in a great tray, either having forgiven me or pitying me too much to stand by. And Lottie, my beautiful girl. She swept a ringlet out of her eyes with her forearm, smiling. The whole spectacle warmed the ice in my heart until it thumped again.

"Wonderful," I said, and turned to my daughter, our self-appointed laborer. "How shall I help?"

"Poor Peter has been peeling down paper for hours," she answered, turning to him. "Do you need a hand, Uncle Peter?"

I smiled at this name she had given him, and he nodded.

"The work is good for me," he said, but he looked even more ragged than before. He had not shaved in many days, and a grayish beard covered his chin. His eyes fell to me and Lenora, our hands still clasped. The same lightning strike I'd seen in Lottie's eyes flashed across his. He leapt down from the ladder and wiped his hands on a rag.

"Excuse me," he said, and then walked by us and out of the room. Lenora let go of my hand.

"He's not himself," Anna said, straightening. "Will, you must eat. Let me bring you something."

"Thank you," I agreed, though I still had little appetite. She had not yet met my gaze despite this offer of kindness. Once she had gone, I took up Peter's post. The labor, in the company of these women who somehow cared for me, settled my nerves. Lenora set up her easel and began a stunning likeness of the room, warmly lit by the afternoon sun.

I did manage a strong cup of coffee and a slice of buttered toast. I thought this might restore my strength, but after three quarters of an hour, I was spent. My arms burned with the effort of removing the wallpaper, and I became so dizzy I was obliged to climb down and rest.

Lottie sat beside me on the sofa.

"You're not well, Papa," she said. "Have you learned something that troubles you?"

"You have your mother's intuition, my girl," I replied, patting her hand. I told her all I'd learned about the strychnine, and my estimation that the teacakes were what had done it. I could not tell her what I'd learned of my mother.

"Oh!" she cried. "A clever deduction. Where are the teacakes? I shall fetch them and we can bring them to Constable Devlin. Perhaps he knows a toxicologist in New York City. They can test for these things now, can't they?"

"Yes, perhaps," I said, but I scarcely had energy enough to retrieve the teacakes, much less travel. "It's a fine idea. I left them in the cellar with her clothing, if a rat has not gotten to them."

"I'll see to it, Papa," she said, and then embraced me. "You mustn't worry."

Within the hour, she had gone, leaving behind a bit of the blessed hope she kept always within her heart.

Chapter XVII

WILLIAM GARRETT'S JOURNAL

January 19, 1889

There is no end to this horror. What a fool I was to believe, even for one blessed moment, that this day would pass without its own nightmares. I sent Lottie off to town with a reply to Mr. Hawkins's letter, confirming we would be pleased to host his interested friend. I could have sent it via post, surely, but I did not want Lottie here when we entombed the child. I am grateful I had this foresight, for what we discovered in the crypt haunts me still.

By the time they'd gone, the sun had burned up all the clouds. It was the sort of day for brisk walks or carriage rides through town, but this was not our lot. Ravenswood does not permit such infinitesimal pleasures.

We all gathered in the foyer, waiting for Wilson to bring the carriage around. The deep circles beneath Murdoch's eyes and the wan look of his cheeks concerned the doctor in me, though I knew there was nothing I could prescribe for him. He'd simply lost the will to continue. I shook his hand. The weakness of his grip confirmed my conclusion.

"If there's anything I can do," I offered, "anything at all, please ask it of me."

"Thank you, sir," he said, bobbing his head but avoiding my eyes. "She reminded me so much of my dear wife, her grandmother. It's as if I've lost her twice." His voice cracked, but he kept himself together.

"Will," Peter called to me from the threshold. "The coffin."

We walked outside together to my carriage, which I'd put at their disposal. Jays screeched down at us from the spires. Before opening the carriage door, he offered his hand to me, which I took without hesitation.

"Thank you," he said. "For allowing my daughter to rest with your kin. I don't know how I would've got on without you and Lenora."

I noted the strange coupling of my name and Lenora's, and the fact that he had used her Christian name, when even I tried to maintain the propriety of addressing her formally to others—and I was master of the house. What had transpired in the months before I had arrived here for a servant to address her so informally? He grasped my arm with his other hand in a gesture of good faith, but I suddenly distrusted him.

When he released me, his eyes turned to the task at hand and he opened the carriage door to reveal the tragically small coffin he had constructed in the days before. Lacquer gave it shine, and fleur de lis flowers had been carved into the sides. It was the finest coffin I'd ever seen. We carried it between us to the house where Lenora had cleared a space for it on the table in the parlor.

Constable Devlin arrived moments later, and I went with him to the cellar to retrieve the body. The coldness of the earth and the unmistakable scent of death gathered around our ankles, lingering about the paintings and sweeping past our nostrils. He removed a bottle of smelling salts from his pocket and offered it to me.

"For the smell," he muttered, but I declined him, wishing to be through with this morose task. He passed the salts beneath his own nose and added, "No one will give this child her last rites, then?"

I could only shake my head. Having received no reply from Deacon Barnes, I assumed he had been unable to set aside his qualms with Lenora. That this innocent girl should be buried without rites was a great shame indeed.

Devlin placed the cork back in the bottle and sighed, his eyes toward the heavens, or the wooden boards of the ceiling, as it were.

"Shall we get on with it, then?" I said, the stench recalling to my mind the evenings of my mother's funeral. I did not wish to think upon such things, but they came to me, nonetheless. I saw her body laid out in the very parlor where we intended to bring young Christine, a bouquet of lilies and a rosary clutched in her pale fingers. Father had assigned me the duty of sitting up with her at night after the others had gone away. He'd insisted on stopping the clocks, so I had not even their ticking to accompany me. These were dark hours, when shadows crept about of their own volition and grief snatched the breath from my lungs. As the constable unfolded the linen sheets, I still felt her cold hand in mine.

I shoved my hands in my pockets, grasping the little trinket so tightly that it might have left its imprint upon my palm. I do not recall the words he spoke then as he laid these cloths around Christine, for I perceived some movement beside Lenora's paintings—nay, not beside, *in*. I squinted in the dim light at a half-finished self-portrait. The paint blistered as if on fire, leaving gaping black wounds in the canvas. I shut my eyes and looked again. This did not cure its disease. Maggots wriggled inside the canvas and fell to the floor as Devlin drew the sheet up over her face.

The other paintings around the room fell forward, one by one, some with such violence that the frames cracked. I cried out, but Devlin carried on.

"Enough!" I shouted, unable to bear this madness any longer. Silence fell over the room immediately, my candle extinguished by a gust of foul breath.

"What's the trouble, Dr. Garrett?" Devlin asked, his candle revealing his face to me, seemingly as pale and bloodless as the child's. Lenora's paintings had been righted again, not a blemish or maggot in sight. I stood motionless, words forming on my tongue but never passing my lips.

"It's nothing," I whispered at last, and we made haste in the silence to finish wrapping Christine in the linens and then carried her upstairs to the waiting figures of her family. My mind, however, remained in the cellar. What the devil had I witnessed? Another consequence of the noxious air within this festering house? This explanation pales, as does the conviction of my own sanity. I cannot bear these waking nightmares.

We placed the body in the little coffin, heaving me from one horror to the next. Peter hovered nearby like a phantom of himself. As Murdoch placed a rosary on the child's chest, I watched an exchang between Peter and Lenora that nourished the bitter seed of jealousy in my heart. She set her hand lovingly on his arm, and he turned and pressed his forehead against hers, taking her face in his hands as if he meant to kiss her. Only grief impassioned him, one could see that plainly in his wretched expression, but she swept her hands through his hair with such familiarity that my jealousy grew still. Dr. Johnston had been wrong to call me a good man. Good men did not fall victim to such wickedness while standing before the dead body of a child. I turned from the lot of them. Anna, who had been lingering near the door, approached me and set her hand on my shoulder.

"You look as wretched as Peter," she said, and then embraced me.

"Cousin," I muttered, this fleeting moment of comfort a blessed surprise. I had believed she harbored some ill will against me, and the lifting of this burden was a great relief. How I could have thought her capable of deceit I can only attribute to my troubled mental state that night.

"I must ask your forgiveness again," I said, releasing her.

"For the earrings?" she said, nearly laughing. "You weren't in your right mind, Will. It is forgotten. You know in your heart I couldn't do such a thing."

Before I could agree with this, Peter stepped up beside me.

"We're taking her now," he whispered.

We made our grim procession, the coffin carried between Peter and I, to my family's crypt. Melting snow and rain soaked the earth, and we trudged through mud that clung to our shoes and slowed our steps.

We reached the crypt at last, breathless and weary. Lenora struggled at first with the old key and then opened the door wide.

Her cry echoed in the hollow room like the moaning wind. Startled, Peter released his side of the coffin and it crashed to the ground, splitting down the side. Christine's blonde ringlets spilled out as her body slid forward. Lenora fell to her knees.

A desiccated corpse lay atop the sarcophagus of my patriarchal ancestor, hands bound in yellowed silk across its sunken chest.

"Christ," I muttered. Lenora reached for the corpse's withered hand but then withdrew. I lowered the other side of the coffin as gently as I could, and then I entered the crypt. Female by the shape and dress, the body had practically mummified in the absence of natural elements. Long dark hair fell over the side of the sarcophagus, and the clothing, though moth-eaten and faded, was of high-quality silk the color of coal.

Constable Devlin stepped up beside me with his hands in his pockets.

"Aye," he said, "I'm starting to believe in this curse. Do you know who it is?"

"No," I answered, but the corpse resembled the woman who had appeared to me in the attic. I could not speak such a thing aloud.

I called for Lenora, but she'd gone.

"Been here about a year, I'd say," Devlin said.

"Mother of God," Murdoch muttered before I could reply, crossing himself as he stepped onto the marble.

"Mr. Murdoch, please." Devlin tried to usher him out, but he'd turned to stone, staring in wide-eyed horror at the corpse.

"No," he whispered. "I don't—we can't leave her here."

Peter grabbed his arms, strangely unaffected, or perhaps only numb.

"Father, where else are we going to keep her?" he whispered fiercely.

"The ground is not so frozen, is it, Constable?" Murdoch asked, desperation thickening his voice. "Let us bury her. Let us be done with this."

"Take them away from here," Devlin said to Anna, and she gathered them like a loving mother, with soft words and assurances. In a moment, the constable and I stood alone, surrounded by the dead.

"I should have listened to Dr. Johnston," I said. "I should have gone back to Baltimore."

"It's too late for that now, it is." He walked around the sarcophagus to examine the body, his hands behind his back. I looked back to Christine's coffin, cast aside at an angle with its front upon the marble and the end upon the damp, dead grass. I could see her cheek through the crack, so I removed my greatcoat and laid it across the coffin.

"Constable," I said, turning back to him. "I think my father killed this woman." I told him about the letter he'd written me but never sent.

He considered all of this for a moment, and then he said,

"Well, he'd gone rather out of his mind, Dr. Garrett. You're aware of that?"

"I haven't been allowed to forget it."

He shook his head and then waved me toward the broken coffin.

"Here," he said. "Help me bring her inside. I can't stand to see her like this."

I retrieved my greatcoat and draped it around my shoulders as we dragged Christine's coffin into the crypt, the smooth pine whispering across the marble. A swirl of leaves blew in behind us as we carefully lowered the coffin, the wind carrying the slightest breath of spring to mock us here in our underworld.

Devlin and I approached the corpse of the unknown woman again, bending to examine her. Fractured light from the stained-glass windows shown upon her in colored shards and glinted off of a tarnished silver necklace.

"Are those initials there?" Devlin asked. I plied the necklace from the withered flesh and unclasped it so we might better examine it.

"Yes," I answered, my voice only a breath. There, delicately engraved on the heart-shaped pendant, were the letters L.M.L.

Chapter XVIII

WILLIAM GARRETT'S JOURNAL

January 21, 1889

Sweet Molly is with us no more. A part of me believes a broken heart took her life, not the lacerations. Without the child to give her purpose, she must have simply surrendered herself to death. At least, this is what I tell myself. I could do nothing for a broken heart. I might have done more for the wounds. The house is colder without her. I did not fully know the comfort she brought me until she was gone.

Lenora did not leave her room for two days. I heard her crying at night, but she would not open the door to me, or anyone. I yearned to ask her about the necklace that bore her initials, for I could think of as little explanation for this as for the woman's spirit haunting the attic.

Murdoch and Peter resumed their usual duties, likely to keep their minds occupied rather than to aid me. I prowled about the house, eating and drinking by the fire with Lottie and Anna, but my mind was with Lenora, my body able to feel only the weight of the necklace in my pocket.

Constable Devlin wrote to report he had sent the teacakes off to an acquaintance in New York, hoping to isolate the poison. He had also been making inquiries into the identity of the mystery woman in the crypt, but to no avail. I was engaged in writing him a reply, alone in my chair, when Lenora emerged at last from her chamber. Her appearance shocked me. The color in her cheeks had gone, along with the gracefulness of her fingers. They trembled now as she picked up her embroidery from my mother's basket and settled on the sofa, as if no time had passed at all. She spoke not a word.

"Are you well?" I asked.

"Fine, thank you," she said, but she did not look up at me. "How are the Murdochs?"

"As well as can be expected under the circumstances."

"*Que bien.*"

"Are you hungry?" I placed my unfinished letter in the drawer of the side table and took what is now my chair by the fire. I feared if I sat beside her, she might spook like a horse and abandon me again. I could not bear another day without her.

"Yes, thank you," she answered. Still, she did not meet my eyes. I rang for Murdoch to request an early supper, and he answered with his usual low bow, but the grief lingered about him like a shadow.

Lenora retraced a failed stitch. The thread tangled in her quivering hands until she cast it aside, frustrated.

"Do you know who she is?" I asked after mustering my courage.

"Should I?"

"You seemed to. You were rather upset for a stranger."

Her bitter gaze pinned me to the chair. "I have never been so surrounded by death in my life, Mr. Garrett. Forgive me for becoming overwhelmed by it."

"I didn't mean—"

"No, no, you never do."

"Lenora," I rose and took her icy hands in mine. "Please, I am as horrified by all of this as you. I only seek the truth. I must find it. Do you understand?"

"I can't help you with that."

"I think you can." I took the necklace from my pocket and dangled it before her. She attempted to snatch it out of my hand, but I, being unable to part with a presumably valuable piece of evidence, returned it to its place in my pocket beside the trinket.

"Where did you find that?" she asked, breathless.

"On the body in the crypt. I intend to give it to Constable Devlin. It is significant, I'm certain." She closed her eyes and turned her face from me, but I pressed on. "Can you explain how this woman came to have your necklace?"

"You know I can't," Lenora replied. She reached again for her embroidery, but I stopped her.

"Please."

"I don't know. I lost it."

"And you have no idea who she could be?" I asked, but I sensed she grew tired of my questions.

"It could be anyone."

"But you never saw another woman here in this house?"

"Never."

Silence stretched out uncomfortably between us as we searched each other's faces.

"I feel as though I'm in a dream, unable to wake," Lenora said at last.

"Yes," I agreed.

"Can you forgive me for abandoning you to it all?" She lifted her eyes to mine, and somehow the obsidian at their center dulled to ash. She was another person, one burdened by tragedy and grief.

I covered her hand with my own. "Are you sure you are well? You're very pale."

"I..." she began, and then drew in a heavy breath. "All of this death has leached into me."

At this moment, a robin chirped in the garden and I thought perhaps this glimpse of spring might cheer her. It became the most pressing matter in all the world to secure even a moment of happiness for her.

"Listen," I said. "The birds are singing for you now, and you must still make good on your promise to help me with the party."

"You still wish to invite your friends into this place?"

I laughed more ruefully than I'd meant. "The people I plan to invite are gossipmongers, waiting for a glimpse of this nightmare house. They're no more my friends than the wolves in the forest."

"Then why invite them at all?"

"Because one of those miserable bastards might like to take this place off my hands. You've made good progress on your paintings. It's fine time to show them off."

"But is it proper to host a gathering when the house is in mourning?"

"Let Peter and Murdoch mourn their kin. I have been in mourning my whole life. I can do it no longer."

January 22, 1889

With our new task at hand, merriment followed us all about the house like a cheerful sparrow. Whether this sentiment was contrived or genuine, I cannot say, but we had thrown the new curtains open wide, and the sun shone warm across the whole of the house. These rare glimpses of springtime lifted my spirits so. I had all but forgotten little Christine, whom we had interred with the corpse of the unknown woman not long ago. The darkness haunting Ravenswood broke away today like so much glass. We swept it out with the cobwebs and the dust.

After breakfast, Wilson took Lottie and Anna into town to procure victuals for the party. They were so like sisters now, nigh inseparable, and the idea of parting them at the end of this nightmare gave me pain. Their shared opinion of Lenora, too, troubled me. While I could empathize with Anna's feelings, I'd trusted that my daughter would not be so easily influenced. Even at breakfast they spoke not two words to her, despite their gaiety with one another. A man, I suppose, cannot have all he desires in this world, and I feared the day when one of them would force me to make a terrible choice.

Lenora, bless her, would not allow me to brood on these matters for long. She swept through the front door with an arm full of daffodils, the blush of winter in her cheeks and spring in her smile. I could only stand before her in the foyer, bewildered by her beauty.

"You mustn't look so contrary, Will," she said, pulling loose the string of her bonnet with the pluck of her thumb and forefinger.

"Where the devil did you find daffodils this time of year?" I asked, laughing because she had pressed them into my arms to remove her cloak and some of the blooms spilled onto the floor.

"Anna brought them from her greenhouse," she answered as we knelt to gather them. She held a yellow flower to her nose and smiled, and I forgot myself again.

"Will you stand beside me at the party?" I asked as she rose, leaving me inadvertently on my knees before her, which drew a little titter from her throat. I hastened to collect the remaining flowers and stood, mere inches from her.

"People will talk," she answered, eyes turned up to me.

"Let them."

I held her gaze for a long while, my poor heart all aflutter. When my eyes fell to her lips, made scarlet with cold, she stepped backward.

"And disappoint the eligible ladies?" she said. "I wouldn't dream of it."

"How many are you going to invite?"

She grinned. "All of them, of course."

"Then perhaps you should also invite all the eligible men to give yourself a proper selection of dance partners, since you won't have me."

The laughter that burst forth from her was both beautiful and mildly humiliating. She salted the wound with a sly, "Perhaps I will invite them."

"Incorrigible." I maintained the good humor in my voice, but disliked the thought of Lenora in the company of other men, especially the eligible ones.

"You have forgotten the aim of this gathering already, then?"

"To spend the evening with a beautiful woman on my arm? Certainly not."

I couldn't help myself.

"Mr. Garrett, I belong on no man's arm. You shall find me in the garden with the birds." She pecked a lighthearted kiss on my cheek, tied her bonnet back on her head, and walked toward the door.

"Planning to fly?"

"Perhaps..." She looked over her shoulder. "Put those in water before they wither, won't you?"

"My mother's vase on the piano will do them justice."

I watched her stroll away with sunshine in her step, her kiss lingering on my skin. How quickly my situation had improved. Only weeks hence I had wanted to be rid of this place as one might cure oneself of a disease. We had planned this party for the sole purpose of finding a poor, unsuspecting soul to take it off my hands. Was that not the aim? Only now, on the heels of Lenora's unusually cheerful mood and the sunny aspect of spring, I couldn't imagine another man in my place, sitting in my chair or leading his horse into my stables. I could imagine no other woman but Lenora sleeping in my old quarters. No, something had changed indeed, for I did not wish to be rid of Ravenswood at all.

I strode into the sitting room with her flowers draped over my arm and her smile in my heart, but when my eyes rose from the daffodils to the piano, I could go no farther.

My mother's vase was gone.

Mr. Hawkins, and his infernal cat, have just paid me a visit, bringing at least one mystery to a troubling close. The whole business has me feeling bleak despite the brilliant sun keeping time along the walls.

My attorney's carriage clattered up the drive at about half-past three, and Murdoch showed him into the sitting room with his usual gallant bow and a promise to warm up the coffee.

"A fine day for travel, isn't it?" he asked as I motioned for him to sit on the sofa. He looked about, stroking his cat as it purred from a satchel that looked rather like an oversized reticule. I agreed with him, and he added, "You've done a fine job with this place, Dr. Garrett. My friend will be pleased."

"Mr. Hawkins, forgive me, but you must have come all this way for a more pressing matter than my redecorating."

"Indeed." He sat at last. "Two matters, as it were."

I waited, sitting on my mother's piano bench. Murdoch arrived with the coffee tray, and another quarter of an hour passed while Hawkins prepared it to his liking and sipped it.

"A bitter roast," he muttered, clearing his throat.

"I prefer it strong."

He returned his cup to the tray, which Murdoch had placed on the table beside him, and settled back into the cushions.

"Well, then," he said. "The prospective buyer will be arriving on the twenty-sixth and would like to view the property the following day, if possible."

"The twenty-seventh then? That isn't much time to spread the word about a party."

"Nonsense. Write up your invitations, and I'll deliver them personally, if need be."

"Thank you, but I'm sure that won't be necessary."

His cat mewed, and he sobered as if the thing had reminded him of something.

"There is another matter we should discuss," he said. "You see, I've come upon some very disturbing news, and admittedly I ought to have led with it."

"Disturbing?"

"Well, I happened to visit Mrs. Cunningham last week, and she was wearing the most beautiful necklace."

I tapped my foot against the piano, waiting.

"I've been your family's attorney a long time," he continued, "so it's no hard task upon the memory to identify an article that your dear mother once wore. I remember it because it caused a scuffle between me and my late wife. She wanted one just like it, you see."

"I don't understand your meaning," I said, though I was rather afraid I did.

"I have investigated the matter, Dr. Garrett," he went on, removing a handkerchief to dab beads of sweat from his forehead. "I am sorry to say that your mother's articles have recently turned up all across town. Mrs. Peterson came upon a fine garnet broach, and one of the Gregory triplets was seen wearing a diamond pendant that I personally assisted your father in purchasing."

"How can that be?"

"Were the terms in your father's will unclear? No items were to be sold from the estate. I've spoken to each of them, Dr. Garrett. Sending your dear cousin to peddle your wares is most unbecoming and, frankly, very distressing."

The moisture in my mouth turned to sand.

I had never catalogued my mother's things, never rescued them from the moldering attic as I'd intended. Anna, it seemed, had taken this task upon herself.

"Mr. Hawkins, you are mistaken," I muttered, my voice weak.

Before he could give me further evidence of my cousin's deceits, she and Lottie bustled through the front door, chatting cheerfully. He took this as his cue to leave, or else did not wish to be present when I confronted the thief.

"We will, of course, need to address this with regard to the breach of your father's wishes," he said, and stood, but he was obliged to sit again after teetering. The cat hissed, angry for having almost been crushed beneath him.

"Are you quite all right?" I asked, going to him as Anna and Lottie entered the room, their arms full of packages.

"Oh, forgive us, Papa. We didn't see you were with company."

Anna said, "How do you do, Mr. Hawkins?" as if there were nothing wrong in the world at all.

"Lottie, could you fetch him a glass of water?" I asked, for I feared he might lose consciousness. All the blood had drained from his face.

"No need," he said, waving me off. "I was just going."

I helped him to stand after further insistence and guided him into the foyer.

"Anna," I said over my shoulder. "Wait for me here. I need a word."

Once the attorney was secured in his carriage and homeward bound, I returned to the house with my aggrieved heart in my throat. Anna waited dutifully on the sofa, her arms folded across her lap. The packages had been cleared away, along with the tray of coffee, though I'd not yet tasted it.

"Did you wish to discuss Dr. Johnston's journal?" she asked when I sat beside her, but I admit I had entirely forgotten it. "I'm sorry, Will, but Lenora was right. There was no more mention of your father."

"No," was all I could manage.

"Has something happened?"

"Mr. Hawkins has just informed me that you have been selling my mother's belongings to the women in town."

She opened her mouth, perhaps to deny it, but must have

seen the pained finality in my expression because she bowed her head and her eyes filled with tears.

"You must hate me so," she whispered.

"I could never hate you, Anna. Only tell me why. There are grave consequences to me and Lottie that you cannot know."

"I'm so sorry, Will," she said, taking my hand. I had been prepared to argue with her, but these piteous tears gripped my heart so. I was ready to forgive her then, before she even implored it of me.

"Why?" I repeated.

"I didn't want you to know." After a moment, she brushed the tears away with the back of her hand and straightened. "Your father's funds have run out, Will."

"What do you mean they've run out?"

"He allotted a certain pension to Murdoch for food, as you know. It's all gone. Murdoch is beside himself."

"How it is gone?"

"It wasn't enough," she answered plainly. "He is as miserly in death as he was in life. And he likely didn't account for my presence—or your daughter's."

"Why did you not come to me?"

"You have been through so much. I know it was wrong of me to sell your mother's things, but I thought if I could manage this one thing for you, you might still cling to your hope."

This confession, while misguided, touched me. Tears burned behind my eyes and in my throat, and for a long while, I could only squeeze her hand.

"I'll get it all back somehow," she offered, and she leaned against me. "Can you ever forgive me?"

The consequences of these actions remain to be seen, but I could neither admonish her nor hold her accountable for these good-natured transgressions. I now had the very real possibility of poverty to contend with, and my father strangled any hope of rising out of it, even from beyond the grave.

Chapter XIX

WILLIAM GARRETT'S JOURNAL

January 25, 1889

The last days have been filled to the brim with preparations. The arrival of Mr. Hawkins's friend is fast approaching, and as such, our dinner party and gallery. I've little concern about the lateness of the invitations, which Lottie took upon herself to write and send, including a handsome notice regarding the sale of the house. Gossip is rampant in these parts, and those who wish to gawk will have no trouble rearranging their engagements, propriety and fashion be damned. Now all of Catskill knows my intent.

We are still woefully unready for guests, as there is much to finish, but the rosebushes and the hedges have been trimmed, the wallpaper is up, and the rodents have been mostly evicted. The doors shut soundly, their hinges freshly oiled, and the new carpet looks charming beneath my mother's piano.

I am grateful to have been engaged in activities other than brooding over murder. After all, it had done no good thus far, and Devlin is no closer to finding the truth than when we carried little Christine's body into the crypt. I fear the whole business has had such a wretched effect on me that I am making enemies of my friends, namely Lottie, who says she sees a great change in me. I cannot deny this, for I feel changed. There is bitterness inside me that seeps out at the slightest provocation.

Peter is cross with me as well, as he has deduced that I mean to keep him from troubling Lenora with his advances. This evening, I gave him a rather harder time than he deserved, I fear.

Completely disregarding propriety, he had the audacity to sit down with us at supper. Lottie welcomed him, but I could not tolerate so brazen a disrespect. To add insult to injury, he pressed his lips to Lenora's hand with an air of defiance about him.

"Peter," I said. He immediately withdrew his hand. A fox caught in the hen house! "Once again, you have forgotten your station."

"How can I forget it, *sir*, when you remind me at every turn?"

"You've been brooding ever since—"

"Since? Since my daughter was murdered?"

This silenced me. Lottie set her hand on my arm.

"Papa, you have been too hard," she whispered. "I have never seen you treat a man this way, no matter the station."

I turned back to Peter, who had risen to take his leave.

"Peter," I said, attempting to meet his eyes, but he would not look at me. "Peter, you are welcome to eat with us, if you wish. I apologize."

"I've lost my appetite," he answered, and he left without another word. My cheeks burned as Lenora stood and followed him, her apple tart untouched.

"You're not the same man you were, Papa," Lottie said in a gentle voice that reminded me of her mother. "You taught me to be fair and kind, and you are neither of those things here."

"It's improper for him to treat her this way," I said, but the barb stuck, and even in my own ear it sounded like a poor excuse.

"Why? She's only the painter. Isn't she?"

I looked down at my plate, unwilling to answer. This was confirmation enough for her.

"Anna was right, then," she muttered. "She is an evil influence."

"I won't have you speaking this slander. Not you, too."

"I can speak in whatever manner I choose. I am not your property."

"You're in my house," I retorted, the silverware rattling as my fist struck the table. She remained as still as a portrait, and she then leveled her gaze on me.

"I thought this was Grandfather's house."

All the fight went out of me. I closed my eyes, and when I opened them, she had gone. I swallowed the remainder of my sherry and strode up to my chamber with my head hung in shame. I do not know myself anymore. I do not know this anger, this violence, until it rattles the bars of its cage and bursts forth to injure those I love. What is happening to me?

Lenora has come to my door, likely to admonish me. I shall finish this entry presently.

I have betrayed her. I've done the thing I swore I could never do again.

Charlotte. I am no longer worthy to speak your name, and so I write it one final time, each letter stinging as the pen scratches it out, as if written in my own flesh. Can I be blamed for seeking warmth in this place of death, for grasping at comfort amid all this putrescence?

The answer, I know, is a resounding *yes*, spoken in Lottie's voice. She was right, after all. I had been beguiled, and am still, but this does not feel like the love I knew with my wife. It is haunted. It is love's dark cousin. I cannot rid myself of it, even if I wish to. In the name of posterity alone, I record this next moment in my life so that I might look upon it and know my own disease.

Lenora did indeed tap upon my door, and when I answered, she did not mention my treatment of Peter. She carried the guttering stump of a candle. The buttons at the neck of her dressing gown had not been fastened, and a shadow pooled in the gentle hollow of her throat.

"I cannot sleep," she said. "I thought I might sketch my room for the gallery, but I require more light. Do you have a candle to spare?"

"You're welcome to them all," I answered and fetched the box from my night table. She lingered there in the doorway even after I'd handed it over and the air between us grew heavy. Lavender wafted up from her hair, mingling with a scent like oleander.

"You could—" she began, her gaze on the floor. "You could accompany me, if you wish."

I could only nod, my tongue as dry as parchment, and followed her into her room. She sat on the sofa and collected a small sketchbook and pencil from the side table. I tossed a log onto the grate, as the fire had begun to smolder. Sparks popped up into the flue.

"May I?" I asked, motioning to the cushion beside her. Her pencil quivered as she set it to the page.

"Artists are not designed to live in the grotesque," she muttered. "When we tremble, so does the drawing."

"The paintings in the cellar," I said. Lenora nodded as I settled beside her, nearly touching.

"They were painted by fear," she answered. "I wish I had burned them."

A tremor shivered through her fingers, so she was obliged to set the pencil flat. I covered her hand with mine, and my wedding ring caught the firelight. For a long moment, she simply regarded it, unspeaking, and then she swept her finger over it, like it was a wound her magic could heal.

"When are you going to let her go?" she asked at last. The answer came to me like the sweeping shine of a lighthouse in the dark. I turned to it, even if it were a mirage, believing I was no longer lost.

"Whenever you ask me to."

Lenora held my gaze as steadily as she held my hand. I smoothed a ringlet of her hair between my fingers, as I had wished to do so many nights before.

"Are you not a spirit, sent to drive me mad?" I whispered. Her breath brushed my cheek, and I struggled to breathe through the tightness in my belly. Her eyes lingered still on mine, large and dark and wanting.

"I am no spirit, Will," she answered, her lips so close to mine I could feel their warmth. Could she hear my heart? I was on the edge of a great chasm and tempted to jump, the void below yawning dark and horrible beneath me. I could not resist it.

"Still, I am mad," I said, and when I kissed her, she sighed as though relieved. My hands slipped along her arms, brushing aside silk and lace to bare her shoulders to the candlelight. I pressed my lips to her neck.

She tipped her head back against the velvet with my name on her lips.

"Is this wise?" she asked, but she did not push me away.

"What does it matter?" I murmured against the swell of her bosom. I cared about nothing. I felt nothing but the warmth of her skin and the sweetness of her mouth as she brought her lips again to mine. In a moment, her fingers had unbuttoned my collar, and in one moment more, the coolness of the lavender air brushed across my bare chest. The candle flame flickered in the darkness of her eyes, and I was lost.

⸎

January 26, 1889

Wakefulness did not dawn upon me gracefully, as it was wont to do in the novels, after a man had spent the evening as I had. I'd imagined waking to Lenora in my arms, warm with the half-light of dawn, entangled in linen.

I woke instead with a start, alone and pursued still by visions of the recently deceased.

The fire had gone out. I wrapped the duvet around myself and sat up, shivering, my chest damp with sweat. Angry, roiling clouds lashed cold rain against the windows and rattled the panes, consuming yesterday's sunshine. I had no real concept of time, though the clock on the mantel ticked away the seconds. I only knew that Lenora had gone, and that I was very hungry. I noted then with some alarm that the clock hands read ten o'clock.

Dressing quickly in my shirtsleeves and breeches, which I was required to retrieve from the floor, I left the room. Anna saw me.

"Will," she whispered, eyes wide. "What have you done?"

I could not speak. Emotion swelled inside me, filling my chest so my lungs could not take air. Tears sprung into my eyes, and I felt my lips move, but no sound issued from my throat.

"Oh, Will," she said. Her shoulders fell, as if I had sealed not only my fate but somehow hers. "Come. We must talk."

"What can I say?" I managed, and she gathered me into her arms.

"You've let her into your heart," she whispered. "Now you must rid yourself of her."

I pulled away. This was not the comfort I sought. I had done a terrible thing, I knew, but I did not wish to be rid of her.

"Let me be happy in my disease," I said, and I turned toward the stairs.

"Your mother would not want this for you," she called after me. These words froze me in place as quickly as a blade of grass beneath the snow.

"You know nothing of my mother," I answered, but I did not turn around.

"I know she only wanted your happiness. She *died* for your happiness, Will. You are not happy."

I spun on my heel at this, anger burning in my cheeks and ears.

"Happy? I cannot know the meaning of it. She made sure of that when she begged me for her laudanum."

Anna's lips fell open, and I knew I had spoken too much. I'd not told a single soul of my sin, not even Lottie.

"You…" but she could not go on, and I could not explain further.

She knew. Despite my horror and shame, I no longer bore the burden of it alone.

"It was mercy, then?" she asked, but I could not answer.

Chapter XX

WILLIAM GARRETT'S JOURNAL

January 27, 1889

The day of our dinner party has arrived at last. I haven't much time to write before the guests arrive, but I wish to record a short exchange I had with Murdoch concerning Lenora.

After breakfast, I'd assigned myself the task of assisting Murdoch in the kitchen. I mangled pastry dough as he prepared a great quantity of rhubarb according to my mother's pie recipe.

"I'm a poor baker," I said by way of apology, for the dough had broken up and wrapped around the rolling pin. He sprinkled flour over it all like faerie dust.

"A bit of practice, sir. You'll have it."

I began again. Old Murdoch's spirit, while as dour as ever, had returned to him at least in part. He went about his duties with his usual severity, which had begun to spark again in his watery eyes. I sought the courage to mention a peculiarity that had been troubling me. After another unsuccessful attempt at the rolling of crust, I wiped my hands and turned to him at last.

"Murdoch," I said, and he looked up from the rhubarb. "May I ask you something?"

"Whatever you wish, sir."

"Peter and Lenora...They seem to have grown close?"

I could see the question disturbed him, but I did not withdraw it. Although Lenora and I had neither spoken of nor repeated the sin we'd committed together, it had hardened my suspicion of Peter. His apparent affection for her troubled me more each passing day.

Murdoch's lips compressed, and he averted his eyes to the floor, which was not his custom when speaking to me.

"A strange question, sir," he answered finally.

"I'm sorry to ask it."

"He's always been alone, you know. Never a proper woman in his life. You won't remember when his mother left us. You boys were only children then. I thought Christine's mother would bring some light into his life, but she was just the same and ran off with a navy man."

The pace at which Murdoch peeled the rhubarb intensified as he spoke, and I let him continue without interruption.

"Miss Laveau," he went on, "she's affected him. He's not the same as he was, sir. There's a shiftiness in his eye that troubles me something awful. He didn't seem to care for her one way or the other at first, but when she returned from her holiday, he turned into a right lovesick dog."

"It appears that way to me as well," I replied. "I am afraid it disturbs her. I do not wish her to be uncomfortable here."

"Nor I, sir." The paring knife quivered in his hand, so I thought it best to continue my questioning at a later time, as eager as I was to learn. We continued our pie making in silence until Murdoch paused and smiled to himself.

"Do you recall, sir, that summer your father went to California," he asked, plucking a shriveled stalk from his basket and tossing it aside. "You were just a child then, you were."

"Very well," I answered, smiling. So many fond memories bloomed in my mind that I could not land on one alone but flitted about them like a moth. I saw myself clumsily herding young chickens into the new coop, or sneaking slices of fresh cinnamon bread from the counter, my mother watching silently as she kneaded another loaf.

"I think often of the day she brought that orphaned fawn into the kitchen. It was a day quite like today."

I put down the rolling pin and laughed, unable to stop myself. To my surprise, Murdoch joined me. Such a merry sound it was.

"That creature went about the whole house wreaking havoc," he said.

"I remember."

"That was the way with Lady Garrett," he said, shaking his head, the rhubarb forgotten. "Always bringing in the strays. She'd instructed me to feed it every night at one o'clock, so it wouldn't starve, you see. But I always found her here in the kitchen with one of your old baby bottles, the poor deer drinking like its life depended on it."

"I didn't know that," I answered.

"Those memories are very dear to me. Forgive me, sir. It seems I've forgotten myself."

"Nonsense. My mother ought to be remembered."

We reminisced further as the morning wore on until the happy memories outshone all else. I was grateful to old Murdoch for that, bless him. At long last, sunshine broke through the kitchen window and revealed how truly hideous my piecrusts were.

"Better let me have at it, sir," he said, and I bowed gratefully as he took the rolling pin. He paused, lost in his thoughts.

"Your mother's death was a great loss," he said at last. "A terrible burden to put on you, sir, but she did what she thought was best. That's all any of us can do."

I could only look at him as he patched holes in the dough.

Had Anna told him of my role in my mother's death? Did he know what I had done? Suspicious now that he knew all, I feigned fatigue and fled to my chamber to sit alone with my own shriveled conscience and write these words. The dinner party begins in under an hour, and I must collect myself.

I'd forgotten how ardently I loathed parties until the first guests arrived, the ladies with their hats and new dresses, the men with their canes and forced gallantry. It was all so tedious. My guest of honor, the friend of Mr. Hawkins, had not yet arrived, and so I was forced to fix my attentions on others.

My mind lingered on Lenora as I shied away from a gaggle of young women, led gallantly inside by Peter. Her paintings adorned the house, in every room. Each of them displayed Ravenswood Hall as I had known it before the sun set upon it— bursting with greenery and spring sunshine. We lined the foyer with oil renderings of the crystal chandelier—unburdened of its cobweb shroud—of the grand fireplace adorned with trinkets, and of sunbeam streamers warming the polished staircase.

My eyes climbed the steps, longing to retreat to the quiet of Lenora's chamber, and my gaze fell on the place where my mother's portrait had been. I have not yet found it, but we shall hold its place with a striking depiction of her lavender fields, which Lenora painted only a few days hence. She is a better angel and a siren all at once. I am as blessed as I am haunted.

The evening we shared together has seemingly been forgotten, at least by her. I shall never forget it as long as I live. She treats me as if our relationship has not been irrevocably changed, so I sometimes wonder if I'd only dreamed it.

I couldn't imagine what was keeping her. She'd abandoned me to do all this miserable welcoming on my own, and God only knew where Lottie had gone off to. I'd kissed so many hands by five o'clock that I hardly knew to whom each belonged.

"Dr. Garrett, you've positively outdone yourself," one of the

Betteridge sisters said with her hand on my arm. She was the uglier of the four of them, with an upturned nose and altogether too much powder on her face. Her mother, ever eager for a morsel of gossip, pulled me aside.

"Where is this woman we've heard so much about?" she asked, her pink cheeks glowing, the first of several chins waggling beneath her face. A very well-to-do lady, she was, to afford such a luxurious diet.

Her husband, built of the same cloth except with less hair, stood at her side a moment later, and said loudly, "Yes, the one your father allegedly murdered. Fascinating stuff!"

"Yes, I'm sure it's all very entertaining," was all I could say. Mrs. Betteridge huffed.

"You'll forgive my buffoon of a husband, I'm sure." She turned to him and stage-whispered, "Dear, where *are* your manners? Clearly Dr. Garrett does not wish to speak of his father's misdeeds."

"I assure you that Miss Laveau is alive and well," I said.

"Likes to make an entrance, eh?" Mr. Betteridge clapped me on the shoulder. I hadn't seen the man in over twenty years and I physically recoiled from the contact.

"Now, dear," Mrs. Betteridge said, her head lifted toward my ear. "I hope you won't mind the intrusion, but we've invited a woman here I believe may be of some use to you. You are familiar with what they call spiritualists, aren't you?" Unable to answer, I lifted my brow and waited for her to continue. "Yes, I see that you are. I've just met the loveliest woman. Ah, here she is. What charming timing."

A woman appeared at my door, clad in a velvet black dress and the longest string of pearls I had ever seen in my life. A large-brimmed hat hid her eyes. She held her hand out to me and curtsied but did not speak.

"May we present Miss Carlotta O'Malley."

"A pleasure, miss," I said, and leaned down to kiss her hand. The tiny scar on her index finger gave her away.

"May I?" I offered her my arm, which she took with more grace than I expected. To the Betteridges, I said, "Peter will show you around the house." He appeared as if by conjuring, and he guided the whole lot of them toward the parlor as gently and efficiently as a border collie without even a glance in my direction.

The crowd thus dispersed, I walked with the supposed Miss O'Malley into the sitting room.

"God, they are horrible," she sighed, letting go of my arm and smiling at me as if I had released her from purgatory.

"Carlotta, eh?" I said, my eyebrow raised, and she giggled. "Lottie, what the devil are you doing? Where have you been?"

She shushed me, my transgressions seemingly forgiven. "I'm in disguise."

I could not help but laugh. "Why on earth? What are you wearing?"

"Exotic, isn't it?" She twirled for me with the fabric of the dress clutched in her hand. "No one will gossip to the host's daughter, you know."

"What interest have you in gossip?"

"People tell all their best secrets to spiritualists. After all, they think we know them already, what with our ability to see the other side." Lottie waved her fingers in front of her face, her whole countenance a picture of mischief, the way she had been as a girl.

"Perhaps," she continued, "someone may know more about Lenora than they're revealing to *you*."

"What do you mean?"

"I still haven't been able to ascertain where on earth she went, but she did not go to Spain. Someone must know something."

She snatched up my hand with such swiftness then that I nearly cried out.

"You've lost your ring," she said, her voice full of despair. I withdrew my hand.

"It's safe," I assured her, but the realization that dawned

across her features, turning down into sorrow, sent another pang of guilt through me. I had taken it off that night. It no longer felt proper for me to wear it.

Her eyes lifted over my shoulder and I turned to find Lenora standing upon the landing of the staircase, her fingers resting gracefully on the banister. When I looked back to Lottie, she wore a smile that spoke more of devastation than of happiness.

"Go to her," she said, and then embraced me. "She brings you something like happiness, and that will have to be enough."

"You're going to give yourself up," I said, holding her tightly. "What reason would a stranger have to embrace me so?"

"You're right," she gasped, pushing me away. "To the Betteridges I go!"

She disappeared into the crowd with a playful wave.

I took the stairs two at a time.

"Running away already?" Lenora asked when I reached her. I'd never beheld a more beautiful creature in all of my life.

A gown of sunflower-colored silk clung to her waist, and sleeves of sheer lace draped her shoulders with as much sweet grace as the song of a canary. She had pinned up her hair but for a few ringlets that brushed her cheeks. I forgave her for abandoning me.

"You…" I stammered. "You look…"

"*Gracias*," she said. "But you will need to do better than that if you want to impress the women downstairs."

"I wish only to impress one." I took one step up to meet her, so that her lips were only a breath from mine. Her eyes searched my face.

"That won't do, Mr. Garrett," she whispered, but she did not pull away. My eyes fell to a glimmer around her neck. She wore the necklace I had taken from the corpse in the crypt. I stepped backward and lost my balance. My fingers clutched the banister as Lenora reached for her pendant.

"I should have asked you for it," she said.

"You searched my room?" I asked, recovering. I had stashed

the necklace in the drawer of my night table, on top of the handkerchief that bore another set of initials. Had she taken that as well?

"It belongs to me," was her reply, and she turned to go back upstairs. I took her wrist.

"Our guests are waiting," I said. She needed only to ask and I would have given her the necklace. Instead, she crept into my quarters, rifled through my belongings, and stole it like a common thief. I saw her as Lottie did then. The veil had been lifted from my eyes.

In my brief absence, a great number of guests had arrived, and all now stared up at us expectantly, no doubt waiting for a spectacle. I recognized some of the faces from the far corners of my memory—old acquaintances from my school days, friends of my mother, and a few of the braver souls from Catskill proper who had been more fascinated by the scandal than horrified. My friends from Baltimore had arrived as well, including Lottie's friend Beatrice and a lady reporter who I thought might write up an advertisement for Ravenswood Hall in her paper.

"My friends," I said, bowing to them all. My fingers tightened around Lenora's wrist so she could not escape. A tight smile creased cheeks reddening by the moment. "It is my honor to present to you the famed Ghost of Ravenswood Hall. As you can see, she is still very much alive."

A murmur of voices echoed around the room. Encouraged, I continued.

"I invite each of you to admire Miss Laveau's art, which we have displayed throughout the house, so you may see this place as I once knew it and know her as I do."

We strode down the stairs to another wave of voices, this time carrying the slightest tone of dissatisfaction, but I could not be sure. The group accosted Lenora with questions and embraces that may have been well-meaning but overwhelmed her in only moments. The tension in her shoulders spread to her smile as Mr. Beasley, one of my mother's friends from Canada, bent to kiss her hand.

"Good riddance, I say," he whispered. "Not to speak ill of the dead, of course, but I'd wager you're glad to be free of him."

Lenora opened her mouth, but no answer formed on her tongue. I inserted myself into the conversation with a hearty handshake. My trust in her had cracked like a terra-cotta pot, but I could not stand to see her in so much discomfort.

"Good God, William, you're his double," he said. I had shaved but the once since arriving. I'd hoped my whiskers would hide my father's influence, but people cannot be so easily fooled.

"So I've heard," I replied, and then I leaned toward Lenora. "Go and see if Murdoch requires anything, would you?" She met my eyes with gratitude and escaped to the kitchen.

"Quiet as a mouse, that one," Mr. Beasley said. "Absolutely stunning, though, simply one of the most beautiful specimens of femininity I've ever beheld."

"I see you haven't broken the habit of studying us mere mortals as anthropological subjects, then."

"Once a scholar, always a scholar."

I looked over his shoulder at a commotion that had gathered around the door. My eyes met Anna's as she stepped inside. She smiled at me as if she knew nothing of my many sins, and then embraced one of the Watson girls, who now looked like a regular spinster. On her heels emerged Mr. Hawkins. He brought his damn cat, dozing in the crook of his arm and flicking its tail. His other arm was occupied by the hand of an elderly woman.

No one else accompanied him. Where was this highly regarded, powerful buyer? No one had written to decline the invitation. I pressed through the crowd toward Hawkins, my head full of noise.

"Ah, Dr. Garrett," he said, stroking the cat. "The place looks grand. Put more of the old elbow grease into it, have you?"

"Indeed," I answered, and shook his hand. "I trust you are feeling better?"

"I'm afraid your coffee was just a bit too strong for me, my lad. Not to worry."

I nodded, and then turned to the lady, dropping my head in a half-hearted bow. The cat looked up at me, angry for taking his master's attentions. "Mr. Hawkins, do you have a moment to speak in private?"

"Not a single moment, sir," he answered. "It is a pleasure to introduce you to Mrs. Amelia Anderton."

Anderton?

This frail old woman was my potential buyer?

The wicked smile that creased her parchment cheek told me in an instant that she was not to be trifled with.

"I see I've surprised you, Dr. Garrett," she said in a voice as thin as newspaper. "I'll save you the awkwardness of asking where my husband is. He's quite dead."

"Well, I..." I stammered, but she held up her hand.

"It is so fortunate that my interest in this property is not dependent on its current owner, isn't it?"

Mr. Hawkins suppressed a chuckle. I, thoroughly humiliated, nodded.

"Yes, madam."

"Would you like to show me the grounds, or shall I set off on my own?"

Someone touched my arm a moment later, and I turned to find that confounded Mrs. Betteridge staring up at me with a mischievous look in her dull eye.

"Oh, Dr. Garrett, I do hope I'm not interrupting," she said. What was I to say to this? I said nothing. She continued without prompting, as expected. "But you see, Miss Carlotta has something special planned for us all. At my request, of course."

"I'm engaged at the moment," I said finally.

"Nonsense," said Mrs. Anderton. "I should like to see this *special something*."

"Very well," I answered, exasperated. Murdoch came around then with a tray of champagne.

"Amontillado for you, sir," he said to me. "A gift for you. I took the liberty of opening it."

"A gift from whom?" I asked, taking up the glass. Lenora appeared out of the kitchen a moment later, her brow creased.

"It was left on the front table with the other gifts. The note there was beneath it, sir," Murdoch answered.

A card sat beneath the glass, which I picked up to read.

To the new master of Ravenswood Hall.

"Peculiar," I muttered. "It's not signed." I swirled the amber liquid in the glass and then took a sip. Despite it being rather bitter for my taste, it was a fine sherry. Mrs. Betteridge, whom I'd forgotten, patted my arm. Lenora and I shared a heavy glance before I allowed Mrs. Betteridge to guide me toward the sitting room, but I could not ascertain what she wished to say.

"I have never met a more charming woman, this Carlotta," Mrs. Betteridge said.

"I've no doubt about that whatever," I answered. "And what exactly has she planned for us?"

"A séance!" she squealed, and then covered her mouth as she entered the room. I halted at the threshold.

"For God's sake," I said under my breath. Lottie and her shenanigans. She perched herself atop a stool before the fireplace. A few chairs and even the sofa had been dragged toward her, guests settling down in the cushions to await my daughter's prestidigitations. The others stood around like patrons at the zoo, and I became so irritated with the whole group that I could scarcely prevent myself from backing out through the door unnoticed.

Lenora, who had been trailing close behind, knocked into my arm when I stepped backward. My glass flew from my hand and shattered on the floor.

"Oh!" she cried. "*Qué lástima.*"

She bent to collect the shards, but I pulled her to her feet.

"It's nothing." As I spoke, Murdoch arrived with a towel, which I relieved him of and sopped up the mess myself.

"I am so sorry," Lenora said again. "I've ruined your drink."

Murdoch collected the glass and the soaked rag with a gloved hand and a nod and disappeared into the other room.

"We shan't proceed without your blessing, Dr. Garrett," Lottie called to me, waiting. I resented the spectacle she was making of me. This was not the time for games. She must have known my mind, however, for she tilted her head at me with a steady smile and I trusted her at once. Anyway, she likely meant to do it regardless of my misgivings. I nodded my reluctant acquiescence.

Mrs. Betteridge pranced about the room and dimmed the lamps as though she'd done it a thousand times before, and once the atmosphere had become satisfactorily ghostly, she planted herself in a wing chair and waited.

"Silence, please," Lottie—or rather Carlotta—said in a firm voice. Quiet fell about the room, settling comfortably in rustling skirts and bated breath. My daughter closed her eyes and bowed her head, her palms open toward the heavens.

"We seek the spirits of Ravenswood Hall," Lottie said. "You are among friends. Make yourselves known to us."

We waited.

A single lamp flickered, but it was nearest to the door. A draft.

My daughter's face contorted as if in pain, and then she threw her head back so violently that she nearly fell off the stool. My heart told me to go to her, but I could not move. The lamps flared all at once and then went out. Murmurs broke the silence, and then every pocket watch in the room ticked in time. I could hear nothing else but the *tick tock, tick tock, tick tock* of time. Impossibly, the lamps sprung back to life.

What trickery was this? She must have put Betteridge up to it somehow. I looked at Mrs. Anderton to ensure that she was not in distress. She looked on with a glimmer in her eye, appearing, on the contrary, rather pleased.

I sensed movement behind me and turned to find Dr. Johnston standing in the doorway.

"Doctor!" I cried. "Good heaven, we thought you'd died." I extended my hand toward him, but he did not take it. He stood with his fists clenched as if in pain. Indeed, his entire countenance appeared sickly and wasted. His cracked lips moved over words as if he meant to speak to me, but no sound issued from his throat. I stepped toward him to hear him better. Everyone turned to look.

"You cannot," Lottie cried, though she did not open her eyes. "He cannot be touched."

"What the devil do you mean?" When I turned back to the doctor, he was gone. Vanished! The guests gasped collectively, absurdly.

I spun back to Lottie. "What's the meaning of this?"

I was answered by a terrible scream. Not from my daughter, but from outside in the garden. Utter silence followed, all eyes upon the door.

"Will!" Peter stumbled through the door with an expression of terror. "In the garden. Quickly!"

I followed him outside into the falling dusk, the whole crowd of guests trailing behind. Mrs. Anderton kept pace, clutching Mr. Hawkins's arm as his cat mewed. We wound around the gravel path to the leaning garden shed. Anna stood beside the open door with her hand over her mouth. Darkness pooled within.

"This door was locked," I said. "Who has opened it?"

A little voice in the back of the crowd called, "It was already open!" The rounder of the Betteridge sisters walked forward through the parted mass like a convict, her cheeks redder than any I'd ever seen. "I just wanted a peek, just a peek. The smell, see..."

"Well, what the devil did you find?" I asked.

Anna said, "I think it's the doctor, Will."

I opened the door wide and the waning sunlight shone on a body. Screams and gasps volleyed as my guests caught a glimpse of the poor town doctor, crumpled in a decomposing mass on the dirt floor. The doctor we had all witnessed only moments before.

"Dear God." I covered my mouth with my arm. Flies swarmed, and a wall of odor billowed out upon us until my eyes stung. "Call for the constable." Anna, all too grateful for the excuse to leave, swept away through the crowd.

"Please," I said, addressing the familiar faces. "Return to the house, all of you."

They dispersed, some more reluctantly than others. I looked for Mrs. Anderton and Mr. Hawkins, but I did not see them. It would be useless for Devlin to interview them all. Based upon the condition of the body, the doctor had been dead for many days.

"What have they done to you, my old friend?" My voice broke, cracking the question into separate pieces. I could no longer look at him nor control my temper. I swung at the door with a cry and gave the rotting wood such a violent blow that its splinters tore into my fist. Lenora, who had been beside me all the while, turned and ran through the garden.

"Where are you going?" I called.

"To send them all home. What use are they to us now?"

She disappeared around the corner of the house. Any hopes of selling this property had died with the doctor. Not a soul in this godforsaken town would pay two dollars to live here, and certainly not a woman as respectable as Mrs. Anderton.

I latched the shed door to prevent wandering eyes but could do nothing about the crawling things that might wish to feast on the poor doctor's body. Unable to think upon such a subject any longer, I turned and walked back to the house with my hands in my pockets, my mind a maelstrom of questions. Lenora met me at the front door and grabbed my arm.

"Will," she whispered, consternation pinching the edges of her eyes. "They won't leave." She pulled me into the parlor where the whole lot of them had congregated into tight groups, whispering among themselves. One voice I heard above the others. Mr. Betteridge addressed ten or so of my guests, all huddled around him and listening intently.

"The murderer could be in this very room!" Betteridge exclaimed with excitement in his voice, which he then lowered to a loud whisper. "We must remain vigilant. The curse of Ravenswood Hall lives on!"

I heard similar conversations all across the room. Lenora clutched my arm either in sympathy or to prevent me from flying at them, but I did not care which.

"Enough!" I yelled above them. All eyes turned to me. "You vultures," I spat. "Have you no decency? How many of you have gone to Dr. Johnston in your time of need? Did he ever turn you away? Did he ever once fail to come to you when you called? How many of you owe your lives to him?"

Silence greeted me, but I could not stop. "And yet here you stand in my house speaking of curses. You!" I pointed to Betteridge. "Will you write to the doctor's daughters and tell them of his passing?" He stared at me, bewildered, and I'd be remiss if I said I didn't take some satisfaction in it. "Or are you all too occupied with your own lives to consider the poor man's family at all?"

"Will," Lenora whispered in my ear. I had said my piece. I wanted nothing more to do with these people.

"Now get out," I said, pointing to the door. "The whole lot of you." Standing beside the fireplace with her hands behind her back, Lottie met my eyes and then squeezed through the crowd.

"Papa," she whispered, staring as if she did not know me.

"Enough of your nonsense, child," I said, forgetting she was now nearly a grown woman and no longer bidden by my will. "I have tolerated too much of this. Your days of dabbling in the supernatural are through."

She curtsied at me, which was near enough a slap across the face. I remembered myself and called after her, but she had joined the rustling skirts of the Betteridges as they gathered their things to leave.

I took Lenora's hand and led her up the stairs, though I had no destination in mind other than *away*. Voices carried behind me in fragmented pieces as we climbed.

"Distasteful indeed! We could at least be allowed our supper."

"His father lives on in that one, to be certain."

"And after we've come all this way!"

I stumbled on the stairs. A curious sensation climbed my limbs, as if lightning coursed through my arms instead of blood. My muscles twitched beneath my flesh like crawling beetles. Lenora said my name. No matter how I tried, I could not rise to my feet.

"I..." I stammered. "I can't..." My jaw tightened so suddenly and severely I could not complete my thought. I knew then what was happening to me as clearly as I tasted the bitterness of the amontillado. A horrible spasm in my legs knocked me again to my knees. I took hold of the banister as Lenora cried out for help.

"Lottie," I ground through my teeth, and then cried out in pain as the muscles in my back wrenched my spine.

Lenora fell to her knees beside me and reached for my hand, but I pulled away for fear her touch would exacerbate the spasms. On all other days I had yearned for it, and now I shied away. Somehow, I had gained the landing at the top of the stairs. My shoulder screamed against the floorboards.

My father had given me an appreciation of pain, and I consider myself well tolerant of it, but what I experienced then made me beg for death. My consciousness ebbed as if fluid, as if I hovered beneath the surface of a great and terrible ocean, each breach calling forth pain as I'd never known it before.

When the episode passed and my body had given up the convulsions, I came to in my own bed with the taste of blood in my mouth and my daughter looking down at me. I could not speak her name, though I felt it on my tongue. Lenora appeared from the other side of the room and reached for me, but Lottie stayed her hand.

"Don't touch him," she commanded, and my heart was so glad to hear her voice that I might have smiled if the muscles in my face were under my control.

"You have no reason to trust me, I know," Lenora said. My consciousness waned, blurring her outline. "But you cannot keep me from him."

"Listen, you fool," Lottie answered with her usual fire. "How I feel about you is of no consequence. External stimuli will aggravate his condition."

Lenora fell back into the gloom.

"Papa?" Lottie said, but I could only look at her. "I'm here, Papa." Darkness greeted me then, and I knew no more.

Chapter XXI

WILLIAM GARRETT'S JOURNAL

Continued by Lottie Garrett
January 28, 1889

My dear father has written in this journal nearly every day since the death of my mother, and so I am bound by his resolve, as well as my own, to continue the narrative.

He has not regained consciousness, except for a few moments of mad thrashing when he cries out for Lenora. Papa and I have been on our own for so many years, I might have thought he should call out for me, or least of all my mother. This woman has invaded even the dark corners of him, which surface only when agonized. I've seen the same in cases of personal hauntings. The obsession takes hold soon after the spirit manifests, leaving the poor victim to drive himself mad, if he was not so already. Only Lenora is flesh and blood, or must be.

This morning, after a breakfast I could only poke at, I

returned to Papa's bedside to find Lenora in my chair. She stood when she saw me and tucked a crumpled letter in her pocket.

"What is that?" I asked her.

"It is for your father," was her reply.

"I am his proxy until he wakes. Whatever you have for him, you must give to me."

I suspected it was some confession of love, and I intended to burn it. In a moment of childishness, I suppose, I tried to snatch the letter and grabbed it at its edge. She didn't relinquish it.

"There is much you do not understand," she said, and then, seeing my resolve, released it and ran from the room.

While I'm often content to respect my father's privacy, my suspicion of Lenora was too great to allow the contents of this letter to reach him without inspection. Besides, it had already been opened. I unfolded it quietly, my hand rising to my mouth as I read. Papa will have to make something of it, for I cannot.

A LETTER TO DR. WILLIAM GARRETT

Catskill, New York, to Ravenswood Hall
Postmarked January 20, 1889

Dear Dr. Garrett,

I believe you are owed an explanation as to why I refused Christine Murdoch her last rites and why I could not reply to your letter or allow Miss Laveau to enter my church. My sacred duties still bind me from divulging this terrible secret in its entirety, for your father begged for absolution, but I cannot find rest until I have unburdened myself of all I am able. I must give you this small warning, or I am undone.

Many months ago, your father came to me in the middle of the night with so great a quantity of alcohol on his breath that I believed he might perish on the spot. He grabbed me by the collar and begged me to follow him home. What I found there I shall not forget until the day I die, and what I did to relieve your father of his mad anguish has damned my own soul. In your family crypt, you will find a body that does not belong there. I can do no more than guide you to the truth, and so that is all I can say.

I could not speak out. I could not warn you, for I had entwined myself in your father's sin. Now, I have denied a young child passage into heaven, and this I cannot bear. I've written to a friend at the church in Linlithgo and he has agreed to do what I could not, if you will accept him. I have resigned my position as deacon.

The Lord our God alone holds true power over death, and He has forsaken Ravenswood Hall as he has forsaken me. I am loathe to think of what dark magic your Miss Laveau has performed, or to what demon she has pledged her allegiance, but there is no soul inside the body that sleeps under your roof, Dr. Garrett. Hear my words, man. Take heed! The Lord Jesus shall deliver you if you renounce the evil that dwells within that house.

I will keep you in my prayers, if the Lord will grant audience to a wretch like me.

Humbly yours,

J. Barnes

WILLIAM GARRETT'S JOURNAL

Continued by Lottie Garrett
January 29, 1889

Another day spent tending to Papa, this one more devastating than the last. This afternoon, a letter arrived from my friend, Beatrice, in Baltimore. I was so pleased to receive it, I didn't imagine for a second how completely it would crush me.

Along with a brief but blessedly kind note that she didn't believe a word of it was a page from *The Baltimore Sun*. Such a damning article it is. I do not know what we are going to do. I do not know what to think, only that it must be slander, or we are ruined.

I have pasted it here in his journal for Papa to read when he is well enough. I cannot bring a thing like this to him now. It might kill him.

BALTIMORE —MONDAY—JANUARY 28, 1889
LOCAL FAMILY PHYSICIAN, A MURDERER!
RAVENSWOOD HALL HEIR ADMITS TO MATRICIDE

WILLIAM GARRETT OF RAVENSWOOD HALL HAS CONFESSED TO THE MURDER OF HIS OWN MOTHER, NEARLY TWENTY YEARS AFTER ITS OCCURRENCE. DEATH BY LAUDANUM POISONING, HE REVEALED TO AN ANONYMOUS SOURCE EARLIER THIS WEEK. AUTHORITIES IN NEW YORK CITY HAVE BEEN NOTIFIED, AS THERE IS NO STATUTE OF LIMITATIONS IN NEW YORK STATE ON THE CRIME OF MURDER.

THE FAMILY ATTORNEY, WHO PREFERS TO REMAIN ANONYMOUS, CLAIMS TO KNOW NOTHING OF THIS CRIME, AND LIKELY THE ONLY SOUL WHO COULD CORROBORATE IT HAS DIED. MURDERED! THE CORPSE OF GARRETT'S PHYSICIAN, DR. JOHNSTON, WAS DISCOVERED DURING A DINNER PARTY AT RAVENSWOOD HALL, WHICH THE AUTHOR OF THIS ARTICLE HAD THE MISFORTUNE TO ATTEND. A TRULY HIDEOUS SPECTACLE IT WAS, AND HORRIBLE TO RELATE! THE BODY WAS LEFT FOR THE RATS IN AN OUTBUILDING, AND IT WAS IN SUCH A STATE OF DECOMPOSITION THAT ONE

OF THE GUESTS NEARLY FAINTED AT THE STENCH WHEN THE DOOR WAS OPENED.

SPECULATION ABOUNDS OF A CURSE ON THE ESTATE, WITH MORE RUMORS STILL OF THE LATE MRS. GARRETT HAUNTING THE OLD HOUSE. WILL JUSTICE SET HER SPIRIT TO REST? ONLY TIME WILL TELL. THIS STORY IS DEVELOPING, AND READERS CAN BE ASSURED OF MORE DETAILS AS THEY COME TO LIGHT.

WILLIAM GARRETT'S JOURNAL

Continued by Lottie Garrett
January 29, 1889

I could not hold the burden of this with just my two hands. Since I could not ask Papa for an explanation, I instead took it to Anna, my most trusted friend and cousin. How blessed I am to have found her after all this time. She has set my heart at ease, though it storms in my mind.

"Anna, I must show you something," I said as I knocked on her door. She opened it immediately and welcomed me inside. I handed her the article, which she read with her hand over her heart.

"Is it true?" I asked.

"Yes," she answered right away. "But not in the way this describes. Not at all. Come, Cousin. Sit down."

We sat on the edge of her bed and she pressed my trembling hand.

"Your father came to me with this confession, but I think it must have been mercy, Lottie. He could not bear to see his mother suffering under his father's hand."

"We cannot go home now, not ever," I said, but the tears choked my voice. Anna held me against her chest, the closest thing to a mother's touch I had known for years. It broke me into pieces, and I sobbed against her.

"You're already home, Cousin," she whispered, stroking my hair. "You must know, I haven't spoken a word of this until now, I swear to you."

I believed her as I rested there, safe but for a moment in this miserable house. Papa tried to warn me, but I did not listen. I never listen.

"How could this come to be?" I whispered.

"Someone must have overheard our conversation."

I knew in my heart what must have happened, and her name wiggled out from behind my teeth.

"Lenora."

Chapter XXII

WILLIAM GARRETT'S JOURNAL

Date Unknown

I only now have the strength enough to write. I do not know the date. I am writing this on the back of a discarded envelope, as my journal has gone missing. Many days must have passed away and with them all that remained of my peace of mind. Those I once counted as friends I now greet with suspicion. Who am I to trust? The fact of the matter is that someone in this house has deliberately and malevolently made an attempt on my life.

I wish to feel the sunshine on my face and fresh air in my lungs, but I am not yet strong enough to walk down the stairs. The muscle convulsions were so severe that my legs have not regained strength enough to bear my weight, but Lottie is with me always should I require aid. Her presence in this place is a breath of fresh air, a small morsel of happiness in a room with ten thousand ghosts.

Lenora has not come to see me, which I do not understand. I wish to tell her that I've forgiven her for taking the necklace. It belongs to her, after all, and such a matter seems small once a man has faced his own death. Perhaps Lottie has told her I must be left to rest. It would do me well to see her and feel her soft hand in mine. The nakedness of my ring finger ought to have afforded me a short visit in the very least, after all we had been through together.

Lottie has been in with the constable, who is as kind and diligent as ever. He has taken my statement, as well as a sample of the amontillado, which was the only refreshment I consumed that evening. I am losing hope.

February 2, 1889

I am ruined.

My daughter has just shown me my journal, and I have read the horrible pages. I know why she chose to keep it from me. I now have only as much strength as I have hope, and I barely have will enough to lift my head from the pillow.

I knew by her face when she entered my room that she wished to speak but could not begin. She set my supper on the bed, a tray laden with cold meats and rye bread she had prepared herself, and then drew a ragged breath.

"Has something happened?" I asked. Tears welled in her eyes.

"You are strong enough now to know all," she said, handing me my own journal. "So much has happened while you were ill. It's all there for you."

She waited while I read, standing over me as though death were about to spirit me away.

"Sit down, child," I said, but her face twisted in an expression of pain. She plucked at a string on her sleeve and shook her head. I continued reading with her eyes upon me, but I soon forgot them as I came to Deacon Barnes's inexplicable letter.

"What the devil," I muttered. "What can he mean?" His letter offered me only more questions.

"There's more, Papa," was Lottie's quiet reply.

And then I read it. The newspaper article that at once brought my life to ruin and spoke of not one betrayal, but two. The author of the article was none other than my reporter friend from Baltimore, who had been a dear companion of my wife. This disloyalty stung me, for we had once been quite close, but the other...

"Bring me Anna," I said, the blistering wound in my heart quickly turning cold.

"She didn't betray you."

"Bring her to me."

Lottie's tears fell freely, and she began to weep.

"I cannot. Oh, Papa, she's dead."

The journal fell from my hands and clattered onto the tray. I could not speak. Perhaps I had only misheard. Lottie wrung her hands.

"We were together in her chamber the night before and nothing seemed wrong with her. Peter found her on the bed in the morning when she didn't come down to breakfast. It's so horrible. I only just got her and now she's gone."

I set my tray aside and gathered her into my arms.

"Hush now. It will be all right," I said, but the acid in my empty stomach hardened into stones. I held her as she wept, shutting my eyes against my own burning tears. "Where is her body?"

"Peter took her to the cellar," she answered, and wiped her face with her sleeve. "I told him you would wish to...examine her when you were strong enough. Constable Devlin will need to know her cause of death. I don't believe strychnine did it. There is no rigidity in her body at all."

"Take me to her."

"You are still ill. You'll faint."

"My girl, I have seen much worse already. My constitution is not so weak as that. I must see her." I threw off the blankets and set my feet on the cold floor. Lottie, perceiving perhaps that she could not prevent me, rushed to my aid and allowed me to drape my arm over her shoulders.

The journey into the cellar might have been one hundred miles. Each step ached deep inside the muscles of my legs, my heart thundering with the effort. When we arrived at last at the cellar door, a sheen of sweat dampened my poor daughter's brow, for she had likely borne more of my weight than I.

"Where are the others?" I asked.

"The Murdochs have gone to inquire after a line of credit at the grocer," she answered, the tang of my own shame on her tongue.

"And Lenora?"

The muscles in her jaw tensed. "I do not know."

She opened the cellar door, which had remained unlocked since Christine's death, and we descended together.

Lottie lit a lamp, and an orb of light formed around the table that once held the child's gruesome remains. A beetle fed upon the soft, putrescent wood, but Anna's body was not there.

A LETTER TO DR. WILLIAM GARRETT

Catskill, New York, to Ravenswood Hall
Postmarked February 2, 1889

Dr. Garrett,

A brief note here to inform you that I have sent for Inspector Gerard, out of New York City. He is a hard but trustworthy fellow and you need not question his motivations. Justice drives him, and justice alone. He's our man for this tangle, you can be assured of that.

On another matter that will interest you, my associate in toxicology was able to isolate the strychnine from the cake sample your charming daughter rode out to me. You, my good man, have discovered the murder weapon. No doubt there are tablets of the stuff in your pantry even as I write. It's a common poison for rats, as you know, so I don't know how much closer to the killer it will take us. The amontillado is next on the docket, and that may offer up more clues in combination with the note that was left for you. I've not given up.

Hope brings me to the next order of business. You must keep it close by so you may draw on it in the days to come. Your daughter has written me about your dear cousin. Be assured, I will get to the bottom of this. If you have trusted me thus far, do so now.

Humbly yours,

Charles Devlin

P.S. I sent Dr. Johnston's body to the morgue in Albany, though a precursory examination gives me an impression of a puncture wound to the heart. You'll be performing no more autopsies if I can help it. A task as gruesome as that has an effect, and you require every last ounce of your strength to get well again. I will write again when it's done.

WILLIAM GARRETT'S JOURNAL

February 4, 1889

I awoke this morning to a knock upon the door, my grief and bewilderment still a stone inside my throat. Lottie peeked her head inside as the clock chimed the hour. Ten o'clock.

"I'm sorry to wake you, Papa," she said. "Inspector Gerard arrived early this morning and has been asking a lot of questions. You are wanted. Constable Devlin is here, too."

"You should have woken me," I said, vexed that a stranger had been permitted into the house without my consent. Dressing as quickly as I could manage in my shirtsleeves and breeches, I left the room with Lottie and walked haltingly downstairs, my bare feet padding on the cold floor. I found Lenora, Peter, Wilson, and Murdoch seated at the dining table with Devlin, along with another man I did not know. His handlebar mustache was as waxed and polished as his bald head, which he mopped with a handkerchief. I sent Lenora a smile, which she returned to me in full. It rose into her eyes for one shining moment, and then was gone. I wanted more from her. I wanted everything.

"I beg your pardon," I said to the man. The constable and the stranger stood in unison.

"Dr. Garrett," Devlin said. "May I introduce Inspector Gerard?"

I took the man's hand and shook it with a polite bow. "A pleasure, sir. Have you been waiting long?" His grip tightened, but he made no other indication that he'd even heard me. Devlin touched my arm and leaned toward my ear.

"Forgive the delay. We had meant to come yesterday. It's my wife. I'm afraid her condition is worsening."

"I am sorry to hear that, Constable."

"You're a doctor...if, perhaps...if you would be willing to come by the house, seeing as how the doctor is... Well, it would surely be a comfort."

"I would be glad to, Devlin," I said, and shook his hand. A wide smile came across his face as though I had promised to save the woman's life. I could offer no such hope. I had so little of my own left to give.

"Please, Dr. Garrett," Gerard said with an accent fresh out of Brooklyn and a tone that suggested such a long journey had peeved him. He motioned for me to sit and pushed a plate of scones toward me, but I held up my hand, my appetite gone.

"You've quite the stack of corpses in your recently inherited estate, haven't you, Dr. Garrett?"

His tone irked me. I replied, "If you mean to accuse me of something, I suggest you make it plain."

"Papa," Lottie warned, her cheeks flushed.

"It is my duty," Gerard continued, "to determine the exact whereabouts of each person in this room at the approximate time of the murders, including the most recent death of your cousin. Would you be so kind as to show me the body, now that you have joined us?"

Lottie stood and said, "It's gone missing."

The muscles in Gerard's jaw knotted, but he made no reply. He pulled Devlin aside and spoke to him in tones lower than I could hear, his gestures both accusatory and, in my opinion, overly aggressive. With a hand gripping his upper arm, and a finger pointed at the constable's chest, Gerard gave the impression not of a lawman but of a schoolhouse bully.

"I've not come all this way for games," he spat, louder. "I cannot investigate this crime without a body."

Devlin resisted, saying, "If this is too great a challenge for you, I will call for another man."

Gerard backed down, and he turned his attention toward me.

"Dr. Garrett, we are wasting time. If you have nothing to offer me in the death of your cousin, we must move on to other matters."

I nodded, still too overcome by it all to speak. Lottie slipped her hand in mine.

"We will sort this out, Papa," she whispered, sitting beside me. "We must."

We looked at each other in silence. Gerard stood over us with his arms crossed, weighing our scales with his eyes. One of us was his man, and we sat beneath his gaze like pheasants waiting to fly at the sound of the gun.

"Have you no other suspects?" I asked at last. "You can't believe that one of us is capable of such heinous acts."

"With respect, sir, I don't know you from Adam, nor any other person at this table. I'll gladly hear if you've another name I ought to be investigating."

"You'll kindly leave my daughter out of it, then." I did not want Lottie interrogated like some common criminal. She'd scarcely had time to mourn.

"It is my understanding that she was present for the discovery of both bodies, the child and the doctor," Gerard said. "And she was the last to see your cousin alive. Am I mistaken?"

"That is correct," Lottie said, straightening defiantly in her chair.

"See here," I said, rising. "You may question whomever you like, but my daughter shall not be involved in these proceedings."

Lottie met the inspector's eyes with such intensity that I pitied him.

"I have nothing to hide, Papa," she said, and then casually selected a scone as if they'd only had a disagreement about the weather.

"Very well," I muttered, and I sat back down. "Your time is wasted on us, Inspector."

Devlin leaned toward me and said, "Even still, it would be wise to cooperate."

Gerard's mustache twitched. "I will be conducting interviews individually. I ask that each of you kindly remain in your seat until you are called."

"Have you any issue with my washing up, then?" I asked, unable to strip the defiance from my tone. What nerve this man had, to enter my house and stake claim like this. I had not even breakfasted.

"Do as you wish, Dr. Garrett," Gerard said. "Only do not leave this house until I am finished with all of you. Miss Laveau, shall we?" He stood, and with a slight bow and gallant wave of his hand, he ushered her out of the room.

I rose from the table and walked into the hall to think, to move, to do anything but remain idle. Lenora's gentle voice reached me from the sitting room as I paced past the door, to and fro, until it occurred to me that I might have a singular opportunity now to eavesdrop. Grateful I had neglected to don my shoes, I paused before the door and leaned toward it, listening.

"Miss Laveau," the inspector said. "Can you tell me how you came to be here?"

"I am a classically trained artist. I came to America to paint and found a position here. The late Mr. Garrett commissioned a portrait in exchange for room and board and a small sum to be paid upon its completion."

"Why, then, did you not leave upon his death?"

"I have not been paid, sir."

"Dr. Garrett has not honored his father's contract, then?"

"No."

She did not elaborate further. She did not explain our agreement or offer anything at all that might cast me in a finer light.

"And his mother," Gerard said. My blood slowed to sludge. I ought to have known I'd be hunted down for what I'd done to my mother, whatever my motives or the years gone by. And did I not deserve it? Still my stomach soured.

"You've read the newspaper article, no doubt?" he continued.

"I have not. I know nothing of these matters."

Gerard sighed, and I heard the springs of the chair pop as he adjusted himself and his line of questioning.

"Did you know Christine Murdoch well?" Gerard asked, tapping his pen.

"No," Lenora answered. "She did not speak to me often."

"And where were you on the day of her disappearance?"

"Here, with Peter."

Another pause stretched out, the tension thick even through the solid oak door. I daren't breath. A rustle of fabric. The clearing of a throat.

"What is your relationship with the master of the house?" Gerard asked.

"The dead master or the living?"

"Let's begin with the living."

Another pause, another rustle of fabric. Why did she not answer him?

And then, "I am his tenant."

"Nothing more?"

"Nothing more."

My heart fell like a stone into my stomach. Perhaps she did not wish to implicate me in any scandal. Surely that was it.

And then, the inspector asked, "And with Peter Murdoch?"

The answer came clearly and without hesitation. "We are lovers."

My lips parted in silent disbelief. I had surely misheard.

"You are, then," the inspector continued, "in a physical relationship?"

"I beg your pardon, Inspector. That is hardly your business."

"Everything is my business. Kindly answer the question."

"Then, yes."

There was no mistaking it. I could bear no more. I flew from the hall and into the dining room.

"A word?" I said through clenched teeth. Peter rose. "Outside."

"What's the matter?" he asked, and I grabbed him by the arm and shoved him bodily into the hall. The frozen porch boards shot ice into my bare feet. Unthinking, I took Peter by the collar and pushed him against the front of the house.

"If you lie to me, I swear to God—"

"Lie to you about what, Will? What's gotten into you?"

"Lenora."

His eyes widened first in surprise and then an instant later narrowed to contempt. The change came over him so quickly that I did not detect it until he had pushed me backward. This only fueled my anger.

"You think because you own this land, you own all of us that live upon it," he spat at me, his hand balled into a fist. "Lenora is a free woman and can make her own decisions."

"Like the decision she made with me the other night?"

The muscles in his jaw clenched tight. "What?"

"Have you not ears?"

I had the wherewithal to dodge the fist he swung at me and launched one of my own, which landed squarely across his nose with a sickening popping sound. He fell down the steps with a curse but regained his footing. We had fought before, as schoolboys do, but this was different. My hand, as if of its own will, grabbed the axe leaning against the wood pile.

I think if Lenora had not run outside at that moment, I might have killed him.

"What are you doing?" she cried, grabbing my arm. Inspector Gerard stood in the doorway, watching.

"Witch," I hissed, and she flew past me to attend to Peter. Blood poured freely from his nose and onto his shirt, the cold rain soaking them both.

"What has he done to you?" I heard her whisper, but he pushed her away so she stood between us both, appearing quite lost. The inspector cleared his throat.

"You've both proven quite thoroughly that you are capable of violence, thank you. Mr. Murdoch, clean yourself up. I shall be speaking with you next. Dr. Garrett, if you'll join me in the sitting room? Ah, you may leave the axe."

Without a glance at my opponent or his *lover*, I dashed the weapon against the porch boards and followed Gerard inside, prepared to defend myself now from less physical assault. Anger fueled me. It filled the dark hollow space inside my chest with fire. When Gerard took possession of my chair, I sent him such a look that he immediately removed himself to the sofa.

"Quite a display you've put on, Dr. Garrett," he began, crossing his legs and flipping open a notebook.

"Yes, well, my father's blood runs in my veins. Or have you not heard?"

He ignored this and asked, "You are a medical man, are you not?"

"I have a small practice in Baltimore with my daughter."

"You're quite familiar then with medicines, tinctures, and the like?"

I did not like where I suspected this line of inquiry was leading. "I was appropriately trained."

"In Maryland?"

"You seem to know everything about me already," I interrupted. "Why bother yourself with the inquiry?"

He only smiled and removed a tobacco pipe from his jacket pocket, which he then filled, lit, and drew upon as comfortably as if he had lived here all of his life.

"I have never been to Maryland," he said, exhaling a long plume of smoke. I did not take this bait, but instead waited for him to come around to the point. "You've lived there for quite some time, I believe."

"Yes, I apprenticed under a reputable physician in Baltimore and then completed my training at Johns Hopkins Medical School. I then worked as a surgeon in Boston before returning to begin my own practice."

"You went there straight away after killing your mother, then?"

"I beg your pardon?" I wanted to stand, to cry out, to bash his skull, but the tightening of my fist on the arm of the chair was the only outward expression I could give to the fury.

"I'm sure someone has shown you the article by now."

"I have seen it," I seethed. "It is slander."

"I think I should like to be the judge of that. It appears to me you've confessed to murder—"

"I did no such thing," I lied, but he carried on as if he hadn't heard me.

"And if a young man can kill a person, surely later in life it would not be so hard a thing to do again."

I met his stare and answered, "I am no killer."

"Death trails you like an old dog though, doesn't it?"

I flicked my eyebrow toward the ceiling and took a long moment to survey the room. "We're cursed, haven't you heard? It has my scent."

My anecdotes did not amuse him. He sat, sucking on his pipe and faintly nodding, occasionally scribbling on his notepad. I drew in a breath to calm the fire in my blood, but it only stoked it.

"Pray tell," he said at last. "Do they use strychnine commonly in Maryland?"

"As commonly as everywhere else in the country," I answered. "As pest control primarily. Some doctors still prescribe it for malaria."

"Have you ever prescribed it?"

"Never."

"But it is fairly easily obtained?"

"I suppose so, yes."

"And how is it that you determined cause of death in Miss Murdoch as strychnine poisoning and not tetanus? I understand the symptoms are similar."

"Tetanus is not extremely common, Inspector."

"And poisoning is?"

"You are a law man. Surely you have seen as much poison in your line of work as I."

He nodded again and twisted his mustache thoughtfully.

"Now, really," I said, standing, "I've had enough of this."

"We are not finished, Dr. Garrett."

"I say we are."

"There is the small matter of your daughter that we must consider." He motioned toward my chair, but I did not sit. "If you were to die or be declared of unsound mind, who stands to inherit this estate?"

I inhaled a slow breath, thick as much with tension as with

the scent of burning pine and tobacco smoke. The logs in the grate popped and snapped and I focused on these noises for a time so as to prevent myself from losing my temper again.

"My daughter," I answered at last. "She was still in Baltimore when Christine disappeared. You're on the wrong track, sir."

"I will, of course, need proof of her alibi."

"That will not be a problem," I assured him, bristling. "I have a letter she wrote me, postmarked from Baltimore."

"Very good. Now, there is your alibi to discuss."

"Devlin will confirm my visit to him at the time of Christine's disappearance."

The inspector made no response to this and only continued to write in his blasted notebook. Hunger pangs cramped the muscles in my stomach. I had not eaten since yesterday morning, and this interrogation was beginning to annoy me.

"Yes, Devlin and I discussed that while you were, ah, sleeping. I am referring to the death of the doctor, of course. I've confirmed that you were the last person to see him alive."

"You had a busy morning."

"I have resources and friends which enable me to obtain information quickly."

I detected the slightest intonation of a threat. The arrogance, while secondary, caused a crinkling around the eyes that was unbecoming.

He asked, "I imagine your visit to him cannot be corroborated by any witness?"

"I don't know. You haven't told me when he died. I've spent most of my time with Lenora. Surely, she will corroborate."

"Alas," he sighed in mock despondency. "She will not."

"What?"

"In her words, she wants no part of it and will not be condemned for merely living in your house."

"Well, I—" Words failed me. The tightness in my throat choked off the sentence I meant to say. I knew now that here, in my father's house, ruin was the only outcome. It had taken everything I'd held dear and ripped it from me as a wolf disembowels its prey. Inspector Gerard shut his notebook with a snap.

"You'll be wanting to find that proof for me now. For your daughter's sake." The sinister smile beneath his mustache moved his ears. "And if I might offer some advice? I would make arrangements should one or both of you be arrested. I always get my man, sir, and to be frank, I like you best for the lot of it."

I stood there, looking at him dumbly and feeling as though there was something I ought to say, perhaps something he expected me to say, but I could not speak.

"That will be all for now," he said, and so I left the room with his gaze upon my back. Peter brushed by me with a sneer, his shirt stained with blood. I trod up the stairs toward my chamber without looking for Lenora. How long ago those mornings seemed when I whiled away the hours, waiting for her to come down so I might catch only a glimpse of her.

What a fool I had been, a love-struck puppy cast beneath his master's boot. If she would not bear witness for me, I should have to do it myself. I had no choice now but to get to the rotten core of it all. How, after all Lenora and I had suffered together, could she betray me so? I had now only to look for the thirty pieces of silver on the steps.

I was so blinded by my anger that I nearly collided with my daughter as I gained the hall to my bedroom. She clutched a book to her chest as reverently as if it were a Bible.

"Oh, Papa," she cried breathlessly. "I knew it wasn't you. It couldn't have been you."

"What the devil are you going on about, child? I haven't time."

"Listen, Papa. Please, for once just listen."

She withdrew a handkerchief from her dress and pressed it into my hand. I unfolded it, and a devilish-looking seed pod spilled out. It was covered in spiny protuberances and contained strange black seeds.

"What is this?" I asked. "Where did you get it?"

"I couldn't stand waiting for that Gerard, so I came into the kitchen. I thought I'd make a pot of coffee to occupy myself. I don't even like coffee. Why would I do such a thing?"

"Speak plainly, Lottie. Come to the point."

"I found five or six of these pods in the tin. And then I remembered something I'd seen in one of Dr. Johnston's books when we were looking for Christine's cause of death."

She opened the book to a page she'd marked and read aloud.

"*Datura stramonium* of the family nightshade is native to the eastern United States and originally referred to as Jamestown weed. It contains a powerfully toxic alkaloid compound known to induce dizziness, convulsions, hallucinations, and bouts of violence."

My mind remained in a fog induced by the remnants of rage, and although I did indeed comprehend that this find was of great significance, I could not on my life discern it. I had been poisoned with strychnine, like Christine. The symptoms were plain enough. What did this Jamestown weed have to do with it?

"Don't you see?" she asked. "You're not mad at all. Someone has been systematically poisoning you. Here is your logical explanation. This is what you've been searching for."

As my daughter spoke, the fog lifted. I remembered the disembodied voices, the hideous visions, and nightmares. Hallucinations, every last one? But who had done it? And why? Although I was relieved to learn of the possibility that my madness was chemically triggered, the fact remained that it had been done *to* me, likely by someone in this very house.

The galloping shame came on the heels of this revelation. I had been bitterly cruel to everyone around me, most especially Peter. For God's sake, I'd been ready to murder him in cold blood only moments ago. Even if this monstrous plant were partially responsible for my actions, it was I who had spoken the words, I who had picked up the axe. I took my daughter's hand.

"Lottie, Peter and I—"

"Did something happen?"

She hadn't seen, then. I thanked whatever cruel gods looked down upon us, for I knew I could never be restored in her eyes after a transgression such as that.

"I'm afraid I've treated him rather poorly," was all I could say.

"No, no, Papa, you were sick. It wasn't you. I knew it couldn't be you. It was this!" She snatched up the pod, and a few of the black seeds dropped onto the handkerchief. I rubbed them between my fingers.

"But, Lottie, you've been preparing my food these last days. Even if I was being poisoned, surely, I'm not under its effects now."

"Not the coffee," she said, her voice so thick with desperation that she could hardly speak. "Uncle Peter made it every morning before I rose. You're the only one who drinks it. The rest of us prefer tea. I didn't think—"

"Peter?" I whispered, and then recalled Mr. Hawkins bout of illness. He had blamed the bitter coffee, and rightfully so.

"The question is," she went on, eyes on the floor. "Why *slowly* poison? Why not murder you outright? And then, why use the strychnine now, after all this?"

"I need to talk to Gerard," I said, turning. "Come, bring the book."

She grabbed ahold of my shirtsleeve.

"We can't accuse anyone without real evidence, Papa," she said. "I cannot prove Peter made the coffee, only that it was one of his usual duties. If you take this to Gerard, you'll only succeed in proving to him that you weren't in your right mind and prone to fits of rage. We need more."

"Someone tried to kill me, Lottie, and Anna's body is missing. There are too many questions. We can't play at detective."

"I think I may know how to find the answers, but you won't like it."

"Tell me."

"You need to talk to him."

"To who?"

"Grandfather. And the woman in the attic," she whispered, and then pulled at my sleeves like a child, dragging me down the hall toward the yawning darkness of the attic staircase. I paused before the door. Lottie turned back and looked at me, first with pity in her expression and then with impatience.

"Now, hold a minute," I said. "I stand by what I said before. I won't have you carrying on with this spiritualist nonsense."

"We haven't got a minute. You said yourself you heard his voice. You know in your heart this is true."

"It was only a hallucination," I said. "You proved that."

She was right, though. Whether or not I was under the influence of some diabolical alkaloid was of no consequence. My father had spoken to me. My conviction of this wavered only in the forefront of my mind, where logic prevailed. In my heart of hearts, I heard his voice still.

I hesitated nonetheless. Lottie picked up a candle from the old claw-foot table and handed it to me. "You mustn't let him frighten you."

"I am not—" But it was hopeless to lie. She knew me better than anyone on earth. She took my hand, and I climbed those stairs as a man might climb the Tower of London, my fearless daughter ahead of me. When we reached the attic, Lottie released my hand and looked toward the rafters.

"This is where you saw her then, is it?" she asked. "The woman who looked like Lenora?"

"Yes."

"Do you believe in what I do?" she asked, and pain rippled in the depths of her eyes. She had never before asked me this question. I'd always believed the whole thing to be a charade, a passing fancy. Yet, before my very eyes I had seen the spirit of Dr. Johnston. We had all seen him. I could not fathom the strength of her belief. I envied her for being so certain. I envy her still.

"Well, I...why," I stammered. "I want to."

"That won't do, Papa. You must believe."

"You will have to teach me, then," I answered.

"Sit," she said, and then she sat right in the middle of the floor, crossing her legs beneath her and closing her eyes.

"What are you doing?" I asked.

One eye opened. She shushed me, and then closed her eye again. I could do nothing but sit across from her, waiting and watching her expression.

"Anyone who wishes to speak may do so," she said, but not to me. I waited, listening, watching the candles light her face. Wax dripped down over my thumb and I drew a sharp breath, sending wild shadows across the room. All at once, a shadow descended upon me, though my eyes did not perceive it. My spirits dampened like an extinguished candle, and I shivered.

"He's here," Lottie said.

I did not need to ask whom she meant. I felt him in my soul.

"Tell him," she commanded me. "Tell him he is no longer master of this house."

"You mean to have me speak to my father's ghost?" I whispered.

"I'm not asking you to believe in ghosts, Papa," Lottie said, opening her eyes and leveling her gaze on me. "Only in me."

I swallowed the tightness in my throat and spoke my father's name.

"This house belongs to me now," I said to the rafters, though I felt foolish.

"You're not going to convince anyone with a tone like that."

"Father," I said, louder, my heart rising in my throat. "I am master now. Whatever you wish to say to me, say it now. You owe me this much, you bastard."

"Better," Lottie said beneath her breath. Her eyes closed again, and the silence gathered like cobwebs around us. The gloom did not lift.

She whispered, "Do you not know me, Grandfather? I've brought your son. You are free to speak."

Did I perceive a slight shifting of the darkness at the edges of my vision, or had I only imagined it? Had I imagined the sudden blaze of the candles, or the standing of the hairs on my forearms? I sat in the silence, watching the expressions wax and wane across my daughter's face, searching for clues. A man of science, indeed! I was no more than a child, fighting the same urge to run or to hide beneath the blankets until dawn.

"Enough!" Lottie cried suddenly, slamming her palms onto the floor. "If you will do no more than rebuke us, leave us so we may speak to the child."

The candle flames dimmed, and yet somehow the room brightened. Who was this woman before me who could command the dead? I saw Lottie then as I had never seen her before, not as my little girl, but as a woman of terrible power. A woman not to be trifled with.

"The child is here now," she said. "I can feel her."

"Christine?"

"Don't be afraid," Lottie said, but I was not certain if she spoke to me. "Christine Murdoch, make yourself known to us. We are friends." She tilted her head, listening, her brow creased. "She's gone to get someone. She wants me to meet her."

"Who is it?"

A long time passed, and I could see her eyes moving behind her eyelids.

"How is this possible?" she asked.

"What? What do you see?"

"Lenora," she said. "Her spirit is here with us. How can that be?" I could offer her nothing, for I had seen this mysterious doppelgänger as well. Her brow creased deeply and she shook her head.

"What's happening?" I called, for she felt far from me. Her eyes flew open, and I held her gaze, tethering her to this earth. The room grew colder, as if we stood out upon the mountain with the winter wind all around us. The candles blew out. Darkness fell over us, and I heard Lottie's skirts as she stood.

"What did you see?" I asked, but she had already fled the room. I ran after her, catching her by the wrist at the bottom of the stairs. "Lottie, please."

"I don't know," she breathed. She took a step backward, asking, "Are you quite certain the woman downstairs is who she claims to be?"

"I'm not certain of anything anymore. Why ask such a thing?"

"Lenora Laveau is dead. Your father killed her."

Chapter XXIII

WILLIAM GARRETT'S JOURNAL

February 5, 1889

Lottie did not come down for supper last night, nor to breakfast this morning. Gerard, ever suspicious, sipped tea poured by a bent and haggard Murdoch. Peter was nowhere to be found.

"Dr. Garrett," he said. "Is your daughter unwell? She will be wanted for questioning."

"This has all been a great shock," I answered. "She will be down presently."

Lenora, who sat beside me but had not so much as glanced in my direction, rose from the table.

"Shall I look in on her?" she asked, likely eager to be away from me. Her presence was an agony to me. The bitter truth that we were little more than strangers weighed heavily on me, even in the face of her betrayal. Still, I wanted her nowhere near my daughter.

"That won't be necessary," I said, and then turned back to Gerard. "I need to speak with Devlin."

"Your man took him home last night, what with his wife being ill. Shall I send him a message?"

"This is a private matter. I'll have Wilson prepare the carriage."

"I can't allow that, Dr. Garrett. Until I have cleared each one of you personally, you are not permitted to leave the premises. You have failed to provide me with the postmarked letter you promised yesterday, which clears your daughter's name, so you say."

I rose, stronger and more defiant than yesterday. Although the Jamestown weed no longer influenced me, my father's rage gladly took up the reins.

"If you wish to keep me prisoner here without cause, so be it," I said. "But I will not allow this madness to affect my daughter."

"It already has," Lenora said, barely louder than a whisper.

"What did you say?" I asked, but she did not repeat herself. Instead, she pushed her chair from the table and walked into the kitchen. Gerard dabbed his mustache with a napkin.

"I have inquiries to make," he said. "I shall be traveling into Catskill proper to look into a number of leads and will return by late afternoon. I trust I need not tell you again to remain in the house?"

Rather than answering him, I threw my own napkin onto my plate and stormed from the room. Murdoch shuffled after me.

"Sir," he breathed. "Forgive me. You've not seen today's mail."

"Later, Murdoch. I haven't time."

"Please, sir."

The tone of his voice gave me pause, and I turned from the staircase to find him clutching two letters, his face a picture of distress.

"Are you ill?" I asked, and he bowed his head. His hands trembled as he handed me one of the envelopes.

"Miss Lottie left this note on the front table," he said. "I discovered it this morning, but she's written yesterday's date on the envelope."

It had been hastily written and torn so forcefully from the book that the bottom of the page had been ripped off completely. Tears smudged the ink. I unfolded it, and it read thus:

Papa,

You must forgive me for leaving you the way I did. I know you have questions and it was wrong of me to flee without explaining. Yet, I cannot do so even now.

Please tell Gerard, if he is looking for me, that I've only gone to Anna's. We had so little time to know each other, and I want to be in her presence again, among her things. I cannot make sense of what Christine revealed to me. If Anna's spirit remains there, perhaps her guidance might be offered beyond the veil. Do not worry for me. I shall be home again in time for supper.

Know this, Papa—you are not mad. You are not your father. I believe we have been the victim of a great deceit and I intend to ferret it out, whatever the consequence. I will explain everything when I have found the words for it.

L.

As I read these words, a fear I had never known grabbed ahold of my throat, choking the breath out of me. I'd thought she'd been shut up in her room all this time. She'd gone out yesterday and not returned.

"Have you seen her?" I asked Murdoch, taking him by the shoulders. "Have you seen my daughter?"

"No, sir," he answered, but looked down at the other letter, wrinkling it with his tight grasp. Tears gleamed in his eyes. "I'm afraid he's involved somehow, sir. What has he done?"

I took the letter from him. Peter had scrawled my name across the envelope. I recognized his hand as easily as Murdoch. Tearing it open, I read with my heart throbbing in my ears.

A LETTER TO WILLIAM GARRETT

From Peter Murdoch
No Postmark

Dear Will,

It's all crumbled to dust. Every carefully laid plan, every dream, all gone to rot. I can't bear the burden of it anymore. Without Lenora, it's all meaningless, and you've staked your claim there as swiftly as with the rest of it.

We were going to fly, you know. We were going to take your money and my daughter and live out the rest of our days in the warm sunshine of Spain, but you and Lenora have ruined everything. Let this letter be my confession. I am in the wind already, and it matters little if you know now. I must purge my soul of it, if not for my sake, then at least for my father's. He knew nothing of it. I will tell you all.

Lenora set her hooks in me after she returned from her Spanish holiday. I can't account for her supposed murder, only that she was so different when she returned that she might have been resurrected from the underworld as a demon and I would have accepted it. She possessed me body and soul, and I was bound to do her bidding.

When she revealed her scheme to me, I could not refuse. She took me up on the mountain and promised all below could be mine. It was a simple plan, really. Lenora was to beguile you into making her the beneficiary of your will, and the two of us together were to slowly drive you into madness. Once you had been sent off to the asylum, the house and all its assets would be transferred under a power of attorney to her—to us—for our life together. Murder was never meant to enter into it, do you understand?

You are likely wondering how my daughter paid the price for our sins. That, I cannot answer. Lenora blamed Anna for my daughter's death. She showed me Miss Meredith's recipe for the teacakes, which called for a secret dash of nutmeg, and I smelled it for myself in the cookies you took from Christine's pockets. I believed her, but now I have seen how quickly Lenora turns to betrayal. She must have made them herself using the recipe to implicate your cousin. Clever, perhaps, but I am no longer blind. Anna has only ever shown me kindness, which is more than I can say for you.

When Anna discovered the doctor's body that day in town, she ran to me for help, but I, as angry with you as I was, came up with a way to use his death for my own gain. It was I who hid his body in the shed, and I who led the dinner guests to it to prevent a sale from occurring before we had achieved our aim. It was I, also, who set my phonograph in your father's room so you might hear voices of the dead, and I who ground poisonous seeds into your coffee each morning. Your madness was a thing of my making, Will, but you alone are responsible for the cruelty you inherited from your father.

You want answers. Lenora has them, all of them. She keeps the evidence locked up in her room. I wash my hands of this. They are too soaked with blood already. Tell my father I am sorry.

Good bye, old friend,

Peter

WILLIAM GARRETT'S JOURNAL

February 5, 1889, continued

I left Murdoch at the bottom of the stairs with instructions to call for Devlin, his watery gaze on my back as I climbed with his son's damned letter crumpled in my fist. When I reached Lenora's quarters, the room I had inhabited my entire young life, I entered as a man possessed. Memories of our evening together gathered like splinters behind my eyes. The threads that bound us together had been uncleanly severed, and now only the rage remained.

I tore the drawers from my old mahogany dresser, dumping the contents onto the bed and scattering them across the floor. I upended trunks and rifled through the wardrobe. I channeled the mad energy that pumped through my veins into destruction.

"Father!" I cried toward the ceiling, throwing my arms wide. "You've had your way, you son of a bitch!"

Only Lottie could speak to him. Silence reigned, and I became so infuriated by it that I grabbed a glass vase from the mantel and dashed it against the wall, a cry issuing from my throat that I scarcely recognized as my own.

Exhausted and gasping for breath, I sank into the wing chair where I used to read and surveyed the chaos I had created. Paintings sat fractured on the floor, their canvases ripped and unsalvageable. Stuffing fell out of cushions. The curtains pooled on the floor, brass hooks snapped and bent. In my blind rage, I had destroyed everything I'd ever found comfort in as a boy.

"Christ," I whispered to myself, running my hands down my face. I was weary of these mysteries, of all of these questions without one single goddamned answer.

I rose, weakly hoping Lottie had only fallen asleep on Anna's couch and might walk through the door at any moment. In my heart, I knew the truth was far more sinister. I could call my daughter's name from the mountaintop and I would not find her. In denial of this fact, and chasing ugly images from my mind, I entered the washroom, which had yet been spared my assaults. I stood before the basin, where I had first kissed Lenora, avoiding my own gaze. I had known fear in my life, but this was torturous. It was powerlessness and anger tangled into a single, hideous skein.

Peter may have been beguiled, but I could see clearly now. Lenora had the answers, so he said, and I intended to uncover them even if I had to choke them out of her. If I could not find evidence of her witchery, she would tell me where I might. As I turned to leave the washroom, intent on confronting her, my eye fell upon a pewter box, inlaid with irises and partially hidden by a hand towel.

Locked. I looked around me. Where would she keep the key? On her person? I opened the bottles of perfume, unfolded towels, and pricked my finger on hairpins gathered in a box. The mere fact that she had hidden the key so well made it all the more imperative that I find it. Surely the contents of the box must be of great importance. I opened the top drawer of the vanity and cast aside compacts of pressed powder and mirrors of various size, but I found no key.

With no other option but to force it open, I snatched up one of the hairpins and set to picking the small lock. In a moment the latch sprung. I drew back the lid, which groaned on its hinge.

No diary lay within, only some scraps of embroidery thread, a sewing kit, and a small framed portrait of a man and women, which I presumed to be her parents. I could see her in her father's eyes and in her mother's raven hair. Beneath the portrait, I discovered a silver trinket set atop a packet of envelopes, and I picked it up, my other hand clasping instinctively around its twin in my pocket. I did not yet understand the meaning of this, only that the discovery was of great significance. It was the key, it was everything. As I dropped it into my pocket with the other, I recalled the words of the woman in town.

They'll be reunited in the end.

My attention turned toward the envelopes, tied together with twine. The first was addressed to Lenora, postmarked from Málaga.

I retrieved it. The envelope had been slit with a letter opener so all that remained for me to do was extract it and read the contents. Each envelope contained two letters—the original in Spanish and a copy in English—though I knew not for what purpose they had been translated. I hesitated, knowing instinctively whatever I found would change everything.

LETTERS FROM CATARINA LAVEAU,
Translated from the Spanish

Málaga, Spain, to Catskill, New York, Post Office, C/O Lenora Laveau
11 May 1888

My dear sister,

What am I to do with what you've written me? Something must be done! Oh, you never should have left home. Why did you go?

Do not tell your employer you are with child, Lenora. Judging by your description of him thus far, he is a villain and I fear what he might do. You haven't told him, have you? Is there anyone in the house you can trust? A housemaid or the cook who can help you get away from him? Damn his portrait and your contract. It is not worth this! Until you find means of escape, stay in your quarters and away from him whenever possible, do you understand?

You wrote me your situation has affected your art, that your paintings are shadowed now with ruin and misery so he has rejected them, but I say this is a lie. Nora, I believe he intends to keep you prisoner there, using the contract as a guise. Please come home at once so you may be among family and not in that dreadful house, alone with him. I will come for you if I must. I've done as you asked by not telling Father, but I cannot keep this secret forever. Please, do write me. I'm terribly worried for you.

All my love,

Caty

1 June 1888

Nora,

In your last letter, you wrote me you could trust the master's sister. Did she agree to help you? Why have you not written to me? It has been three weeks. I had to tell Father. If we do not hear from you soon, I fear he will come for you. I have never seen him so angry. He says he is going to kill him. Can you forgive me? Please do write.

7 July 1888

It has been a month since we have heard from you. Father leaves port tomorrow. If you are receiving these letters, if we have misunderstood the situation, please write before Father does something he cannot undo. I miss you with all of my heart. I cannot sleep nor eat for fear something terrible has happened to you. For God's sake, please write.

Caty

WILLIAM GARRETT'S JOURNAL

February 5, 1889, continued

The situation unfolded before me—the disappearance, Lenora's utter hatred of my father, but...a child! No, I could not accept it.

And what had become of her father? Had he murdered mine in a fit of rage?

The web in which I had become inextricably entangled had begun to weave a hangman's noose around my neck, a sentence for the sins of my father and not my own.

Beneath these letters, I found one from Dr. Johnston, and it was addressed to me. Under this still were two sheets written in Lenora's hand. It took only a moment to realize these were additional pages from his journal.

A LETTER TO DR. WILLIAM GARRETT

Catskill, New York, to Ravenswood Hall
Postmarked January 13, 1889

Dear Dr. Garrett,

Your last letter lingers with me, and I cannot sleep at night for thinking I ought to have been more forthcoming with you. I had said I could not comment on matters of law, but you are missing, in fact, the beginning of this story, which is the skein from whence I believe all other events have unraveled. I kept it to myself because it was not my secret to tell, but I fear now I may be too late. I cannot explain this sense of foreboding that grips me, and only I hope you receive this in time.

Lenora Laveau came to me early last year, quite in the middle of the night, extremely distraught. After swearing me to secrecy, she revealed Mr. Garrett had forced himself upon her some months back and she now suspected she was with child. Perhaps you will think me surprised at such a revelation, but after what he had done to your mother, I was not. Your father was a villain, William, a villain of the worst sort—that is, a man lacking morality but not money. I thank the heavens you take after your mother.

I examined her, and I determined she was in fact pregnant. I advised her to seek further counsel from the police. I have never seen such horror on the female face. I remember it still, and I could not help but feel I had given her a sentence of death rather than of birth. She rued the day she had come to paint Mr. Garrett, she said, because the features of his face would haunt her until death came to carry her off. Every wrinkle and whisker! Artists have such peculiar, fantastical ways of speaking, but that is what she said. I remember it exactly.

William, I believe something horrible has occurred, but I cannot explain—I do not know what part your father played in Lenora's disappearance or reemergence, only that the guilt of it haunted him until his death. It was this guilt, I believe, which caused the fever in his brain.

I hope you will at last solve the mystery plaguing your family these months past. I have given you all I know. I pray it is enough.

A. Johnston

DR. A. JOHNSTON'S MEDICAL JOURNAL

Copied from shorthand by Lenora Laveau
21 November 1888

Tonight, I received word of Oliver Garrett's death. One of his relations, Anna Bell, called upon me to sign the death certificate, but as I could not determine cause of death—there was no body—I merely wrote *suicide*. He had apparently flung himself onto the rocks, and the animals tended to the corpse, as they do.

A strange occurrence transpired while I was there, which I will put to paper should the cause of death come into question in the days to come. Young Christine Murdoch verily crept up upon me as I leaned over the widow's walk, employed in the gruesome task of scouting the scenery from above for human remains.

The girl tugged on my coat frantically and then pointed to a place on the floor inside the room. It appeared a rug had been recently removed, one that had held its place there for a long while before.

"Did you see something, child?" I asked. I knew she could not speak. Her father had brought her to me several times on that account. She merely nodded. "You saw Mr. Garrett jump?" This time, she shook her head, and then appeared extremely agitated, dragging me into the house. Then Miss Laveau came in to inquire after my progress, and the girl scurried away, as silent and quick as a frightened mouse.

"She is an odd little thing," Miss Laveau said.

I asked her if Christine had been in the house when Mr. Garrett died, which she answered in the affirmative. No evidence contrary to suicide exists, but the cause of death on that certificate troubles me so. If we might only convince the poor creature to speak, I believe we could know once and for all.

WILLIAM GARRETT'S JOURNAL

February 5, 1889, continued

What was I to do with all this information? The shivering threads of this grotesque web did not intertwine but instead carried on independently, telling different tales as I grasped for them.

The latch of the door disengaged as I stared at the documents. My fingers clenched around the papers. The door opened. I waited with as much trepidation as a man with a noose around his neck before the floor drops out beneath him.

"Will!" Lenora cried, her hand flying to her heart at the sight of me. Her eyes shifted from my face to the ruins of the room, and then to the letters, an expression of horror frozen into her features. We stared at each other like hunted foxes, each of us caught with no escape.

When I did find my voice, I could not manage greater volume than a whisper.

"What have you done, Lenora?"

I expected the fight of a cornered animal, but she strode into the room and sat upon the bed, eyes fixed on her hands. I questioned her again, my voice stronger.

"It's not what it seems," she said at last.

"Peter's gone," I said, and I took up his letter and waved it toward her. "He's told me everything. Where is my daughter?"

"He told you all he knows, which is only half the truth. You do not understand." She rose again and walked to the window.

"Then *help* me to understand."

"Will, I copied those entries from Dr. Johnston's journal. I translated all of those letters. I did it for you. I came here now to give them to you."

She said this as though it might absolve her of any wrongdoing, as though it would sew together the tattered bits of sinew that kept me from coming apart. I did not believe her. The violence inside me pulsed in my neck and flared my nostrils, but I could not succumb to it, not until I knew the truth.

"This has gone far enough. I don't care what happens to me," she added, without even troubling herself to look at me.

"Why did you not give them to me before?" I demanded.

"There are things about what's happened here that you don't know, things you cannot know."

"Was it your father, then, who killed mine?"

"No, for God's sake." The window reflected her face as she shut her eyes, hiding.

"Then who?" I asked. "I can take no more of this, Lenora. I've lost everything to this place."

"Not everything," she cried, and when she turned to me, tears streamed down her face. "Not yet. Don't you see? That's what I'm trying to tell you."

"Speak then!"

"I tried to tell you," she cried, backing against the window. "I have been trying to tell you somehow all the while. I thought, after all we had become to one another, you might show me mercy and allow me to return to Spain."

"After all we had become?" I repeated, incredulous, the words like a vise around my head. "And what is that, exactly?"

She leveled her gaze on me, but she did not answer the question.

"I killed your father." The admission burst forth from her trembling lips. "I shot him in the head with his own pistol."

The pieces of this tale came together violently, cracking like pressured glass, the sharp edges drawing blood. I closed the distance between us, an action she met with defiance. She lifted her chin and squared her shoulders as if prepared to meet her own death.

"It's true, then?" I said, a breath from her. "That's where

you went when you disappeared? To have your child? And you returned to murder him?"

"*Madre de Dios*," she groaned. "You have it all wrong."

"Does the child live?"

"Please don't. I can't bear it." She averted her eyes, but I took her arm.

"You owe me the truth. I have a right to know."

"A right?" she repeated, standing tall again, her voice sharp with ice. "And what, you have inherited this *right* from your father? What more could you possibly take from me?"

"What does that mean?"

"I should have let you drink the amontillado," she spat, tearing herself free from my grasp. She slipped by me and stood before the fireplace.

"You poisoned it?" I asked, and as this discovery fell upon me, the full weight of her role in my undoing crushed me like a mouse beneath her heel. What a fool I had been! But she shook her head, so I pressed. "Then you know who sent it."

"I may be a witch," she replied into the fire. "But I could not let you die. *Tal vez*, I was wrong."

"And Christine? Peter wrote—"

"Peter knows only what I have allowed him to believe. He didn't know I had been trapped."

"Trapped by whom?"

"Your cousin!" She shouted this at me as though I had insulted her, the words thick with resentment. I laughed, the sound so sardonic and full of malice that fear passed across her face.

"Anna is dead. How dare you."

Lenora, seemingly exhausted, fell upon the sofa.

"Are you such a fool that you haven't realized?" she murmured. When I did not respond, she looked up at me and said, "Anna blames me for her mother's death. She hates me even more than she hates you. She was going to tell them what I had done, all of them. This town would burn me alive if they knew. *Como no ves*? They already believe I am an *hechicera*. They would have needed no more proof. I had no choice. I was bound by her will."

"If you were so frightened, why did you not run?" I asked.

"How could I? I have no money. Anna turned the whole town against me. I could find no man brave enough to carry me on his horse or lend me a dollar."

"You are accusing Anna of starting the rumors?"

"It was always Anna. It still is. *Dime*, have you found her body?"

"You know we have not," I answered, but her meaning came through with enough force to push me back against the window. I leaned on the cold glass, shaking my head, my memory replaying these last weeks beneath the sheen of this sickly new light.

"I do not know how she fooled us all," Lenora continued. "But once her body disappeared, I knew what she had done. She used me, and I used Peter, all to ruin to you. To drive you mad like we did your father."

"The Jamestown weed," I muttered to myself, and she shot me a look of surprise.

"You knew?"

"Lottie found the seeds in the coffee tin. Very clever indeed."

"Lottie," Lenora whispered, closing her eyes. "Oh, you never should have come back here. Anna assumed you were dead. We all did."

"Yes, I know."

"You weren't supposed to come back."

"Speak plainly, woman," I said, weary.

"Ravenswood Hall was Anna's until you came home. She thought she was your father's only remaining relation, and then she learned you had a daughter." Her hands fell into her lap as if she had simply lost the will to go on. She shook her head and fell against the cushions.

"She asked Lottie to come," I said.

"She had to bring her here to complete her plan. Will, you and Lottie are still in her way."

My world froze. Heretofore, the danger to my daughter had been faceless, a vague threat on the horizon. Now I saw clearly. Now I believed.

"Jesus Christ," I said, and ran toward the door. Lenora ran after me and grabbed my arm.

"Where are you going?" she asked. I attempted to break free from her grasp, but she would not release me. "You don't know where she has gone."

"We looked for her body not knowing she had legs to walk."

"Do not leave me."

Unable to move my tongue or think of words for all the pounding in my head, I pried her fingers from my arm and glared at her with such violence that she fell back.

"Will!" she called after me. "Don't tell her what you know, I beg you. She'll have me killed!"

But I paid her no mind.

Chapter XXIV

WILLIAM GARRETT'S JOURNAL

February 5, 1889, continued

Apart from the stinging rain, I do not remember the journey to my cousin's house. We had not thought to search it—she was dead, so why would we? I knew not what she had hoped to accomplish in staging her own demise, nor how indeed she had accomplished it, but Lottie's intuition had led her to the old farmhouse, and it was all I had left to follow.

As I drove the horse down the mountainside, a terrible fear descended upon me, greater than any I had ever known in all my life. I had but one soul on this godforsaken earth who remained dear to me, one soul who loved me as I loved her. I tried not to allow my mind to journey beyond the charge of reaching my daughter, though these fears seeped through, nonetheless. As I spurred my father's horse on into the driving rain, I battled specters of Lottie in the throes of convulsion, or worse, but I did not yet have the full truth. There were horrors in store for me beyond this.

I did not tie my horse, nor did I knock, but instead I burst into the house. There she stood before the fire, stoking it with an iron poker. She straightened but did not turn around.

"Hello, Cousin," she said, and it was all I could do not to strangle her. She leaned the poker against the bricks.

"Where is my daughter?" I grabbed her by the shoulders and forced her to look at me, repeating the question.

"You've finally figured it out, then?" she asked, and I tightened my grip on her arms, but she did not react at all.

"I know everything, you conniving witch. What have you done with my daughter?"

"Release me."

I did as she asked, if only because I depended entirely upon her to locate my child.

"Now," she said, rubbing her arms. "What's this about Lottie?"

"I'm in no mood for games. I know it was you who tried to kill me."

Anna looked at me with finely crafted offense and said, "After everything we've been through together?"

"If it weren't for Lottie and I, you'd have everything," I said. "The house, the land, and the ghosts, the whole lot. If it means so much that you'd kill your only living family, you might have asked."

"Family?" she repeated, a cruel laughter bubbling in her throat. "I have no family. Momma is dead. You weren't supposed to come back at all, but isn't that just like you? Greedy for more even when you already have everything."

"That's not fair," I said. "I never wanted this house. I came to be rid of it."

"You never once considered, after everything Momma and I did for Uncle, that I might have a right to it?"

"I can't imagine why you would want it. It's brought us

nothing but pain."

"No, Will," she replied. "You and your father alone are responsible for the pain. Do not blame the house. Its only fault is being made of stone, like you. You're no different than him."

Although she aimed this barb at the heart, I was not so easily wounded. If I could not purify myself of my father's blood, I would use it against her.

"How did you do it?" I asked. "Lottie saw your body."

"Although very pleasant to the senses," she recited in a singsong voice. *"Drinking it in double the quantity makes the person out himself for three days, and in fact it kills him if the quantity is multiplied by four."*

"What the hell does that mean?"

"You don't know it? Dioscorides's *De materia medica,*" she answered. "A passage concerning nightshade. My mother was a botanist, Will. I know the nature of every plant, even those whose toxin mimics death."

Atropa belladonna would have lowered both her heart rate and respiration until nearly undetectable. Lottie would not have known the difference. And how could she have guessed at all this horror?

"But why?" I asked.

"I simply did what needed doing. It was the perfect time. You were in no condition to examine me, and Lottie is not as well trained in the medical arts as she believes. I could resurrect myself after you were either carted off to the asylum or arrested for murder and then collect what I am owed."

"Someone would have found you out."

Anna shook her head. "I was just another victim of attempted poisoning, and then I awoke in the dark, cold cellar..." She lowered her voice theatrically, as if telling a ghost story by the fire. "I ran for my life and hid here, for you had left me destitute and without any prospects."

"A fine tale."

"Easily told. Easier to believe."

Anna moved to the other side of the fireplace. She opened an intricately carved wooden chest beside the iron poker. From it, she withdrew a human skull.

"You comprehend only a fraction of what is happening, Cousin," she said, shoving the skull into my hands. I ran my finger over the bullet hole, recalling my supposed episode of madness in the forest. "It was all real, you know. Except Christine. She was long dead before she appeared to you in the woods. You'll have to account for that on your own."

"You murdered an innocent child," I murmured.

"Oh, she was everywhere and nowhere all at once," Anna replied with an exaggerated and petulant sigh. I saw the monster inside her then, the ugly thing living behind the girlish smile. I placed my father's skull on the table with enough force that enough force that it cracked. I could bear to see neither it nor my cousin, and so I set my eyes on the crackling fire behind her.

"That girl would've ruined everything. She witnessed both Lenora's and your father's murder."

"How? She was just a child."

"Yes, and her favorite place to read was the linen closet adjoining your father's quarters. The nosy little minx watched him through a rat hole in the paneling."

Her gaze followed mine, landing almost wistfully upon the burning coals, and she went on. "When I learned you had somehow coaxed words from her mouth, I knew it was only a matter of time. All I had to do was set the teacakes beside her bed. It was my mother's recipe, except for the strychnine, of course. I thought it would be a proper way to honor her."

"You're mad."

"I didn't even have to hide her body. She went about playing make believe in the brambles, and that was that."

I thought of the excruciating pain that had overtaken me and the violent convulsions that jarred my bones when I'd been in the throes of her poison. I remembered the aching depth of my fear, but I'd had my daughter by my side all the while. Little

Christine died alone, in the bitter cold, with no one but the dog to mark her passing. My throat swelled at these thoughts, and my eyes stung.

"Why was she a threat to you?" I asked, swallowing hard. "The girl posed no real danger to you if Lenora had murdered my father."

"She knew the part I played in your father's descent into madness, and who do you suppose told Lenora where to find the gun?" she replied, turning back to me with a wry grin. "Lenora— as you call her—could implicate me, and she *would* implicate me to save herself. In that, and in other acts, too. And I can't inherit your estate if they hang me for murder, can I? The two of us were locked in a cage of our own design. Her part could not be revealed without also revealing my own. If the child had told what she knew, all would have been lost."

"So, you spread the rumors about her murder and the hauntings. You made everyone believe she was a witch, and so she believed she might be vanquished like one—at the stake?"

She returned to the chest, tossing aside blankets and wooden toys. "How else was I supposed to keep her under my control? She wanted out when you arrived, but I had come too far. Everyone in this town is so superstitious, beyond even reason. Sell off a few cursed pieces of a dead woman's jewelry, and it's all anyone can talk about. It was no great challenge to manipulate them—or her."

I could not reply to this. I needed to know it all, every last detail of her sordid plan if I had any hopes of finding Lottie, but desperation quickly chipped away at my patience.

"Please, Anna," I said through my teeth. "Just tell me what you've done with Lottie."

"What do you suppose is the most effective way to drive a man insane?" she went on and then paused her rummaging to look over her shoulder at me. "See, some people say it's guilt. That certainly seemed to be the case for your father. I think, though, it's grief. You have to break a man apart so the lunacy seeps into the cracks. Not being of sound enough mind to control an estate will do, after all."

"This is madness, Anna. This can't be true."

"You always were as dumb as stone, Will," she murmured with a sigh and bent into the chest to reach the bottom. "The woman you call Lenora is not who you think she is. Ah, here it is. We decided it would be best if I kept this for safekeeping. If you or your father had discovered it, well..."

With a one-sided shrug, she handed me a miniature portrait of Lenora and another woman who shared her features, exact enough to be uncanny, with only a slight variation in the eyebrows to differentiate them. Twins.

On the back of the miniature, two names had been written in elegant script: *Lenora & Catarina*.

The dark portraits in the cellar, and Caty's letters, came at once into my head along with the ghostly visage of Lenora's simulacrum hovering above me. A terrible, amorphous idea formed in my mind. As it took shape, I thought of all I had learned. Then I heard Lottie's voice.

Lenora Laveau is dead. Your father killed her.

"There," Anna said, and she settled herself down into the sofa as though she had not a care in the world. I clutched the trinkets in my pocket and understood. "Now you see. It was a stroke of fortune, really. Caty came to Catskill in search of her sister, and the driver brought her here, either by mistake or because he was too much of a coward to take her all the way to Ravenswood Hall. In either case, Christine had made such a fuss about her murder it would have been foolish for Caty to believe her sister still lived. We had a singular opportunity to devise a plan together. She for her revenge, and I for mine. My mother deserved better."

"Your mother?"

"Momma worked herself to the bone for Uncle. She was master of Ravenswood. It should have belonged to her."

"So, you and Lenora—*Caty*—poisoned him with Jamestown

weed to drive him mad, and Caty posed as Lenora."

"As her ghost, to be precise. The nail in the coffin. Everything was moving according to plan—"

"Aunt Meredith allowed you to do this to her only brother?"

"Oh, Momma hadn't a clue. She thought Uncle had been too influenced by Lenora, and they argued about her all the time. Caty was supposed to haunt him into madness, to frighten him, but she possessed him like a demon, the same as she's done to you. That's her wont, I suppose. After Uncle turned us out, Momma lost her will to live. She'd given everything to him, and he abandoned her."

"You're forgetting a rather significant portion of this plot, Anna," I said. "Even if my father were committed, the estate would default to me."

"Yes, well, I didn't know that at the time. I thought you were dead, but here you are."

"So, you kept up the plan, the same one you used against my father, and hoped it would work on me."

I wanted to sit, for my legs grew weary of bearing my weight, but I did not trust myself enough to sit beside her. Every word that left her mouth brought my intent nearer to murder.

"Put simply, yes," she answered. "You were so dead set on selling the place, I had to take measures into my own hands. If that miserable old woman had bought it before the plan came to fruition, it would've all been for nothing."

"You sent me the amontillado," I said. "To finish what you started before it was too late."

"Yes, but ironically you had something Uncle didn't—a daughter."

I met her eyes, and I realized then that her plans had never included me or Lottie leaving this place alive.

"We'd become so close, after all," she went on, nearly laughing. "I knew she would come here to *communicate* with me. Such a predictable little creature. What a surprise I must have been, alive and well and waiting."

"Where is she?" I whispered, my voice raw.

"You're too late, Will." At that moment, she lunged for the iron poker and swung at me, screaming like a ghoul, her hair whipping around her face. The weapon made contact with my shoulder, knocking me off balance as the miniature flew out of my hand and skidded across the floor.

She flew at me again, cracking me across the skull. White light exploded behind my eyes.

"Enough!" I cried, stumbling. I lifted my arm to protect my face from another assault. The hook of the poker ripped into my forearm. This set loose something inside me, something I hope to never feel again as long as I live. I wanted blood. I wanted to kill her.

I took her by the hair and dashed her against the wall, my arm at her throat. She gasped, clawed at me, but I would not release her.

"Where is she?" I asked again, my face so close to hers that I could see her heart pulsing in her temple. I ground my arm into her neck until tears sprung from her eyes.

"The crypt," she gasped. "She's in the crypt."

I think it was Lottie that stopped me from killing her then. I heard her voice in my mind. *You are not your father.*

"What have you done?" I whispered, releasing her and backing away. Anna clutched her throat, hissing.

"Have you ever heard the sound of a shovel cracking a human skull?"

"No," I whispered, backing away. "No."

"Such a dull, vacant sound," she said, and then she laughed.

Time was out of joint. In one moment, it had frozen, and in another I was on my horse again with the miniature in my pocket. I spurred the horse into a gallop and I set off toward the crypt, the rain lashing my face, mud splashing on my shoes and trousers. The heat in my face and the pounding of my heart gave rise to a kind of fever I was powerless against. It throbbed in time with the hooves of the horse as we climbed the mountain, higher and higher, until at last the dark, skeletal figure of Ravenswood Hall rose up through the weeping trees.

Through the gates I flew, down the gravel drive, beneath the shadow of the house, and up to the bolted doors of the mausoleum.

I dismounted, removing the ring of keys from my pocket. The key was gone. Had Lenora returned it to me after we interred Christine? I could not remember.

"Lottie!" I cried, slamming my fist against the door. She did not answer me. Half blinded by rain and tears, I grabbed a stone angel that adorned the entrance and bashed it against the door. I called my daughter's name again and again until my voice was hoarse and the stone cut through my palm. The statue grew slick with my blood, but I felt no pain.

The wind carried Lenora's voice to me—she must have been watching for my return from the window. A moment later, she crested the hill, her dress clinging to her legs, a soaked black shawl wrapped around her hair.

"Will, stop!" she cried, but I did not. I could not. "You're bleeding."

"Where is the key?" I asked in answer, but I hadn't time to lose as she search her memory. "Never mind, bring me the axe!"

I struck the door again and again until Lenora returned to me, and then I tore the axe from her grip with so much force that she fell to the mud with a cry. She made no other move to stop me as I brought the axe down into the splintering wood, drawing sparks from bleeding iron nails. Such a lifeless sound. It haunts me, even now. I thought back to the night I had this same wretched task in mind—to exhume my mother for proof of her death. What a cruel circle of chains had I wrought.

I tore the ruined door from its hinges with my bare hands, aching with cold, my muscles quivering. Lenora remained where she fell, her expression empty, as I stepped inside.

Lottie slumped, unmoving, against the far wall. Dark blood matted her hair, coagulating in a hideous, gaping wound at her temple. A circle of spent altar candles was strewn about her like a faerie ring and wrapped around her shoulders was the moth-eaten remnant of a burial shroud. It seemed she had survived Anna's attack and opened her ancestor's sarcophagus in an effort to keep warm. The remains of this ancestor stared up at me, all sunken eyes and grotesque grins as I skirted Christine's coffin and the corpse of the real Lenora Laveau.

"Oh, God," I whispered as I ran to my daughter, gathering her in my arms. She was so cold, her lips as pale and bloodless as the marble floor. Tears blinded me. I could not breathe.

This was the stuff of Poe and penny novels. This did not, could not, happen to my daughter—not my daughter. In my mind, I heard her call for me. I watched her shiver in the darkness, alone with the dead. I had come too late. Oh, God!

"Lottie, please," I sobbed, lifting her into my arms and rocking her.

Her arms twitched against me. Was I not too late after all? I spoke her name, louder this time, shaking her by the shoulders. She breathed, and her fingers clutched my coat.

"She's alive!" I called, though I knew not to whom I spoke. I only wished to proclaim it.

"Papa?" my daughter said, scarcely audible above the rain.

"I'm here, my girl." I brought her to my chest and stroked her hair, sobbing and showering her with kisses. I never should have involved Lottie in this nightmare. I will never forgive myself for it.

"I'm so sorry, child," I said over and over.

"Anna," she whispered, shivering. I removed my coat and draped it over her shoulders. The dried husks of moth larvae fell from her blanket.

I hushed her. "I know."

"I'm sorry, Papa," Lottie said. "Lenora—Lenora's not—there's another one. There are two."

"That's what you saw in the attic," I said, rubbing her hands to warm them, and she nodded. "Can you stand? We must get you warm."

I helped Lottie to stand, but her legs buckled beneath her.

"Shall I carry you?" I asked, and she held tighter to me but shook her head.

"I can manage. I can't be here a moment longer."

We stumbled outside. Through shivering curtains of rain, the candle flickering in the window of the sitting room appeared miles away. My own body ached with the thought of making such a journey, and I could not fathom how Lottie proposed to do it. But she had inherited her fortitude from her mother, who fought her own death with such ferocity.

We set out, the both of us trembling and struggling to find our footing on the mud-slicked earth. I looked over my shoulder. Behind us, Lenora stood at the threshold of the crypt. The expression of absolute human misery carved into her features haunts me still. Had I known then the intent that had fastened itself upon her, I might have pleaded with her to come away with us to the house. I turned my back instead and left her alone with her dead.

With my daughter clinging to me as she had when she was a girl, we made our way toward the guttering candle flame like a pair of soaked moths, and when at last we found purchase on the steps, she broke into sobs.

"Hush, child," I whispered, holding her close.

Once secured together on the sofa, the fire forcing back the biting cold, Lottie turned to me and held my gaze.

"I saw her, Papa," she murmured. Blood returned slowly to her face. I pulled my soaked kerchief from my pocket and dabbed away the tears.

"Who?"

"Momma," she answered, her lip trembling. "She came to me in the crypt. All these years I've been trying to contact her. All this time, Papa. Every séance I held, I hoped she'd come through to me. I needn't have become a medium after all. All I ought to have done was die."

There was no drollness in this revelation, no sarcasm. I believed her without question.

"Did she say anything to you?" I asked. She shook her head.

"She only looked at me, looking and looking, as if she were surprised to see me."

"Perhaps she was. It was not your time to be there," I assured her, pulling her close and smoothing her matted hair. Lottie rested her head against my chest and wrapped the blanket tighter around herself.

"I wanted to go to her, Papa."

This admission cut into my heart.

"I'm rather glad you didn't," I answered, but she didn't appear to hear me. A long while passed before she spoke again.

"I walked to Anna's to try to make contact with her spirit," she said at last, shaking her head. "Spirits haunt the places they frequented in life. And she was there, but alive. She told me she had solved it all, but she feared Lenora would kill her, so she staged her own death." She broke off here to wipe her eyes and draw in a deep, ragged breath. "The key was the body in the crypt, she said. She had to show me what she uncovered. I believed her. I went with her. What a fool I was."

I imagined this scene playing out before me, and it was not the murderous criminality of it that staked my heart, but the cruelty. Lottie had loved my cousin as much as she might have loved a sister.

"A fool would not have survived the night, Lottie," I muttered. "Forgive me, girl. It took me too long to find it all out."

"You came," she said, nestling closer against me. "All is well."

I allowed the tears to fall freely down my cheeks, dropping onto her hair. The wound in my arm, which I'd forgotten, ached fiercely, but it mattered little. I lifted my eyes to the heavens in gratitude, to my wife, for protecting her.

"Lenora is still out there, Papa," she said, her tremors lessening as she sat up. "She's going to run. You must stop her."

"I won't leave you."

"I'll look after her, sir," Murdoch said, appearing in the doorway. "You needn't worry."

Lottie smiled at him, and then at me.

"I'm safe now," she said. The sound of the front door slamming open against the wall startled the lot of us. "That will be Gerard," Lottie said. "Go. He'll be wanting her."

approached the crypt for the second time, Gerard at my heels. Dread grew within me as I neared the open door like a malignant tumor inside my chest.

Lenora knelt before her sister's body, her face so utterly devoid of expression that I did not know her. Her weak shadow stretched over the withered corpse. My heart hardened at the thought of all I must explain to the inspector, and all I knew now. It was all too fantastical. He would not believe me. I had no recourse but to show it plainly to him.

"A knife, Inspector Gerard," I said to him. We stepped inside through a curtain of rain pouring freely from the roof.

"I beg your pardon?" he said.

"No!" Lenora cried, somehow knowing my aim in her heart. She draped herself over the corpse. "Leave her be, for God's sake!"

"You will have your truth, Inspector," I said.

He handed me an ancient-looking pocketknife, likely a family heirloom, and I considered how utterly I was about to ruin it. There would be no passing it on after this.

I grabbed Lenora by the arm and flung her aside. Gerard held her as she clawed at me, and such a moan erupted from her throat that she might have been a fox or a forest sprite and not a woman.

I opened the knife and thrust it into the corpse's womb, prying open the desiccated flesh with my bare hands. Reaching inside the cavity, I closed my fingers around a tiny, round object.

I extracted it with my eyes closed, for I did not wish to see what I beheld.

An infant skull, partially formed, monstrous.

"What have you done?" Lenora cried, fists tearing at Gerard's coat as I turned to them. "What have you done?"

She sank to the floor, burying her face in her hands. Gerard looked at me with fear in his eyes, like I had become a savage animal. I gave him the skull and the knife, and he handled both as if they were diseased.

"This woman and her child are dead by my father's hand," I said, rain flying from my mouth like spittle. "My father strangled her. A series of letters will confirm that Lenora Laveau did in fact disappear. Some months later, it was Catarina Laveau who came to Ravenswood Hall in search of her sister."

"What are you going on about, man?" Gerard asked. I looked to Lenora.

"Speak, then, if you've courage enough," I said. "Tell us your name."

"You know who I am!" she yelled, her voice hoarse from crying.

"Damn you, woman!" I pulled the miniature from my pocket and cast it before her into a puddle of rainwater. She rushed to it, scooping it up and attempting in vain to dry it with her soaked shawl.

"Bastard!" she cried. "This was the only portrait I had of her."

"You have a mirror, haven't you?" I asked. The harshness of this startled even me.

She stumbled to her feet, hair clinging to her pale face, knees stained with earth. I wondered how I ever thought her beautiful.

"My name is Catarina Laveau," she said at last, her chin high. I heard Gerard mutter an exclamation. "The woman you have desecrated is my sister, Lenora, and her child."

Gerard stepped forward, his mustache drooping over his baffled frown. Neither I nor my daughter would go down for this—not in my father's name, and not in Lenora's, whose name was not Lenora at all.

"My father impregnated a Spanish painter named Lenora Laveau," I explained, cross he hadn't yet solved it. "When he found out she was with child, he murdered her. When she did not respond to her sister's letters, their father came to fetch her. Is that plain enough?"

"Well, what happened to him?" Gerard asked.

We looked at Caty.

"They found his body in New York City, killed for the money in his pocket. He never arrived here." When she looked at me, I recognized the old, fiery hatred I had seen in her eyes when we first met. "Your father took *everything* from me."

"It wasn't enough to simply murder him, then? You had to drive him mad, force him to believe your sister had returned to haunt him?"

My father's blood cried out to me now, from the earth where he had fallen and from my own heart, where he continued still to poison me.

"I didn't want to kill him, Will," she said. Her teeth chattered with cold, biting her words into pieces. "*Pero*, Anna told me about the gun in his room, and I...I was so *angry*."

"You shot him when he turned his back to you," I finished. "Was it too difficult for you to look him the eye when you took his life?"

"I am not a killer," she said, her tone revealing she meant to convince herself and not me. Tears sprung into her eyes, her brow contorting as if in physical pain. "I only wanted to find my sister, to let her rest in peace. I didn't know where he had hidden her until that day we brought Christine—"

"Who helped you throw my father's body off the balcony?" I interrupted. Her agony affected me deeply. It echoed throughout my very spirit, but I could not allow myself this weakness, not after all she had done.

"Anna," she answered. "We were going to share the money. I

was supposed return to Spain with my sister's body and be done with all of you."

"And Peter? You promised to take him with you."

"I did care for him, but then you came, and...and I—"

"Don't," I said. I held up my hand, cutting this sentiment short. I didn't want to hear it.

She turned to the desiccated corpse of her sister, laid atop my ancestor's sarcophagus, and caressed the dust-laden hair.

"*Perdóname, hermanita,*" she whispered. "*Te he fallado.*"

"It was you, then, who murdered Dr. Johnston?" Gerard said behind us, keeping pace at last. The rain dripped from his mustache. He still held the infant's skull in his right hand, entranced by it. In his left, he grasped the open knife.

"Of course not," she answered. "Peter told me Anna found the doctor's body, but you can be certain she killed him. I could not speak, don't you see? If she'd told the people in town what I'd done, they would either kill me in the night or I'd be hanged for murder. I couldn't die here, thousands of miles from my homeland, alone."

"Anna wasn't going to tell anyone a thing, you fool," I said. "She was too afraid you'd drag her down with you. You've been manipulated like everyone else."

Her eyes widened for an instant and then hardened to flint.

"I loved you," she whispered as her shoulders drooped. I flinched at this, as if she had struck me. "But you loved my sister. Do you think I can live her life forever?"

Her eyes fell to the skull in Gerard's hand and the knife held loosely in the other, and then lifted wearily back to mine. Then she lunged toward Gerard and snatched the knife. I braced myself, waiting for her to fly at me, but I was not her aim.

"Lenora, please," I whispered, the name slipping from my tongue before I could amend it. This, the sound of her sister's name and not her own, sealed her intent.

"Don't," I pleaded. I could not move to stop her as she brought the knife to her own neck. That fraction of a moment stretched into eternity. I heard the rain drops on the roof and the cry of a fox atop the cruel mountain.

"I can haunt this place no longer," she said, and then she plunged the knife into her neck.

"No!" I cried. Blood poured freely down her dress. With a sputtering cry, she summoned her remaining strength to reach for her sister and collapsed onto her corpse with a sickening crack of dried flesh.

I gathered her in my arms, my hand pressed to the wound. Blood gushed from the artery and poured out between my fingers. Gerard's voice reached me as if from another plane of existence, my agony so profound that I erased everything but her from my memory. I know he was there for it all, but I cannot recall him.

I sat with her, with this woman I had loved, and her twin, lifeblood pouring into my hands. Darkness fell. Her eyes lifted to mine, and then she was gone.

I held her lifeless body until the rain stopped and the blood dried on my hands, and then I laid her down atop her sister and walked home, to my father's house.

Epilogue

WILLIAM GARRETT'S JOURNAL

May 1, 1889

I have only a few more notes to add in closing, and then I am finished with this wretched tale forever.

I have found no true justice for my father's murder, but if we are to abide by the "eye for an eye" idiom, the scales appear to be balanced. Did he not bring his fate upon himself? Did he not bring it upon me? Lottie says I should forgive him, not for his sake but for mine, but I am a long way from there. I have not yet found it in myself to exonerate him for driving my mother to suicide, nor have I accepted my part in it, as it was this action of mine that set all others into motion. I told Lottie every dreadful detail of my mother's death shortly after I'd written the last entry in this journal. She has shown me more mercy than I deserve.

Inspector Gerard, with naught but a journal-entry confession written under the influence of a toxin, was obliged to let the matter rest, even if I cannot. I suspect he is keeping a close watch on me, though, ready to begin an inquiry anew should I misstep. For now, I find solace in the fact that I have prevailed despite my father's efforts to ruin me, and in the knowledge that in only a few months more, I will have waited him out of the inheritance I am owed.

Mrs. Anderton offered a great deal more than that, though, to bring Ravenswood Hall to the ground so she might reform its bones into her grand hotel. She'd found the whole ghastly business of murder too enticing to pass up and believed she could turn it all to her advantage. People do love a good ghost story.

In the end, Lottie and I could not return to Baltimore. My old friend's article in the newspaper and the sensational tabloid headlines have done their damage, and the ugliness wrought there cannot be undone. Father's pride is still alive and well inside me, and I could not return to watch all we had built molder to dust. Catskill, after all, was in need of a doctor.

I am slowly restoring my reputation to the good people here. Though many have carved their opinion of me as permanently as if in the mountain rock, there are others still who see my heart and accept me not as master of my father's estate but as a friend. I am not him, and Ravenswood Hall will no longer be haunted by his misdeeds—or mine.

Catskill will understand by and by, with Lottie's help. She is as effortlessly kind and gentle as my mother and as feisty and stubborn as her own. The whole town adores her already, including the new deacon. He's a respectable man—not prone to superstition or prejudice—and Lottie seems to fancy him. He has attended every one of her séances, which she hosts every other Sunday. Lottie has been indispensable to Devlin as well, who recently lost his dear wife, in both offering her comfort at the deathbed and her unique talents should he wish to speak with his love again. Her sweetness has endeared her to all.

Many years will pass before I can practice medicine as I once had, but I now have clients enough to make a living. Though, soon neither Lottie nor I will want for anything. It is the final nail in my father's coffin that I should wrench success and happiness from the horrors this place had held within its cold, stone walls.

Mrs. Olsen, our housekeeper, is adjusting nicely to her move from Baltimore. She's brought her son, a boisterous lad of seven, who terrorizes Lottie's chickens and drives our long-suffering Mr. Murdoch properly out of his mind. He and Wilson are all that remain of the former Ravenswood Hall. My trusty driver has been forgiven for his unwitting role in Anna's plot. He confessed that Anna threatened to have me turn him out if he refused to transport Dr. Johnston's body, and I have seen her clutching influence. There is no doubt in my mind that Wilson believed he had only one choice.

I know it is futile to dwell on all I have lost when such welcome good fortune greets me each morning. Still, I struggle. The events described herein appear to me in nightmares, when the sun has set upon the day and I am alone again with the ghosts of all I have come to know. It is then that I reach for the pair of trinkets at my bedside. Lottie has nightmares, too. I hear her at night, crying out for me and muttering her cousin's name.

Anna has not been found. There was a report of her boarding a train in Boston, my mother's remaining jewels furnishing her escape, but it seems she's abandoned her prize and vanished. No doubt she has seen her face on the posters. Perhaps she's only biding her time. Someday Anna may return to claim what she believes is hers, and it is this thought that keeps my windows and doors securely locked. It keeps me awake at night, every creaking board and groaning pipe a threat. I see her face in crowds. I feel her behind me, waiting for just the right moment. I can only remain vigilant and pray that someone turns Anna in. The pruning of this branch on our family tree might have allowed it to grow up from its infested stump, but until then, I think back on our childhood together with great regret.

As for Peter, my old friend? Without the funds for his

escape, he was easily apprehended and now stands accused of conspiracy to murder and awaits his sentence. I read about it in the papers. I often wonder if things would have been different if I'd only treated him like a friend. A part of me wishes to see him one last time and to ask him what sort of love had driven him down the path he chose, but I know. The line between love and death is only a silken strand in a spider's web. When the one side trembles, the other will quiver in its turn. As surrounded by horror as I was, I fell unwittingly in love with Lenora—or with Caty. I can't say anymore. A terrible love it was, intoxicating and malevolent, like poison. I can still feel her sometimes in the rustling of dead leaves upon the lawn, in the withered petals of the roses beneath the heat of the sun, in the wind that blows down from the mountains to chill my bones.

Lottie believes I witnessed the spirits of Christine and Lenora and that they tried to guide me to the truth, but I am not so certain anymore. I have no way of knowing what was real and what was orchestrated, either by Anna or by my own mind. My cousin was right about one thing—the surest way to drive a man to insanity is not guilt but grief. I was so full of it already that I might have believed anything if it saved me from accepting how utterly alone I was there. Losing Lottie would have broken me.

When I think back on those days, my memories are moldered and faded, like the paintings that remain still in the cellar. One day, when I have the courage, I will burn them. I'll watch them all go up in flames, Lenora, Caty, and my father, until the canvases blister and curl to ash. No longer among them is my mother's portrait, which I discovered beneath a dusty sheet, hidden by Lenora's failed portraits of my dead father. She has been restored to her rightful place, not on the staircase, but above the mantel in the foyer, where she can better keep her watch. Whoever calls upon us will know who we honor here.

The curse of Ravenswood Hall fades even now from the lips of the townspeople, but there are indeed spirits that guard this place, two great stone wolves among their ranks. I remember their names now, but it doesn't matter.

No one tells these stories, not anymore.

About the Author

After a decade of working in the publishing industry, H. B. Diaz is now a stay-at-home mom and gothic mystery/horror writer. Her short stories have been published by Flame Tree Press, Ghost Orchid Press, The NoSleep Podcast, and Pseudopod, among others. Her collection, Nocturne: A Collection of Dark Tales was released in 2020 and her southern gothic novel, Wildefell, is forthcoming from Cemetery Dance Publications. She holds a BFA in creative writing and is a proud member of the Horror Writer's Association. She lives with her family in a historic, and likely haunted, town on America's East Coast.

You can find her on social media via:
Website: authorhbdiaz.wixsite.com/fiction
Twitter: @HollyBDiaz
Instagram: @HBDiaz
Facebook: facebook.com/HollyBDiaz.